"You're not going to make this easy, are you?"

"Why the hell should I?" It was a harsh, bitter cry torn out of her. "You used me. You made me fall in love with you, then threw me away when you didn't need me anymore. Give me one good reason why I should make it easy for you! Just one!"

He was staring at something across the valley, his profile like stone. "There isn't one, Megan," he said quietly. "You've got every right to hate me. There isn't any easy way to explain it, but there was a reason for everything I did. And you've got to believe I didn't set out to deliberately hurt you. That was the last—"

"I don't want to hear it," she said in a flat, dull voice. "If you want absolution, find a priest— because you're never going to get it from me."

Dear Reader:

February has a reputation for being a cold and dreary month, but not at Silhouette Intimate Moments. In fact, so many exciting things are happening this month that it's hard to know where to begin, so I'll start off with *Special Gifts* by Anne Stuart. Anne is no doubt familiar to many of you, but this is the first time she's done a novel for Silhouette Books, and it's a winner. I don't want to tell you too much, because this is definitely a must-read book. I'll say only that if you think you know everything there is to know about love and suspense and how they go together, you're in for a big surprise and a very special treat.

Another name that many of you will recognize is Linda Shaw. In *Case Dismissed* she makes her first appearance in the line in several years. If you've been reading her Silhouette Special Editions, you'll know why we're so glad to welcome her back. This is a book that literally has everything: passion and power struggles, dreams of vengeance and, most of all, characters who will jump off the page and into your heart. Don't miss it!

Award-winning writer Kathleen Creighton treats a serious subject with insight and tenderness in *Love and Other Surprises*, the story of two people who never expected to find love again—much less become parents!—but are more than capable of dealing with such unexpected happiness. Finally, welcome bestseller Naomi Horton to the line. In *Strangers No More* she gives us a whirlwind romance and a momentary marriage between a heroine you'll adore and a hero who is not at all what he seems. Figure this one out, if you can!

No matter what the weather's doing outside, February is hot at Silhouette Intimate Moments!

Leslie J. Wainger
Senior Editor
Silhouette Books

Strangers No More

NAOMI HORTON

Silhouette Intimate Moments

Published by Silhouette Books New York

America's Publisher of Contemporary Romance

NAOMI HORTON

was born in northern Alberta, where the winters are long and the libraries far apart. "When I'd run out of books," she says, "I'd simply create my own—entire worlds filled with people, adventure and romance. I guess it's not surprising that I'm still at it!" An engineering technologist, she presently lives in Nanaimo, British Columbia, with her collection of assorted pets.

Prologue

There wasn't even time to scream.

She was so intent on her work, she hadn't heard them come up behind her, didn't know she wasn't alone in the dark, late-hour stillness of the old office building until some movement made her glance up. The black-garbed figure stepped from the deep shadows of the room into the circle of her lamplight like something out of a nightmare, and she stared at it without comprehension.

She wasn't even afraid for that first split second, too taken by surprise to feel anything but blank astonishment. But then bewilderment gave way to fear, and fear to terror. She started to rise, opening her mouth to scream, but it was already too late.

There was movement behind her, sensed more than seen, then something soft and moist clamped tightly across her mouth and nose. Already sucking in a breath to scream for help, she'd inhaled the bitter fumes deeply into her lungs before understanding what it was, had felt her head start to spin even as she panicked and started to fight for her life.

But the first figure caught her flailing hands and held them easily and the second sank his fingers into her thick hair and wrenched her head back, holding her still. She tried to hold her breath but they simply waited until her aching lungs betrayed her and she drew in one, then a second, deep burning breath. Reality started to tilt and gently whirl, then side-slipped swiftly into darkness.

Then there was only oblivion....

It would be dawn soon.

The wind keened down the empty streets, knife-edged with cold. Taggart shrugged his shoulders a little deeper into his worn leather jacket, burrowing his hands into his pockets. The sound of his footsteps echoed back at him from the tall, dark-windowed buildings rising on either side, loud above the rustle of dead leaves along the gutters. A capricious puff of wind sent an empty soft drink can clattering along the sidewalk and he tensed for an instant, then relaxed again with a rueful shake of his head.

It would be dawn soon.

The banshee hours, Lucas had called them. The long, cold hours just before the sun came up and made the world a sane place again. It was a dangerous time, when a man's reflexes were chilled and slow, his muscles stiffened from hours of inactivity and fear. Hunkered there in alien jungles a million miles from home, a man was tempted to draw into himself, to let his mind wander to sweetly remembered things, leaving his back exposed.

It had been Charlie's favorite time, that last cold hour before dawn. The killing hour. They'd come then, ghost-silent, slipping past dozing sentries and trip wires to slit an unprotected throat, to slip cold steel into a man so swiftly, so cleanly, he'd die without even realizing what had brought death.

They'd find them in the morning. Sometimes there had been just one, sometimes more—humped, motionless forms that had seemed to be merely asleep until an impatient shake had sent them sprawling like stringless puppets, blood-soaked and cold.

Taggart shivered involuntarily, the muscles across his back tightening. He glanced over his shoulder, smiling grimly even as he did so, knowing the street behind him was as empty as the street ahead, yet unable to stop himself. This wasn't Vietnam; there was no VC sapper back there slipping through the shadows with killing on his mind. Only an empty city street, a stray cat or two and a lot of bad memories. But still he looked. Old habits die hard.

As do old soldiers.

He smiled faintly again. Strange, how easy it had been to fall back into all the old patterns. Instincts he'd long thought dormant had sprung to life fully alert, skills he'd hoped he'd forgotten had come back effortlessly.

Because of Lucas.

And now Lucas had her. Had his Meggie. And he had to get her back....

Chapter 1

First, there was the darkness.

Thick and silent, it pressed down on her like a shroud as she drifted in and out of consciousness. And Megan started to wonder, in an idle, don't-really-give-a-damn sort of way, if she were dead or if she had merely been buried alive.

She felt heavy and sick and stupid. Her mind had to fight its way through layers of fog as it attempted to make some sense out of what was happening. She was in a small room, lying on a narrow cot under a wool blanket that smelled freshly laundered. For some reason her mind latched onto that fact and clung to it, finding reassurance in the domestic familiarity of it.

Either she'd only imagined the shroudlike darkness, or during one of her lapses into unconsciousness someone had turned on the light. The bare bulb shone bravely, if ineffectually, from the center of the ceiling, casting more shadow than illumination.

But it was enough to show Megan that she was in a storeroom of some kind. Metal shelving units along the walls were crammed with crusted paint cans, gardening tools, ancient flower pots, a pair of scuffed ice skates, and two big cardboard boxes with Xmas Ornaments scrawled on them in black felt marker.

And she wasn't alone.

There was a man there, sitting on a straight-backed chair beside the closed door. He'd tipped the chair back on two legs so it was leaning against the wall and he leafed through a magazine with the air of someone who would have preferred being somewhere else. He glanced up just then and gave a grunt when his gaze met Megan's. The front legs of the chair came down with a bang and he tossed the magazine aside and got to his feet, stretching and yawning. Then he opened the door and vanished through it, pulling it closed behind him.

The lock clicked, overly loud in the silence. Megan simply lay there staring at the closed door, knowing she should be battering at the thing with her fists and screaming at the top of her lungs. But her throat was too sore for screaming and she was so groggy that even sitting up took a lot of effort.

She managed it finally, but was so dazed and sick that she didn't even hear the door open, and it wasn't until a steaming mug appeared in front of her that she realized someone had come in. She looked up slowly.

He was tall and very thin, every feature standing out in relief in the harsh overhead lighting. He was dressed entirely in black, the effect only emphasizing the waxlike pallor of his skin. Even his eyes were black, small bright bits of glass in a pale, pitted face. "How do you feel?"

Megan closed her eyes and shook her head, swallowing. Her head was still swimming, but it was her stomach that demanded her attention, threatening to rebel momentarily.

"They tell me a bit of nausea when you first regain consciousness is normal." His voice was deep and resonant, almost reassuring. "We had to keep you drugged for hours—we couldn't take a chance on your waking up during the

flight and causing trouble.'' He draped the blanket around
her shoulders like a parent protecting his child from a chill,
then pressed the mug into one of her hands. ''Drink this. It
will help.''

Megan stared at the steaming liquid numbly. There was a
tiny clear voice way in the back of her mind that was shouting at her impatiently, telling her to toss the mug aside angrily and start demanding explanations, to insist they release
her immediately and take her home. But she felt too sick to
do more than simply sit there watching the steam rise.
Slowly, his words sank through the fog cluttering her mind.
Flight. He'd said something about a...

''Flight?'' Her throat was so raw her voice was no more
than a croak. She coughed raggedly.

''Drink.'' He gave her hand a nudge and Megan meekly
lifted the mug to her mouth and took a sip of the hot liquid. It tasted faintly medicinal. ''We're in the State of
Washington. A hundred and fifty miles from Seattle, in the
mountains. The only reason I'm telling you that, is to fore-
stall any ideas you might have about trying to escape. Even
if you did manage to get past my people, which is unlikely,
there's nothing out there but wilderness and snow. Nothing
at all.''

It made no more or less sense than anything else had. She
took another sip of the liquid, gratified to realize it was, as
promised, settling her unruly stomach. Her head seemed
clearer and she dared lift it after a moment, relieved when
the room didn't start spinning. ''Who are you?'' Her voice
sounded childlike, almost petulant even to herself. She took
a deep breath to still the waver in it. ''Why did you bring me
here? What do you want?''

He chuckled. ''I'm sure you've figured that out on your
own by now, Miss Kirkwood. We—'' He stopped as the
door swung inward.

A man looked in. ''Sorry, sir. But Curry called and said
there's a problem.''

"Problem?" The word was softly spoken, but the voice vibrated with authority.

"The inbound carrier vessel had engine trouble and reached Vancouver five hours behind schedule.

"So our courier hasn't arrived with the merchandise."

"No, sir. He left Vancouver an hour ago. And Curry indicated that the contacts at this end are uneasy."

"Uneasy."

"That was his word, sir, yes."

The fox-faced man breathed a mild oath, frowning as he looked thoughtfully down at Megan. "All right. Get them on the phone—I'll talk with them. What's ETA for our courier?"

"Nineteen hundred hours, sir."

"And he had no difficulty at the border?"

"No, sir. Our man was on duty, as planned. The courier identified himself and the shipment was brought through without a hitch."

"Good." The fox-faced man paused at the door and turned to look at Megan. "I won't be long, Miss Kirkwood. I suggest you lie down and rest. There's a bathroom behind you with everything you should need—feel free to take a shower if it will make you feel better. The bathroom door latches but doesn't lock, for obvious reasons, but no one will disturb you. And if you continue feeling ill, just call out. There'll be someone stationed outside."

Megan started to say "thank you" from habit, but swallowed the words before they were out. She sat there for a long while after he'd left, taking an occasional sip from the mug without really thinking about it. Her mind, free now from the dizzy residue of drugs, found itself in an even deeper tangle of confusion.

They'd gone to a good deal of trouble to bring her here. They'd kidnapped her out of her little Des Moines accounting office, had carted her halfway across the country—all of which indicated someone thought she was pretty important.

Except that she wasn't.

Megan drew in a deep breath. In fact, Megan Kirkwood wasn't anybody at all. She worked for a very mundane accounting firm in downtown Des Moines that handled nothing more exciting than tax records and a handful of local business accounts. The most interesting account *she* handled was Albertson's Mortuary and there certainly wasn't anything about it, or any of her other accounts, to warrant getting kidnapped.

She had no other information anyone could want, either. After all, she never went anywhere, never did anything. For nearly five years, she'd been too busy caring for her mother to do much else, and after her mother's death two years ago, she'd spent her days taking care of the small house and concentrating on her work. She had a few friends, people she'd grown up with mainly, but they were becoming fewer as they married and had children or moved away.

There was no family fortune she could be bartered for, even if there was someone left to do the bartering. Her father had died when she was barely fourteen, leaving his wife and two daughters comfortably but hardly lavishly provided for. And her sister, Peggy, had been killed in a car accident seven years ago.

There was nothing—absolutely *nothing*—that she knew or had that anyone could want.

Unless...

Megan frowned. No, it couldn't be that. It had happened about a year ago. The dream vacation she'd given herself on her twenty-seventh birthday, the man she'd met...

Megan caught the thought before it went any further. The pain and shame the remembering always brought washed over her but she ignored it. This was no time to let herself wallow in self-pity and recriminations. God knows, she'd done enough wallowing over the past eleven-and-a-half months to last a lifetime. Not only was it over and done with, but she had more urgent things to concern her right now than having made a complete fool of herself over a man she'd hardly known and would never seen again.

Married, a sly little voice whispered from the shadows of her mind. It sounded like her mother's voice. *You didn't just make a fool of yourself, Megan Kirkwood, you married him. A man you didn't even know. A man who walked out on you the day after the wedding.* Megan squeezed her eyes shut, trying not to listen. But the voice wouldn't be silenced that easily. *Not that you should be surprised. What was surprising is that you actually believed a man like that could love you—you, dreary little brown mouse Megan. If it had been Pretty Peggy, he'd have stayed. Pretty Peggy never had a man walk out on her. . . .*

This time Megan did manage to silence the voice. She slammed her mind down across it brutally, refusing to listen. Her cheeks felt hot and flushed and her knuckles were white where she was gripping the mug. For a moment or two, her anger at the memories forced away the fear. But then it was back, raw and rancid, and she looked around her small prison with a shiver.

Then she drew in another deep breath. The odd-flavoured brew the man had brought her had done its job. Her head had cleared miraculously and her stomach no longer heaved rebelliously every time she moved. Feeling stronger—and braver—she got to her feet and explored her small cell block. Not that there was much to explore. There were no windows or other doors, and the bathroom was little more than a closet.

But the water was hot, and they'd thoughtfully supplied her with soap and clean towels. She washed her face, splashing cold water on her cheeks and eyes to clear away the last of the cobwebs, and when she was finished she paused to look at the pale, wide-eyed woman in the mottled mirror above the sink.

She and mirrors had never been close companions. She'd avoided them whenever she could when she'd been growing up, hating what she saw when she did catch an unexpected, unwanted glimpse of herself. She was pure Kirkwood: mud-brown hair, dark eyes, olive complexion. Not like Peggy. Pretty Peggy, everyone had called her. Flaxen-haired, with eyes the color of delft china, she'd been a throwback to some earlier strain of the family that hadn't been seen in nearly three generations.

Why her, Megan found herself thinking suddenly. Why couldn't I have been born tall and blonde and beautiful? This nightmare wouldn't have happened to Pretty Peggy. Bad things never did.

It was one of those bizarre thoughts that sometimes hit her out of the blue, always managing to take her by surprise. She frowned, giving her head a shake, and turned to leave, carefully avoiding her own eyes in the mirror.

The fox-faced man was waiting for her. There was something in his calculating gaze that frightened Megan and she stood with her back against the wall, arms crossed tightly.

He smiled very faintly and nodded toward the cot. "Please sit down. Are you feeling better?"

"What do you want with me?" Her voice was hoarse and Megan wondered if he could hear the terror in it, could hear the pounding of her heart. Her mouth tasted dry and coppery, and she swallowed. "Why am I here? Who are you?"

He stared at her for an assessing moment or two, eyes narrowed. "I've been wondering, purely as an intellectual exercise, how you were going to play this. Indignation or tears were the obvious choices. And I'll admit I was expecting tears."

It was so preposterous that Megan very nearly laughed. But she knew the laughter was too near hysteria to be trusted, and the tears he seemed to want were too close behind *that*. And for some reason, it suddenly seemed very important not to give him the satisfaction. Control, she reminded herself desperately. Her very life could depend on how well she controlled herself.

"You were, I presume, working with him right from the beginning. How we missed the obvious, I'll never know. But it was only after we'd tracked him to Des Moines on one of his visits that we figured out how he'd gotten back into the country without one of our people knowing about it. It was brilliant—as the simplest things usually are. And it would have worked. If he'd stayed to the shadows as he'd been trained—as *I* trained him—he could have eluded us for another year."

"I don't know what you're talking about," Megan whispered. "You've obviously mistaken me for—"

"Oh, I have the right person," he said with a chuckle. It was a cold sound, like water running over stone. "Megan Kirkwood, twenty-seven, an accountant employed by the firm of Abington, Cambie and Finch of Des Moines, Iowa." He paused, as though letting it sink in. "Your real name, of course, is Megan Welles. And you're Taggart Welles's wife."

"Taggart Welles?" she echoed stupidly. She searched her mind frantically for some clue as to what he was talking about, repeated the name a dozen times, hoping it would jar some half-forgotten memory loose.

Nothing. Until now she'd managed to hold her fear to a manageable level, convincing herself that the mistake would be discovered and that she'd be set free. But simple fear was threatening to explode into full-blown panic at any instant and she struggled to hold it in check, telling herself that logic and cool reason would accomplish more than hysteria.

She realized that his frown had deepened, as though her silence annoyed him. "Megan," he said with chilling patience, "I haven't the time to play games. I want Welles. You'll tell me where he is, sooner or later, so why not do us both a favor and tell me now? It would save a lot of unpleasantness."

Unpleasantness. The way he said it made Megan go cold. She swallowed, fighting panic. "But you've got to believe me! I don't know any Taggart Welles! I—"

"We know all about it," he interrupted impatiently. "How he met the tour in Singapore, using the name Michael Walker. How he slipped through our surveillance in Hawaii, how—''

But Megan wasn't listening anymore. All she could hear, echoing through her mind, was the name. *Michael Walker*.

The room started to tilt suddenly and she closed her eyes, put her hand out blindly to steady herself as the nightmare rose without warning. She fought it off and opened her eyes again, finding the stranger watching her emotionlessly.

"He . . . he left me." It was her voice, but so thin and distant that Megan scarcely recognized it. "The day we docked in Honolulu. He said he was going to get our luggage, but he...never came back." She hadn't said the words aloud in nearly a year, living silently with her shame and pain. No one knew. Not one person aside from a handful of uninterested Hawaiian police knew the humiliating secret she'd been hiding. "I have no idea where he is. . . ." Or even who he is, she added to herself, numbed. Taggart Welles. So that was his real name.

"Megan, Megan," the man sighed with what sounded like honest disappointment. "It was a clever twist, his disappearing like that to protect you. And it might have worked, too, if he'd resisted the temptation to see you."

"See me?" The words were a whisper, filled with confusion.

The tall stranger smiled humorlessly. "We've had you under surveillance from the moment we traced Welles to that cruise ship. I'll admit I wasn't expecting much—the two of you were playing it *very* close to the vest." There was a note of admiration in the cool voice. "So close, in fact, that when four months had gone by and Welles hadn't made contact with you, even *I* was starting to believe that desertion story you'd told the Honolulu police. But I'm a patient man. Welles should have remembered that. I left the surveillance team in place and they finally spotted him coming out of your house in late June, but by the time they realized what was happening, he was gone. He's been back since, but he managed to get in and out without my men even touching him.''

Again, there was a flash of that humorless smile, a hint of admiration. ''He's good, Megan. One of the best. But even the best have their weaknesses—and you're obviously his. In the end, he just couldn't stay away, could he?'' The smile faded, leaving his mouth thin and hard. ''That's why government agents should *never* get involved. Nothing messes up a good agent's concentration like a woman.''

It was like being caught on a merry-go-round gone mad, whirling faster and faster until the world was just a blur. Megan felt herself start to slip, put her hand out and caught the back of a wooden chair, clung to it desperately to keep from being flung off into the darkness. ''Agent?'' Her voice cracked.

The stranger's eyes held hers speculatively. ''One of the best, until he switched sides. Did he tell you what happened to send him running, Megan? Did he tell you about the three operatives he double-crossed and had killed? Did he explain that every agency in existence is hunting him? The DEA, FBI, CIA—you name it, they're after him. When he set those three operatives up, he signed his own death warrant.''

''I don't know what you're talking about,'' Megan said in a low voice. ''Are *you* with the CIA?''

His smile was filled with small, sharp teeth, making his narrow face even more fox-like. ''Something along those lines.''

''Then you must know I'm not—''

''Frankly, Miss Kirkwood, it's irrelevant to me how you fit into his plans. It's him I want, not you. If you know where he is, you'll tell me. But even if you don't know where I can find him, it doesn't matter. The mere fact that I have you will flush him out. Either way, I'll get him.''

Megan shook her head slowly, fear starting to trickle through the shock as she realized he didn't understand. Or simply didn't believe her. ''It won't work,'' she whispered.

"He won't come. Not for me. He doesn't care anything about me. I was just handy, that's all. Just someone he used."

The man gave a snort of quiet laughter. "He risked his life a number of times over the past eleven months to see you, Megan. That doesn't sound like a man who doesn't care, does it?"

"But he didn't! Whoever told you that was wrong, because—" She was interrupted by a soft tap at the door.

It opened, revealing the same man who had interrupted them before. "Sir, I'm sorry to intrude, but Curry's on the phone. The buyers are getting increasingly nervous at the delay, and—"

The fox-faced man whispered an oath, then nodded abruptly. "Have Jacoby fire up the chopper, and advise Curry I'll be there in thirty minutes."

"Yes, sir." The man's gaze drifted to Megan. "And her, sir? What if he turns up before you get back?"

"You know my orders. Kill him only as a last resort—I want to know where those damned files are, and if he's dead we'll never find them. Double the security patrols. And don't take any chances, Hanson. If he slips past you again, you may as well put a bullet through your own head and save me the trouble."

"Yes, sir." The man vanished.

The fox-faced man looked around at Megan. His narrowed eyes glittered malignantly. "I *will* get him, Megan. Taggart Welles is mine." Then he, too, left.

"I don't understand," Megan whispered to the closing door. "I don't understand...." Then she lay down on the cot and closed her eyes.

He had the greenest eyes she'd ever seen in her life.

That had been the first thing that she'd noticed about him, that his eyes were the color of polished jade. They'd been filled with warmth and amusement and gentle laughter that first afternoon when Janie Rodgers had brought him over and introduced him, and they'd crinkled slightly at the outer corners as he'd smiled down at her.

That had been the second thing she'd noticed, that lazy, off-center smile, canted higher on the right side than the left. He had a crooked tooth there, one overlapping the next just slightly, and she found herself liking him all the more in that instant for the imperfection.

He was smiling now. And even from right across the stateroom the expression in those eyes made her blush.

And, as it always did, her shyness made him laugh.

It was an easy laugh, as lazy and relaxed as the man himself. Like the cat-green eyes and lopsided smile, his laugh was just one of the many things she loved about him. The way he moved was another. He was as fluid as a shadow, light on his feet, and silent as a ghost. It had disconcerted her at first, how he could be here one moment and there the next without so much as a breath of disturbed air to betray his going. Sometimes, in the darkness, he melted so completely into it that it was as though he'd never existed, and she'd find herself holding her breath, suddenly terrified she'd only imagined him. Then he'd materialize beside her, tall and reassuringly solid, chuckling quietly as he slipped his arm around her or kissed the side of her throat, and she'd laugh at her silly fears.

Because he *was* real. And he was hers.

Megan found herself smiling as she watched him slip off his dinner jacket and hang it up. She never tired of watching him. Even though she'd memorized every tiny detail of him, right down to the small, uneven scar under his left eye where a piece of flying glass had nicked him in a car accident when he was sixteen, she still found it impossible to keep her eyes off him.

It would be hard not to, she reminded herself, even if she weren't so hopelessly in love with him. It was little wonder Janie Rodgers had spotted him among the throngs of people in that dockside market in Singapore. He was the type of man who caught women's eyes wherever he went, and

Janie, Megan had discovered very early in the cruise, had a sixth sense where single men were concerned that was positively spooky.

Janie had adopted Megan on the third day of the six-week South Seas cruise, and within minutes had made plain her intent to find Megan a man. "You said this cruise is your dream of a lifetime," she'd said, "which means—if you're to do it properly—you need a passionate love affair. You don't have to take him home with you," she'd added in response to Megan's protests.

"And stop looking so scandalized! I may be seventy-three, but I'm hardly fossilized. I'm not suggesting you sleep with the entire crew or pick up a different man at every port we hit, though heaven knows I've know women who have. I'm simply saying that you need at least *one* good fling. And if *you* won't put some effort into looking for a suitable man, I *will*!"

It had taken two weeks for Janie to make good her threat. Although it certainly hadn't been for lack of trying. She'd trolled each port of call for eligible bachelors like a cruising barracuda, and Megan gave a sigh of relief each time their ship, the *Paradise Orchid*, lifted anchor and headed back out to sea.

Then they'd reached Singapore. They were there for three days, and an hour before the *Orchid* left port, Janie had disappeared into the crowd in the market with an exclamation of discovery. Megan hadn't paid a lot of attention, thinking the older woman had spotted a bargain in Malay batik or Thai silk. Until she'd appeared minutes later with what was probably the most ruggedly handsome man Megan had ever seen in her life. A man her sister would have called a "real hunk".

He was a scant inch under six feet, wide-shouldered and slim-hipped. The shantung silk suit he was wearing fit too well to be anything but custom-tailored, and he had a smile that Megan knew instinctively could be lethal under the right circumstances. His name was Michael Walker, Janie said

with a Cheshire-cat smile, and he was joining their cruise.
Business had kept him from leaving from Honolulu with the
rest of them, so he'd decided to pick it up in Singapore. *And
he's all yours,* her smile told Megan.

He had wavy hair the exact shade of ripe chestnuts and it
had glowed like fire in the hot Singapore sun as he'd smiled
down at her. She'd smiled back politely, knowing from experience that in spite of Janie's best-laid scheme, Michael
Walker was not going to spend the rest of his vacation with
a tongue-tied little accountant from Des Moines. He was
Peggy's kind of man, not hers. The type of man who usually didn't even notice her, he was so busy watching Peggy.

But Peggy wasn't here. Peggy was dead.

There was just her, and a tall, green-eyed man who, when
he smiled down at her as he was doing now, made her feel
as though she were the most beautiful woman on earth.

Three-and-a-half weeks later, they were married.

Megan glanced down at her left hand again, gazing in
wonder at the gold band encircling her finger. As she'd done
a dozen times that day, she ran her fingers across it, marveling at the dull, rich gleam, the intricate Malay carving. It
had been there all of three hours and it still took her breath
away when she looked at it.

"You're going to wear it out," a soft, laughing voice
murmured above her. "You keep rubbing it as though
you're expecting a genie to leap out and give you three
wishes."

"He could give me three hundred and there's not a thing
I could want that I don't already have." Megan looked up,
her heart giving that familiar little leap as his gaze met hers.
His eyes were warm and gentle and they seemed to draw her
into their sheltering depths. "I'm still having trouble believing it's real. That you're real. That I've been so lucky..."

"I'm the lucky one, Meggie," he said gently. He cupped
her face in his palm, caressing her cheekbone with his thumb
almost absently as he gazed down at her. A frown tugged his

brows together and his eyes held an odd expression, half bleak despair, half wistfulness.

She'd seen that look before sometimes, when she would turn unexpectedly and catch him watching her. That and something she had only just started to realize was deep, gnawing worry. The look appeared more and more often lately, and the nearer they got to Honolulu the more impervious it became to even her best efforts to dislodge it for longer than a few minutes at a time. Once or twice she'd been on the verge of asking him about it, but at the last instant she'd always hesitated that moment too long, sensing he wasn't quite ready to talk about what was worrying him.

Trust, that's what it all came down to. She had to trust him in the same way he was trusting her—heaven knows, there were things about herself she hadn't talked about yet. After all, they'd just met three weeks ago. And they had the rest of their lives to sort through all the secrets of the past.

"You're a very special woman, Meggie," he murmured, his gaze caressing her face feature by feature. "You have some sort of magical aura that makes a man feel safe and whole and alive when he's near you. As though anything is possible...."

Megan reached up and touched his cheek. "I love you," she whispered, wanting more than anything to ease the worry in those dark green eyes. But instead of easing it, her words had almost the opposite effect. Something she could have sworn was pain flickered across his face and he opened his mouth as though to say something, his narrowed eyes riveted to hers.

Megan felt a sudden unease run through her, but before she could ask him what was wrong he gave a rough, sudden oath and pulled her into his arms. "I know," he growled, voice ragged with some emotion she could only guess at. "Damn it, Meggie, I know you do! I just hope I don't wind up breaking your heart, angel."

"Don't be ridiculous," Megan told him with a soft laugh. "You've made me the happiest woman on earth. How could you possibly break my heart?"

He didn't say anything, just tightened his embrace even more, his breath stirring her hair. She rested her cheek in the hollow of his throat, feeling the strong, regular throb of his pulse and breathing in the warm, musky scent of him.

That was just one of the many delights she'd discovered in the past three weeks, that earthy scent of warm, male skin. She'd never dreamed anything could be so subtly erotic. That, and the texture of wind-tangled hair between her fingers, the sandpapery feel of his cheeks against hers, the taste of him when he kissed her in that slow, deep way that always made her feel drugged and faint.

"Things happen sometimes, Meg. People get hurt...." He drew in a deep breath, as though steeling himself, and eased her away from him so he could look down at her. The frown was still lodged between his brows, deeper than ever. "Damn it, Meg, I—" He stopped, gave his head a shake. "There's so much about me you don't know."

"There's a lot about me that *you* don't know," she teased gently. She reached up and rubbed the frown with her fingertips, ignoring the little shiver of apprehension his words sent through her. "Michael, I love you. I know a lot of people would say I'm crazy, marrying a man I met on a cruise ship barely three weeks ago, a man I know nothing about. But I know how I feel about you. And I trust those feelings."

And if her feelings were wrong? The question hung between them as clearly as if she'd spoken it aloud. She knew he was thinking the same thing, felt that tingle of fear dart through her again, refused to acknowledge it.

"Please, Michael," she whispered, almost pleading. "We're docking in Honolulu tomorrow night. Until then, let's just pretend the rest of the world doesn't exist. Let's not spoil the magic until we're back in the real world again, please? After we're home, you can tell me what's been bothering you and we can deal with it then.''

"Meggie..." It was almost a warning, growled under his breath. Then he slipped his arms tightly around her again.

The fear was back, a hard, cold knot in her stomach, but Megan took a deep breath and forced her mind away from all the horrors it was conjuring up. "I love you, remember?" she said calmly. "Whatever it is, it can't be so bad we can't work through it together. Not if we love each other."

"I want you to promise me something, Meggie." He rested his cheek against her hair, arms tightening. "Promise me that if things go wrong you won't hate me too much."

"Hate you?" Megan pulled back to look up at him in astonishment. But the man looking down at her wasn't Michael. For a moment it was someone else standing there, someone tall and dangerous, and the eyes looking down at her were the eyes of a stranger. There was a glint of something in their green depths that chilled her to the bone. "Michael, you're scaring me to death!" She tried to laugh but it came out a gasp. "What on earth are you talking—"

"Promise me, damn it!" He gave her a shake. "Promise me that much, Meggie. Please."

Megan swallowed, feeling as though she were balanced at the edge of some nightmare that could rear up at any moment and swallow her alive. But suddenly she didn't want to know, didn't want to hear whatever it was that could put that look on a man's face. "I promise," she whispered.

He stared down at her as though only half believing she meant it. Then, suddenly, all the tension left him and he gave an abrupt, rough laugh and pulled her into his arms again. "I'm sorry, Meggie—I didn't mean to frighten you. It's just that...so many things can go wrong."

"I love you," she whispered again, saying the words as one might an incantation to ward off whatever evil was out there, lurking. "Nothing will ever change that. *Nothing!*"

Megan awoke with a start, still tangled in the last shreds of her nightmare. It took her a disoriented moment or two to remember where she was. Then, remembering, she sat up slowly and pulled the blanket tightly around her, trying to stop the shivers.

As nightmares went, it hadn't been as bad as most. At least she hadn't wakened crying. She usually did when one of the bad dreams sneaked up on her like that. Sometimes it was Michael waiting to ambush her in her sleep, sometimes it was Peggy or her mother. Or both. And once all three of them had been there, Michael, Peggy and her mother in a circle around her, all smiling their sly, mocking smiles, reminding her what a fool she'd been to ever think he could have loved *her*.

She caught the direction of her thoughts and stopped them in time, wondering how long she'd been asleep. She started to pull her jacket sleeve back to look at her watch before remembering she'd taken it off and put it beside her desk calendar. It would still be there, between the plastic palm tree Adam Cambie had brought her from Tahiti a few months ago and the tiny wooden shoe he'd brought her from Amsterdam last year.

It would still be there on Monday when she didn't come in to work. Beside the half-completed ledger sheets from Johansen's Ice Cream Parlor, the ones she'd been working on when—

Megan shivered suddenly, trying not to think of the two black-clad forms that had appeared in her office. They'd been experts, each knowing exactly what to do, not a motion or word wasted between them. Whoever these people were, they knew exactly what they were doing. And why.

Megan drew in a deep breath, letting the name ease itself into her mind: Michael Walker.

The man she'd loved. The man she'd married.

The man who didn't exist.

She blinked at the sudden unexpected bite of tears and pulled the blanket tighter, throat aching. Damn it, it wasn't fair! She'd spent eleven-and-a-half long months getting him out of her mind and heart. Eleven-and-a-half months of shame and misery. And now, when she was finally starting to heal, when she was finally at the point where she could go entire days without thinking even once of him or what he'd done—*now* he was back in her life again as dramatically as he'd left it.

They'd docked in Honolulu the day after she and Michael had been married. The cruise dock had been a madhouse of milling people, and Michael had gone to find a cab and get their luggage organized. She could still remember the way he'd paused halfway down the gangway to turn and grin up at her, the breeze ruffling his hair. Could still feel the way her heart had done one of those foolish double cartwheels when his eyes had caught and held hers. He'd turned and had made his way down into the throng of people on the dock, the sun glinting off his hair. Then he'd vanished into the crowd.

She had never seen him again.

The police had at first been helpful and sympathetic. But as the days had gone by, their calls had become fewer, their sympathy more strained. Then, finally, they'd sent someone around to her small hotel to tell her they were closing the case.

Because Michael Walker, they'd told her, didn't exist. He had appeared out of nowhere in Singapore to join the cruise, then had ceased to exist just as abruptly in Honolulu. They had contacted the FBI, who had sent someone around to talk with her. And in the end, it had been this man who had urged her to get on with her life.

"Whoever this guy is," he'd told her dispassionately, "he's on someone's most-wanted list—maybe even ours. He needed to get into the States undetected, and what better disguise than as a man returning from his honeymoon cruise?"

Megan had denied it. He'd smiled pityingly, his eyes taking in her tangled, mouse-brown hair, her small, pale face, her eyes red-rimmed from crying, and it hadn't taken much imagination to know what he was thinking.

She'd tried her best to convince herself that he had it all wrong. She'd stayed in Honolulu for another ten days, walking up and down streets that all looked the same, eyes searching the crowds for a flash of auburn hair, a familiar set of broad shoulders. Hoping against hope that she'd look up and see him coming toward her, smiling that wayward, lopsided smile, his eyes glowing with the love she'd once imagined had been there. But in the end she'd known it was no use. And finally she'd used the last of her money to buy a one-way ticket back to Des Moines, knowing she'd never see the tall, green-eyed stranger called Michael Walker again.

It had taken eleven-and-a-half months, but she'd finally gotten over the worst of it, had started picking up the pieces of her life again.

And now . . . this.

Damn it, what had he gotten her into? Megan shivered violently, feeling hot tendrils of anger work their way up through the layers of confusion and fear. She welcomed them, relished them, knowing almost instinctively that if she gave in to the terror she was finished.

There was a loud, metallic click that startled her, and the door swung inward. It was the fox-faced man again, only this time he brought someone else in with him, an older man with wire-rimmed glasses and an air of brisk competence.

"Well, Megan?" The fox-faced man smiled down at her, a friendly smile that showed his teeth. "It's time we talked."

"I don't know where Taggart Welles is," Megan said with quiet emphasis. She stared up at the two of them almost defiantly, clinging to the anger, taking strength from it. "I already told you that he walked out on me in Honolulu and I haven't seen him or corresponded with him since. If someone thinks they saw him in Des Moines, they're mistaken. He used me to get back into the States, that's all. There's no reason for him to contact me. No reason at all."

She lifted her chin, refusing to admit the hurt that last admission brought her.

It seemed to amuse the fox-faced man. He smiled slightly and eased himself into the folding chair. "I'd really hoped you were going to cooperate, Megan. But love always complicates things. If you didn't love him, you wouldn't have this heroic urge to protect him. Ordinarily, I'm a great admirer of heroics, but in this situation they're doing nothing but wasting time I don't have."

"I don't love Taggart Welles," she replied with quiet venom. "Believe me, if I knew where he is I would have told you by now. Nothing you could do to him can even come close to what I'd like to do to him myself."

He smiled tolerantly, then nodded to the other man. It was only then that Megan realized the second man was carrying a small metal tray. He set it on the end of the cot and Megan stared at it, feeling reason start to slip. There were two hypodermics on it, unprotected needles gleaming, a handful of small glass vials filled with pale amber liquid, and two or three cotton balls. He picked up a vial and snapped the end off it expertly, then reached for one of the hypodermics.

And that's when she started to scream.

Chapter 2

For some reason, she kept dreaming about dragons.

Black, coiled dragons, with small, clawed feet, reaching for her. And glinting green eyes. Eyes like emeralds...

She thought of other things too. Silly things, disjointed memories drifting in and out. At times her world almost made sense and she'd find herself eating without feeling hungry, half-aware of others in the shadows, watching. But then it would all fade out, dreamlike, and there would be voices, whispering, the sound of a woman's weeping, and, once or twice, a man's voice raised in impatience. She felt as if she were adrift in fog and through it all the only thing that made any sense, the only thing solid enough to cling to, was the memory of a tall, green-eyed man who, for some reason she couldn't quite remember, it seemed very important to hate.

Then, gradually, the mists started to recede. And finally she awoke one day remembering who she was and why she was there.

So. It hadn't been a dream after all. Megan glanced around the room dispassionately, surprised to realize she wasn't even afraid any more. Maybe there was a limit to how much fear the human mind could comprehend. Or maybe she just didn't care any more.

She sat up, wincing slightly at the dull throb in her head. The sleeves of her wrinkled, once-white blouse had been rolled up and she looked down at the vivid bruising on the inside of her left elbow. The puncture marks were red against the purplish discoloration, and she touched them curiously with a fingertip.

So that part of it hadn't been a dream, either. They'd used drugs, trying to get her to tell them something she didn't even know. Heaven knows what sort of idiocies she'd babbled in reply to their questions, but it couldn't have been what they'd wanted.

So now what?

She didn't want to even think about that yet. One thing at a time.

It was only when she stood up and made her way into the bathroom that Megan realized how weak her legs were. How long had she been lying there, she wondered with a little shiver, drugged and raving? Hours? Days? She rinsed her face with cool water, suddenly annoyed at how easily they had stolen those hours from her. They'd gone rummaging through her memories like burglars ransacking a summer cottage, pawing through everything that was personal. She felt dirtied somehow, as though the sanctity of her innermost thoughts had been left smudged with careless fingerprints, the drawers and cupboards of her mind left ajar.

Damn it, enough was enough! CIA or not, they didn't have the right to put her through this just because Taggart Welles had played them all for fools for the past year.

She was still seething with anger as she left the bathroom. Her prison was still silent and empty and she stood in the middle of it for a moment or two, looking around. "I've had enough of this!" She blinked as her voice reverberated through the small room. A loud, strong voice, nothing at all like her usual half whisper. It rang with anger and impatience and—yes—even authority.

She took a deep breath. "I want out, do you hear me?" It was even louder this time, the kind of voice that demanded—and got—immediate attention. To back it up, she picked up the folding chair and flung it forcefully against the door. "I want out of here!"

To her surprise, it worked. There was a flurry of running footsteps outside, a growl of querulous profanity, then the rattle of a key in the lock. It swung open and the man called Hanson stepped into the room. "What the hell do you want?"

"I *want* an explanation of what is going on here," she said with as much imperiousness as she could muster. "And I *want* out of here. Now!" Her forcefulness seemed to take him by surprise, and Megan pounced at what might be an advantage. She took two strides toward him, hands planted firmly on her hips. "I want to talk with whoever's in charge of this operation."

But her outburst didn't have much effect, beyond making him smile faintly. "He had to leave. But when he gets back, I'll pass on your message. Now why don't you lie down like a good girl and keep quiet?"

Megan's cheeks flushed with anger. "No, I will *not* lie down and be quiet like a good girl," she snapped. "I don't know who you people think you—" She stopped dead, mouth still half-open, and stared at the revolver that had appeared in his hand.

"Honey," he said calmly, "don't give me a hard time. I'm handling things until the man in charge gets back, and I don't want any more shouting or chair-throwing, got it? I don't know what tricks of the trade Welles taught you, but forget about trying them on me—I've forgotten more martial arts than you could possibly know." He smiled pleasantly. "Annoy me too much, and I'll kill you. Understand?"

There was something in his eyes that chilled Megan right to the bone, and it took all her willpower to stand there, face-to-face with him. "You won't kill me." She forced herself to say it, forced herself to believe it. "He needs me, remember?"

His smile was still pleasant. "We've got your husband." He paused, as though giving her time to think about it. "He's damned good, I'll give him that much. Got to within a hundred feet of the place before he tripped a sensor." His smile was cold now. "So you see, Mrs. Welles, we don't need you anymore."

Megan felt herself grow cold and still. "Don't call me that," she whispered.

Still smiling that faintly mocking smile, he pulled the door gently closed and locked it, leaving her alone once again. Slowly, hardly aware of what she was doing, Megan walked back to the cot, her mind trying to take in the enormity of what he'd just said.

They had him. They had Michael.

Taggart, she had to call him now. Taggart Welles.

Liar. Double agent. Killer.

Husband.

The word seemed to mock her. *For better or for worse,* she'd promised. *To love and cherish and honor, till death do us part.*

They had him, and they were going to kill him.

The thought made her heart give a little twist, as though some small, treacherous part of her still gave a damn. It didn't seem possible, after what he'd done to her. And yet...

Megan's knees suddenly gave way and she sat down on the cot with a thump. She took a deep breath, feeling very shaky. They weren't just going to kill Taggart Welles, she realized very calmly. They were going to kill her, too.

The thought was bright with urgency, and she was on her feet in the next instant, heart hammering at her ribs. What in heaven's name had ever made her think these people were CIA—or any other legitimate government agency! They were whatever Taggart Welles was, denizens of some shadowy, never-never land of cold-eyed killers and men without names. And they were going to kill her with as little conscience or hesitation as Welles had had when he abandoned her.

And no one would even miss her. The few people in Des Moines who knew her would just presume she'd done something silly like running off on another cruise. When she didn't return, they'd shrug and agree that it was strange, all right, but she always *had* been the quiet, private one. In a few years the family lawyer would tidy up the few loose ends she'd left behind, and she'd be forgotten. Just one small, unimportant mystery no one really cared about.

She had to escape.

She walked to the door and stood there, listening intently. There was nothing but silence, but she had the distinct feeling that someone was just on the other side, relaxed perhaps, but still on guard. And dangerous.

She took a deep breath, glancing around the room again. But slowly this time, her accountant's mind calculating and assessing, instinctively noting pluses and minuses. The door was out, unless she could distract whoever was on guard. In the movies this part was never a problem. She'd rig up some sort of explosive device and blow the door into kindling, stunning the guard, and in the ensuing confusion she'd slip out, fire up a handy helicopter and fly herself to the nearest police station.

Easy. If you could recognize an explosive device when you saw one. And could rig it together without blowing yourself to bits. And knew anything at all about helicopters.

She gave the bathroom a hasty but thorough search, turning up nothing she hadn't already seen. Back in the main room, she went through the storage boxes as quickly and quietly as she could, but aside from bundles of old Christmas cards and ornaments, tattered schoolbooks and boxes of old toys, there was nothing. She even eased one of the metal shelving units away from the wall to see if it was hiding another door, but all she managed to do was scrape her knuckles on the concrete wall and send a carton of plastic holly spilling across the floor.

She swore under her breath and stuffed it back in the box, praying no one had heard the noise. This wasn't getting her anywhere! There was no way out but straight through that door, past the guard and who knew how many others. And then what? she asked herself bitterly. They weren't going to leave a car out there for her, all warmed up and ready to go!

She was still considering—and rejecting—options when someone unlocked the door and pushed it open. It was Hanson again, looking smugly satisfied about something. He picked up her suit jacket and tossed it to her. "Put this on. We're leaving in a couple of minutes."

"Leaving?" Megan stared at him. "Where?"

"Away from here, that's all you have to know. Come on, come on—I haven't got all day!"

Numbly, Megan started pulling on her jacket, and Hanson gave her an impatient push toward the door. He seemed keyed up and tense, and he grabbed her by the arm and hurried her up the stairs leading to the upper level.

The door at the top opened into a spacious pine-and-brick kitchen. It was flooded with sunshine from a vast expanse of glass at one end that looked out over a panorama of forested hills and snow-topped mountains. Beyond the kitchen was a huge living room filled with overstuffed furniture, thick rugs and heavy pine furniture. Hanson gave Megan a push toward it.

There were two men there, one standing by the fireplace and the other by the big picture window overlooking the spectacular view. The man at the window glanced around when Megan stumbled into the room, then turned his back on her again. But that brief glimpse of his face had been enough.

It was mottled with green-and-brown paint to match the jungle camouflage clothing he was wearing, but it hadn't been that which had made Megan's heart skip a beat. It had been his eyes, as cold and dead as glass. And the heavy rifle cradled tenderly across his chest.

The other man was similarly dressed. There was a vivid bruise across his left cheek and his nose had been bleeding recently. He was still dabbling at it with a handkerchief, looking annoyed and impatient. He glared at Hanson. "I still don't like this! He told us to stay here until he got back."

"We got what we came up here for," Hanson said impatiently. "There's another shipment coming in today and he'll need us at the warehouse."

"He's got ample firepower without us. His *orders* were to stay."

"Until we got Welles." Hanson started pulling on a green army jacket. "Saddle up—and make sure nothing of hers is lying around. Tiger Jack and I will take the two of them down in the chopper. You bring the van."

"I'm telling you this is a big mistake!"

"Jacoby, I call the shots up here, remember? We've completed this part of our objective, now we take care of the rest of it. The sooner this operation is wrapped up, the happier he'll be. He hasn't been able to put a hundred percent into the business end of things for nearly a year and a half because of Welles. With him finally out of the way, things will be back to normal."

"But he wanted to talk to Welles. Find out what—"

"At the warehouse. Khiem's there. We turn Welles over to Khiem for interrogation and when we have what we need, Tiger Jack takes the two of them out in the boat and..." He shrugged. "Now get your gear together and move out."

Jacoby opened his mouth as though to argue, then subsided with an oath and wheeled away, obviously displeased. Ignoring him, Hanson bent over the low coffee table and started gathering up a handful of loose papers. It was all the opening Megan needed. She turned toward the door, intending to make one reckless, desperate lunge for freedom. But she stopped dead, breath catching in her throat, as her eyes met those of the man standing by the window.

He was watching her, his expression curiously anticipatory, the fingers of his left hand idly stroking the barrel of his rifle. There was a predatory watchfulness to him, like a cat poised to spring, and Megan realized with sickening certainty that he *wanted* her to run.

"Behave yourself, Mrs. Welles, or I'll give you to Tiger Jack to play with." Hanson sounded amused. "His idea of fun would be to turn you loose and give you a half-hour start before setting out to hunt you down. That's what Tiger Jack likes—the hunt."

"What difference would it make?" Megan asked dully. "You're going to kill me anyway."

He smiled faintly, not even bothering to deny it. "I don't think you'd like the way Tiger Jack plays, honey. Have you ever watched a cat play with a mouse before killing it? Fun for the cat; not so much for the mouse." He gave her a push toward the fireplace. "Want to say goodbye to your husband while there's still time? After Khiem's finished with him, he won't be in any shape to appreciate a farewell kiss from his beloved wife."

It was only then that Megan saw him. He was sprawled between the raised hearth and the end of a big, deep-cushioned sofa, all but hidden in shadow, silent and still.

He was lying on his side, knees drawn up as though to protect his belly, one arm thrown across his face. His jeans were caked with mud and grass stains and, where the denim was ripped across his left thigh, a wetness Megan knew was blood. There was blood on his heavy flannel shirt, too. A lot of it. One sleeve had been all but torn off and his muscled arm was oozing blood. His shirt gaped where the buttons had been pulled off and Megan could see more livid bruising. She slowly realized from the blood and cuts on his fists that he had put up a terrific fight before being brought down.

She stared at him, feeling the universe start to slowly wheel. It couldn't be Michael, she told herself with immense calm. Michael wouldn't have come after her. So who...?

He groaned and rolled onto his back, drawing one knee up as though in reflex to a jolt of pain. Slowly, he drew his arm back from his face, wincing. He had a good mouth, even through the blood and swelling, and Megan found herself staring at him, taking in the firm, square chin, scraped now and badly bruised, the hard-hewn cheekbones. He opened his eyes, squinting slightly, and gazed up at Megan through a haze of suspicion and pain.

He had eyes of pale golden-brown, not the emerald green of Michael's. Nor was his thick, sweat-tangled hair the deep auburn she'd half expected, half dreaded. The stranger's hair was as pale brown as his eyes, streaked with blood from a gash on his forehead.

It had probably been that blow that had brought him down, she found herself speculating. It was deep cut, already swelling badly, and she wondered if he'd been caught by a deliberately aimed boot or a rifle butt. Whichever it had been, it was a wonder it hadn't killed him on the spot.

She drew in an unsteady breath, feeling oddly empty after all the anticipation, and looked around at Hanson in confusion. "Who is he?"

"You can stop pretending now, sweetheart. He may be a little bloodier than the Taggart Welles you married, but he has no one to blame for that but himself. It was crazy, trying to fight the two of them when they had the drop on him."

Megan swallowed. "This might very well be Taggart Welles, but he's not the man I married."

Hanson's eyes narrowed. From the other side of the room, Jacoby turned to look at her. He glanced at Hanson. "You don't think—"

"No," Hanson snapped. "She's just trying to protect him."

"I've never seen this man before," Megan said quietly.

"Damn it, Hanson," Jacoby said, looking worried now, "if there's the slightest chance she's telling the truth, we—"

"My name's Patrick Kirk," the man lying at Megan's feet said, his voice hoarse and strained. He sat up very slowly, wincing, and shook his head gently as though to clear it. "Dr. Kirk. I'm an entomologist . . . Department of Zoology at Washington State. Up here looking for a rare species of *Sempervivum arachnoideum*. I was minding my own business when these two guys came at me with—"

"Shut up," Hanson barked. "Tiger Jack, get him on the chopper."

"And if he ain't Welles?" It was the first time Tiger Jack had spoken, and Megan shivered. His voice was just a whisper, as cold as wind off ice. "We screw up, Hanson, he ain't gonna be happy."

"Tiger Jack's right," Jacoby said with soft urgency. "Odds are it *is* Welles, but I couldn't swear to it. I only met him once in Nam. He joined our team for a special patrol—just the one night. It was pitch black, raining like there was no tomorrow and he was in bush camouflage—hell, I wouldn't have recognized my own grandmother! Can you swear it's him, Hanson?"

Hanson stared down at the man for a long, hostile while, then finally breathed an oath and shook his head. "Who the hell else would it be, prowling around up here this time of year?"

"Perfect time to find *Sempervivum arachnoideum*," the stranger put in painfully. "They're a ground borer—only hatch once every six years when the conditions are right. This spring the—"

"Shut up," Hanson growled irritably.

"Jacoby's right," Tiger Jack said in that hollow death-whisper. His fingers still caressed the rifle, moving slowly on the oiled metal as though it were a woman's flesh. "If it's not Welles—and the *real* Welles turns up while we're taking this guy down..." He left the rest unsaid, his meaning crystal clear.

"It's *got* to be Welles," Hanson said through his teeth.

"You want to take that chance?" Jacoby licked his lips. "You want to explain why we're bringing him some absent-minded bug professor while Welles is still running around loose?"

They must be talking about the fox-faced man, Megan decided. The way they referred to him only as *he*, in hushed tones of reverence, made her shiver. She slipped the stranger an uneasy glance, found him watching her, his face and eyes expressionless.

"What about Boomer," Hanson finally growled. "He knew Welles in Nam. And he was part of the surveillance team staking *her* out." He nodded at Megan. "He should be able to tell us if this is Welles or not."

"He's out on perimeter patrol with Shortstop."

"Get on the radio and get him back here on the double."

"They're on the other side of the ridge," Tiger Jack said. "Take a couple hours, easy, to get back."

"We'll wait," Hanson snapped. "Take the woman back down to the basement. And toss him in with her."

It was pointless to fight. Megan made no protest as Jacoby nudged her back toward the kitchen again. She made her way down the steep steps leading to her small basement cell, not even turning around as a scuffle broke out behind her on the stairs. There was a snarled oath, the sound of flesh meeting flesh in a meaty blow, then a soft groan. She stepped into the storage room wordlessly and a moment later the stranger came staggering in behind her, off balance from the brutal shove Tiger Jack had given him. He careened into the low cot and fell sprawling, his mouth and chin bright with fresh blood, and Megan simply stood there and looked down at him as the door slammed closed behind them and a key turned in the lock.

The stranger lifted his head and looked around, narrowed eyes alert. Seeing no one there but Megan, he eased himself to his feet with surprising speed, wincing slightly but obviously less seriously injured than he'd pretended. He ran his tongue along the inside of his lower lip gingerly, then turned his head, spat a mouthful of blood, and wiped his mouth with the back of his hand. He looked at her for a moment or two. "Thanks," he said calmly. "You probably just saved my life."

But Megan simply stared at him wordlessly, taking in the strong, battle-scarred face, the cowlick of oak-brown hair tumbling over his forehead. His eyes held hers evenly, amber-hued and slightly wary.

She'd taken the four steps that separated them and had drawn her arm back before she even realized what she was doing. Her palm struck him on the left cheek with an explosive *crack* that made him stagger back a step, and Megan felt her arm go numb all the way to her shoulder.

She was trembling, but not with fear this time. The rage was white-hot and so real she burned with it, relished its heat as it crested and spilled through her, cauterized even the worst of the terror and pain. "You *bastard!*" she whispered, her voice shaking. "By rights I should kill you myself!"

Chapter 3

Taggart eased his breath out between his teeth, wondering how in hell he'd ever thought this was going to be the easy part. Somehow he'd convinced himself that she'd be over the worst of it by now, that eleven-and-a-half months would have done its healing. But the pain and anger were still there, as raw as though it had all happened only last week. And suddenly he found himself wanting to pull her tightly against him, to hold the madness around them at bay while he tried to explain, tried to ease the hurt in those wide, dark eyes....

It caught him off guard, that desperate wanting. Left him staring at her, filled with a deep, aching emptiness so strong that for a moment it almost frightened him. He fought it off, brutally ignoring the other feelings that danced through him just at seeing her again. "Are you all right? They didn't...hurt you, did they?"

"I haven't been beaten or raped, if that's what you mean," she said bitterly, the hostility in her eyes almost palpable. "They kidnapped me and drugged me and threatened to kill me, but to people like you that probably doesn't count for much. All considered, I guess I'm lucky your friends don't play rough.''

"They aren't friends of mine," Tag said harshly, the simmering rage that had been gnawing at him all week threatening to break loose once and for all as he thought of her here, alone and terrified, tormented by an evil she didn't even understand. At least they hadn't abused her, that was one small mercy he could be thankful for. That never had been Lucas's style, but circumstances and people change and he'd had no way of knowing how much leeway Lucas was allowing his men these days. Drugs were bad enough, though. There was no telling what they'd used on her. Something new and improved, no doubt, the latest in chemical wizardry brought to you by the boys in the brain-washing department.

Tag fought down another surge of fury, reminding himself that giving in to his anger now would probably just get them both killed. There would be ample time for revenge after Megan was safe.

He strode across to the door and gave the knob a twist, not surprised to find it as solid as rock. The door was even more solid, heavy wood reinforced with steel, and it fit flush in the frame without even a protruding hinge that could be pried loose. Breathing an oath, he turned to survey the small room, wincing as his bruised ribs protested the sudden movement.

Megan was still standing with her arms wrapped around her as though keeping out a chill, watching him with wide, bewildered eyes. They were so filled with a tangle of hurt and anger and confusion that he felt it tear at him like a physical pain.

He ignored it, brushed by her and stepped into the tiny bathroom. "Is there any other way out of here? A door or a—"

"You used me."

It was more a sob than a whisper, filled with accusation. Taggart felt the muscles across his shoulders tighten, opened his mouth to tell her they didn't have time to talk about that now. But then he saw her eyes. And realized that this, at least, was going to have to be dealt with before they could go any further.

Better to get it over with. He forced himself to hold her gaze. "Yes."

Something shadowed her eyes, bleak despair maybe. Had she expected him to lie? Or had she secretly hoped, down deep in some hidden part of her, that it had been just a terrible mistake?

"You knew all along, didn't you?" Her voice cracked and she swallowed. "Even while you were marrying me, you knew that you were going to leave as soon as we docked."

"Yes." He wondered, even as he said the word, if it was the truth or just another lie. There had been so many, he'd long ago lost track of what was truth and what merely expedience.

Her eyes were very bright and he suddenly realized they were filled with unshed tears. Again, for a split second, he ached to reach out and comfort her; again, he fought it down.

"It was all lies, wasn't it? Everything you said to me for those three weeks was just . . . lies."

The expression on her face made something twist inside him. "Meggie . . ."

"Don't call me that," she said sharply.

That's what my father always called me, he remembered her saying with a shy smile the first time he'd used it. She'd made it plain that no one else ever did, and the fact she'd allowed him to call her Meg, and even Meggie, had touched him as nothing else had. Maybe that's when it had started, he found himself brooding. Maybe if he'd caught it right then . . .

He gave himself a fierce shake. Damn it, they didn't have time for this! "We can talk about this later," he growled. "Right now we've got to get—"

"Damn you, don't you turn your back on me! Do you really think you can just appear out of nowhere like this, twelve months after vanishing from my life, and not even—"

"Damn it, Megan, we don't have time!" He wheeled around to face her, his voice echoing sharply off the walls. It made her flinch, but he brutally ignored the flicker of fear in her eyes. Maybe it was better if she *was* afraid of him, he told himself ferociously. At least that way she wouldn't want answers he didn't have, explanations he only half understood himself. "You bought us some breathing space, but time's running out, Megan. It's not going to take that bunch upstairs long to realize they've got the right man, and when that happens it's going to be game over, understand?"

"Why should I give a damn about what happens to you?"

"I don't know," he said bluntly. "No reason at all, I guess. Except you cared enough to cover for me upstairs awhile ago. You could have told them then and there they had the right man." He looked down at her, holding her eyes searchingly. "You knew, didn't you? The minute you looked at me, you knew."

She didn't say anything. But she didn't have to. Her gaze slipped from his and she looked down, her mouth sullen. "I . . . wasn't sure."

"You were sure," he said softly. "I saw it in your eyes, Meggie. You could have told them, but you didn't." Why, Meggie, he asked silently. Why didn't you just tell them and let them kill me? You must have been tempted. Don't tell me you weren't tempted . . .

She gave her head a defiant toss, as though knowing exactly what he was thinking. "I was playing for time, that's all. If they'd known it was you, they'd have taken us down to Seattle and . . ." She shrugged. "They're going to kill me, too, remember. It's not as though I don't have a stake in what happens."

He had to smile. "Damn straight, Meggie. Which is why we've got to find a way out of here, and fast."

She looked at him, still defiant, still angry. "I'm not going anywhere with you. I'll help you find a way out, but that's it. Once we're outside, I never want to see you again."

"Except I'm the only chance you've got of getting off this mountain alive," he reminded her impatiently.

"Why should I believe you? They said you're a murderer. That you used to be a government agent of some sort until you switched sides and killed three CIA operatives in Thailand."

She stood her ground defiantly, as though daring him to admit it, but he could still see the fear in her eyes as she faced him. It filled him with a weary, despairing anger and for a moment he found himself wondering if any of this was really worth it. Eighteen months of hell, with God knows how many more ahead. And for what? A knife between the ribs or a bullet out of the silent darkness some night when his attention strayed, or something distracted him, or he simply got too damned tired to care anymore.

Then he looked down at her small upturned face and remembered why this part, at least, *was* important. "Megan, I don't have time to argue with you. I came up here to get you out of this mess, and—like it or not—you're coming with me. It's going to be a hell of a lot easier if you cooperate and use your own two feet, but if I have to lay you out like a deck of cards and toss you over my shoulder, I'll do just that."

She drew in a small shocked breath and took an involuntary step backward, her eyes widening with as much indignation as fear. Smiling grimly, Tag reached out and cupped her chin in his right hand, forcing her to look up at his bruised, bloodied face. "I didn't cut myself shaving, angel. These guys mean business—and they're going to kill us both."

He watched her fight it, common sense battling anger and mistrust, found himself coolly calculating where and how hard to hit her should she tell him to go to hell. Slugging her on the jaw and fighting his way out of here with her slung over his shoulder like the spoils of war wouldn't be his first choice—but he'd do it if he had to.

Then, just as he was steeling himself to do just that, her shoulders slumped and she nodded almost imperceptibly, her gaze sliding from his. "There's no way out except for that door. I checked behind the shelves, but the walls are solid concrete. The boxes are full of toys and Christmas junk—nothing useful, except for a can of spray paint. If you sprayed it in someone's eyes..." She shrugged, still not looking at him. "The fuse box is over there. I thought of turning the power off and trying to get out when they came down to check, but I figured they'd know what was going on and be ready."

Tag looked down at her in surprised approval and her mouth tightened, her eyes hostile again. "I didn't believe for a minute that *you'd* turn up, so I decided I had to get out on my own."

The scathing anger in her voice made him flush. "Damn it, Meggie, did you really think I wouldn't come for you after—" he caught himself, knowing exactly what she'd thought. "The hell with it," he growled abruptly, wheeling away. "So the only way out of here is straight up those stairs?"

"Yes. They always have someone stationed outside this door, though. They seem to think I'm dangerous or something...."

Tag found himself smiling faintly. Too bad he hadn't been half as astute himself twelve months ago, he thought wearily. Too bad he hadn't realized just *how* dangerous until it was way too late....

He shoved the thoughts away impatiently. Waste much more time, and the question of which was more hazardous to his well-being—Megan Kirkwood or Jack Lucas—was going to be purely academic.

"Okay, angel," he said brusquely, "time to rock 'n' roll. We're only going to get one chance at this, so let's do it right." Swiftly, he outlined his plan, half expecting Megan to balk. But to his intense satisfaction she took it all in as swiftly as he explained it, nodding now and again as she listened intently.

His admiration took another leap as she took her place by the door without saying a word, and he found himself wondering, as he had countless times, if he hadn't made a mistake twelve months ago by not confiding in her when he'd had the chance.

Too late now, he reminded himself roughly as he arranged himself facedown across the cot. The minute you start second-guessing things you *could* have done, you're dead. You just go with gut instinct and pray it's on the money. And if it isn't, you just keep plunging ahead, doing the best you can, until sooner or later things work out...or kill you. Simple.

He took a deep breath. "Okay, angel. Let's get it done."

Any final doubts he may have had about how Megan would hold up under stress vanished in the next minute or two. She started screaming right on cue, and battered at the door with her fists as though fully intent on breaking it down.

There was a sharp blow on the other side of the door. "Hey! Hold it down in there!"

She gave him a quick, frightened glance and he nodded reassuringly, not wanting to push her too hard but knowing they didn't have time to waste. "Come on, Meggie," he murmured gently. "Get him to open the door. You can do it, angel."

She closed her eyes and nodded, drawing in a deep breath. When she opened them, her eyes were still dark with fear but the panic was gone, replaced by grim determination. She wet her lips. "He's...he's sick," she called through the door. "I—I think he's had a heart attack!"

Tag blinked in surprise. *That* hadn't been in the script.

There was a querulous mutter from the other side of the door. Megan leaned toward it. "I said I think he's dying! Please, you've got to help him. It's his heart! He—"

A key rattled in the lock and Tag hastily dropped his face against the pillow and closed his eyes, remembering in the nick of time to clutch the left side of his chest. He heard the door open and tensed, fought to remain perfectly still.

"Keep the hell quiet," a man's voice growled, "or I'll—"

"*Please!* He started gasping something about his heart, then he grabbed his chest, staggered over to the cot and fell down! You've got to do something. He said he has pills, but I couldn't find them and—"

"Shut up!" Footsteps crossed the cement floor and something hard and cold jabbed him in the small of his back. A gun barrel, most likely. Tag stayed limp. "Hey! You!"

"He's not dead, is he?" Megan's voice rose, quavering with panic. "Oh, my God, he's dead! He's—"

"I said shut up!" The man gave Tag another painful jab in the back.

"Hey, Tiger Jack," another voice shouted from the distance, "what the hell's going on down there?"

Tag groaned inwardly. He'd been hoping to get just one of them in here. But if the other one came down...

"The broad says he had a heart attack or somethin'."

"So what? It'll just save us the trouble of killing him."

"And if it ain't Welles? Send Hanson down here."

"He isn't here—he took the chopper out to pick up Shortstop and Boomer."

Tiger Jack muttered an obscenity. Tag could sense him standing beside the cot, trying to decide what to do next. *Bend down,* Tag urged silently. *Lean a little closer....*

"You've got to do something," Megan wailed. "It's not Welles, I told you! You can't just let him die!"

"I told you to shut up," Tiger Jack muttered menacingly. He prodded Tag with the gun again, then leaned down and grasped his shoulder and started to roll him onto his back.

Tag flipped around like a cat, slamming his right foot up into the man's solar plexis even while he grabbed the barrel of the M16 with both hands. Tiger Jack gave a whistling groan, knees sagging, and for an instant Tag thought he was going to go down.

But he didn't. His face contorted with rage and pain and he gave a bull-like bellow as he swung the rifle butt around hard. Tag reared back an instant too late and the rifle clipped him on the right cheekbone, nearly making him lose his grip on the weapon. Head spinning, he aimed a vicious kick at the man's groin, but felt his foot hit only solidly muscled thigh as Tiger Jack blocked it expertly.

Tag gave the rifle such a ferocious twist he almost succeeded in getting it out of Tiger Jack's meaty fists then slammed the butt up under the other man's chin. He heard teeth click together and a snort of pain, but knew instinctively it hadn't been hard enough to do more than enrage his enemy. "Megan, get the hell out of here! Now!"

Tiger Jack tried to swing the rifle around, but Tag hung onto it grimly, jackknifing his knee viciously into his opponent's unprotected groin. Tiger Jack's breath whistled, his face going a faint green, but Tag realized even that wasn't enough to stop him as he turned sluggishly, eyes murderous, and reached for Tag's throat.

Then, abruptly, he stopped. He seemed to hang over Tag for what seemed like an eternity, motionless. Then his eyes glazed and he sagged across the cot with a wheezing groan and Tag found himself staring up into Megan's terrified eyes. Both hands were still clamped around the sizable piece of firewood she'd smashed across Tiger Jack's skull, and she was staring down at her victim in disbelief.

"Good girl," Tag groaned, trying to heave Tiger Jack's dead weight off. He felt blood trickling down his cheek where the rifle butt had struck him, wondered dizzily how much more of this he was going to be able to take. It had been a long time since he'd suffered this kind of physical abuse. A long time since he'd been locked in hand-to-hand combat with an enemy intent on killing him.

There was a scuffle of footsteps on the stairs behind them and Megan spun around, the firewood flying out of her grasp. The second man hit the door at a dead run, revolver already in his hand, and Tag struggled desperately to free the M16. But both he and it were pinned under Tiger Jack's dead weight and Tag watched in bemused fascination as the man stepped into the room and lifted the revolver.

Then suddenly Megan was there again, wheeling gracefully toward the man. The spray paint hit him full in the eyes and he gave a howl of pain and threw his arms up instinctively to protect himself, the gun flying out of his hand as he tripped over a folding metal chair and went sprawling. Megan was on him in an instant, playing the jet of spray paint over his face and hands as he scrambled frantically to get away from her, blinded and half-wild with pain.

Tag finally managed to shove Tiger Jack's unconscious body onto the floor and struggled to his feet. He wiped the blood out of his eyes and grabbed up the revolver lying near the cot, then he crossed the room swiftly and gently grasped Megan's hands between his. "Let up," he said quietly. "Come on, let up...."

Gently, he pried her fingers off the spray button. The can fell from her hands and Tag could feel her start to shake. "It's okay, angel," he murmured. "You got him. He can't hurt you now. He can't hurt you...."

The man was inching himself across the floor, gagging and whimpering, and Megan stared at him blankly as Tag efficiently knocked him out. She'd gone the color of chalk and Tag rose and put one arm gently around her shoulders, feeling her tremble like a deer.

"Take it easy," he murmured, tugging her gently but firmly against him. She took a convulsive breath and stiffened but he tightened his embrace. "Hang on, babe," he whispered against her ear. "Come on, Meggie, don't give out on me now. You're doing fine, angel. You're doing just fine."

She took another deep breath, this one almost a sob, and he started rubbing her shoulders and back, murmuring to her, soft meaningless words meant only to reassure her. He could feel her breath curl under his shirt collar, warm and moist, felt the convulsive shivers run through her as she fought to control the tears.

A minute later she lifted her face from the hollow of his throat and swallowed, her fingers still knotted in his shirt front.

He looked down at her. "Better?"

Megan nodded. "S-some rescue. I h-have to d-do all the work." She was still pale, but she'd lost that wild, panicked look and it was only then that he realized he still had his arms locked around her.

And he also started to realize how good it felt just having her there again. She fit well against him. That was one of the first things he'd ever noticed about her, how perfectly she fit into the circle of his arms. And he into hers, he couldn't help but remember. Even as tiny and shy and inexperienced as she'd been, he'd fit to her and into her as perfectly as a man could fit to a woman. She'd surprised and delighted herself with the newfound possibilities of her own body, and he'd spent the night teaching her to take as much pleasure as she gave.

A familiar stirring in his groin brought Tag back to the present with a jolt. He gazed down at the top of Megan's head with a kind of despairing amusement, marveling at how his body could respond so vitally to a year-old memory when it was so bruised that even taking a breath hurt.

Marveling, too, at how careless it made him. He let his arms drop from around her and turned away abruptly. "We've got to get the hell out of here before the others get back."

Swiftly getting his mind back on business, Tag rolled Tiger Jack onto his belly and searched him, finding a heavy hunting knife at his waist and another one in his left boot.

"Is—is he dead?"

Tag glanced over his shoulder. Megan was staring down at the unconscious man nervously. "You didn't kill him," he said quietly. "Find me something to tie him up with."

Tag pulled Tiger Jack's arms onto his back and tied his wrists tightly with a strand of Christmas-tree lights that Megan found in one of the boxes. He pulled the man's heavy combat boots off and tied his knees and ankles together, then rolled him under the cot and secured him to that as well. Then, as an afterthought, he stuffed a towel in the slack mouth and tied the gag tightly with strips of torn sheet.

"That ought to hold him," he muttered as he double-checked the knots. Getting to his feet, he picked up the heavy assault rifle and made his way over to the other man.

Tag knelt beside the flaccid body and started stripping off the man's clothing. "Get out of that skirt," he said over his shoulder. "Leave your panty hose on—it'll be some protection from the cold."

"What?" Megan's voice was just a squeak.

Tag straightened and tossed the man's wool flannel shirt and heavy cotton drill jeans onto the cot. Megan was staring at him with openmouthed astonishment. "Y-you can't possibly expect me to wear a dead man's clothes!"

"Oh, for—!" Tag caught himself. "Contrary to popular opinion, Megan, I'm not a cold-blooded murderer. If someone tries to shoot me, I'll shoot him first if I get the chance. But I don't kill someone when he's down and unarmed." *Not anymore,* he added silently, a sudden memory of jungles flickering through his mind, gone before he could even identify it. "I just knocked him out. Now get out of that damned skirt and into these pants. Socks, too. Pull the shirt on over yours and button it up—I'll try to find you a coat. Boots, too," he added, glancing at her bare feet. "Damn it, you've got such tiny feet...."

"I—I'm not going to put on—"

Tag was across the room in three steps. He took her by the shoulders, towering over her, eyes narrowing grimly as he saw the raw fear on her face. "This isn't a damned committee meeting, lady! I've wasted all the time talking I'm going to waste. From now on, you just do what I tell you, got it?"

Numbly, Megan nodded. His fingers bit into her shoulders, bruising her even through her suit jacket, but she ignored it, mesmerized by the lean, handsome face looming close to hers. His eyes glowed with lambent fire, boring into her.

Michael's eyes.

Yet not Michael's. Michael Walker was gone now, whatever and whoever he was gone with him. There was only this tall, cold-eyed man left. The stranger called Taggart Welles.

"Yes," she managed to whisper.

Something shifted deep in the cold eyes. Almost magically they gentled, warmed with the remembering. The muscles in his face relaxed slightly, an almost imperceptible change that only someone who knew him as well as she did would notice.

And suddenly, impossibly, it *was* Michael standing there. Time flickered, shifted, and the small, damp basement room vanished and she was standing in the stateroom aboard the *Paradise Orchid* again, gazing up into Michael's face, three hours married and so much in love it hurt. It was her wedding night and in a little while she'd be lying in his arms in that ridiculously huge bed with its silken sheets and canopy of lace, joined forever to him in all ways, heart and body and very soul. The eyes locked with hers said all the things that words never could, and as she watched his mouth drop toward hers she knew, finally, that all the happiness she'd ever dreamed of was here, with him. . . .

And then, in the next heartbeat, it was over. The skin around his eyes tightened and he went motionless, not even breathing. Then he released her abruptly and turned away with a soft curse. "I told you to get that skirt off. Do it, or I'll do it for you." His voice was abrupt and clipped. He picked up the unconscious man's clothes and shoved them into her arms. "These boys are armed and mobilized like an assault battalion. We haven't a hope in hell of getting out by road, so we're going cross-country, on foot. Odds are we'll get wet—there'll be rain, maybe even snow this time of year. And it gets cold as hell up here at night. You won't last twenty-four hours in that getup. And I didn't risk my neck coming in here after you just so you could freeze to death on some mountain ledge in a late snowstorm!"

Megan said nothing, still too shaken by what had just happened to trust her voice. It had shaken him, too. That's why he was angry, lashing out at himself and some perceived weakness as much as at her.

And he didn't have that right, damn it. If anyone had the right to be angry, it was *her*. She turned her back on him and wrenched the skirt zipper down, using the anger as a bulwark against a tangle of half-formed feelings she didn't want to examine too closely. "All we have to do is phone the police, for crying out loud. They can have a SWAT team or something up here before—"

"It's not that easy, trust me," Tag cut in roughly. "This is government action, angel—or made to look that way. The local cops would turn us back over to these guys so fast we wouldn't know what had hit us."

She turned to stare at him, her mind blank with shock. "What in God's name are you mixed up—?"

"Later," he growled. "Right now the only thing you have to worry about is doing what I tell you, and I'm telling you to get into those clothes. Now!"

He'd give her credit for one thing. When she finally stopped fighting it, she took orders as well as any man in the field. It was as though that sharp little accountant's mind of hers had tallied up all her options and, when the final bottom-line figure was in, she'd accepted it without further question or argument.

She moved swiftly, without wasted word or motion, and in less than five minutes she was outfitted as warmly as possible. The stolen pants were way too large for her but she'd simply knotted the webbing belt tightly around her waist to hold them up and had rolled up the cuffs a turn or two before stuffing them into the heavy wool socks. Ignoring the too-large boots he'd stripped from one of their captives, she calmly reached into one of the storage cartons and pulled out a pair of boy's winter boots that she'd seen earlier. Padded with a second pair of socks, they fit perfectly. She topped it off with a heavy army jacket he found upstairs and although Tag had to stifle a laugh at the picture she made, he was satisfied that she'd be reasonably protected from the cold.

He paused only long enough to collect what weapons he could find—another revolver and a half dozen full magazines for Tiger Jack's M16—and then they were out the door and sprinting hard for the trees. Shouting at Megan to keep going, Tag dodged across to where the van and Jeep were parked. He tore the wiring out of both, then thumbed the M16 to rock 'n' roll—automatic fire—and emptied a magazine into the tires and engine compartments. Releasing the spent magazine, he slapped a fresh one home and pulled the bolt back to put a round in the chamber. The action was still automatic, even after all this time, the weight of the weapon almost comfortable in the curve of his arm. Even the pistol grip felt right, his hand molding around it, finger looped lightly around the trigger. Instinct.

Leaving both vehicles smoking, he raced after Megan, found her crouched in the shadows under the tall pines, white-faced and anxious. She'd been watching him, he realized, and he had a flash of sympathy for how she must feel, seeing the man she'd once thought she knew, the man she'd once loved and trusted and lain naked with, handle an M16 with the easy competence of someone familiar with killing. Little wonder she looked at him with fear in her eyes, flinched whenever he moved too quickly or too near.

It made him feel very old and very tired for some reason. But he fought off an impulse to give her a reassuring smile and brushed by her without a word, heading toward the valley where he'd hidden his gear.

They walked for hours. At first Megan had been able to keep up pretty well, falling behind a bit on the steeper slopes but catching up again on the flat stretches. But as the afternoon wore on and Tag's pace never slowed, she started finding it more and more difficult. She was drenched with perspiration under the layers of clothes Tag had insisted she wear and she was panting for breath, her lungs burning, so light-headed that she lost all track of time or direction. The world seemed to contract until it consisted of nothing but the tiny spot of forest floor directly ahead of her. She found herself concentrating on it fiercely, willing her leaden feet forward one stumbling step at a time, aware of nothing but the ache in her legs and the harsh sound of her own breathing.

And finally, she simply reached the end. Halfway up a steep, crumbling slope, she stumbled over an exposed pine root and fell heavily. She lay there for a moment or two, trying to catch her breath, then slowly pulled herself to her knees, managed to get one foot under her before the moist earth gave way under her boot and she started to slide back down the slope, too exhausted to do more than claw weakly for a handhold.

A hand grabbed the back of her jacket and stopped her descent, then she was physically hauled to her feet and half carried, half dragged the rest of the way up the slope. Tag released her and she simply collapsed in a heap at his feet, shaking her head slowly.

"I can't...go...on," she panted hoarsely, dragging each breath into her aching lungs with an effort.

He squatted beside her and she heard him sigh, but didn't even have the strength to pull away when his hand settled firmly between her shoulder blades. "You have to, Meggie,'' he said quietly, starting to massage her back and aching shoulders. "It's not much farther. A couple of miles, three at the most."

She shook her head again, not even making the effort to look at him. His hand was moving in slow, relaxing circles and she leaned against it gratefully, wanting nothing more than to curl up and sleep forever. "I can't," she whispered, dismayed to realize she was dangerously close to crying.

"Here. Drink this." He uncapped the canteen and held it against her mouth. The water was lukewarm and stale but it tasted like nectar, and she drank greedily. "It's the altitude that's getting to you mainly—your lungs and heart aren't used to working this hard."

"*I'm* not used to working this hard," she panted, rolling wearily onto her back. The sky was a bright, hard blue, piled high in the west with a towering meringue of cloud. "I'm an accountant. I run computers, not marathons."

Still squatting on one heel beside her, Tag smiled. "You're doing fine. In fact, considering what you've been through these past five days, you've held up better than I'd hoped."

"Five days?" she whispered. "I only remember one... maybe. Bits and pieces..."

A muscle rippled along his bruised, dirt-smeared jaw as he stared across the valley below them. His eyes narrowed slightly. "He'll pay for that, Megan," he said in a soft, chill voice. "I swear I'll make him pay for every minute of it."

His profile was hard-edged against the sky and Megan traced it with her eyes, suppressing a little shiver. It was almost impossible to believe that this man and her Michael were actually the same person, impossible to imagine that thin, hard mouth ever laughing, those cold eyes ever looking at a woman with gentleness or love. Michael had been comfortable in expensive silk shirts and elegantly tailored dinner jackets, but this man looked frighteningly at home garbed in jungle camouflage with a bloodstained strip of cloth tied around his forehead as a makeshift sweatband,

and the worn grip of a hunting knife protruding from his belt.

He exuded an essence of raw danger that was only heightened by the dried blood and bruises on his face and the latent tension in every inch of his body. Even at rest, he was as alert and watchful as a cat. His eyes moved constantly as he scanned the tree line on either side of them, the valley stretching below, the steep hillside they'd just climbed. The big army rifle lay nonchalantly across his knees, but he had his right hand firmly on the pistol grip, ready to bring the weapon up and around at the slightest movement.

He turned his head just then, catching her watching him, and one corner of his mouth lifted fractionally as though he knew exactly what she'd been thinking. "Not exactly Singapore, is it, angel?"

Chapter 4

It hurt less than she'd imagined it would, that careless reference to a time and place she didn't even want to think about. Or maybe she had just gone into emotional overload these past few days and couldn't react to *anything* anymore.

She sat up wearily. "Michael, did you—"

"Tag." She looked up and he smiled slightly. "My real name's Taggart Welles. There is no Michael Walker."

"And Professor... what was it? Kirk?"

Again, it elicited a faint smile. "You caught me off guard stalling for time like that. For a second or two I figured you really didn't recognize me, then I realized you were giving me an opening and I said the first thing that popped into my mind."

"And all that stuff about *Semper*... whatever?"

"Oh, the *Sempervivum arachnoideum* really exists—it's a plant of some kind that my mother has in her rock garden. The rest I made up."

"You're good at that, aren't you? Making things up, I mean."

He may have winced. "Meggie, I—"

"I told you not to call me that."

He eased a tight breath from between his teeth. "You're not going to make this easy, are you?"

"Why the *hell* should I?" It was a harsh, bitter cry, torn out of her. "You used me. You made me fall in love with you, then you just threw me away when you didn't need me anymore. Give me one good reason why I should make it easy for you! Just one!"

He was staring at something across the valley, his profile like stone. "There isn't one, Megan," he said quietly. "You've got every right to hate me after what I've put you through. There isn't any easy way to explain it, but there was a reason for everything I did. And you've got to believe I didn't set out to deliberately hurt you. That was the last—"

"I don't want to hear it," she said in a flat, dull voice. "I'm not interested in your excuses and your apologies. What you did to me can't be erased by a bunch of words. If you want absolution, find a priest—because you're never going to get it from me."

Tag looked at her then, filled with an immense weariness. She was sitting there staring at her hands, shoulders slumped, her face tucked down so a wing of hair had fallen forward to hide her expression from him. He put his hand out to brush it back, suddenly wanting to touch her, but he managed to catch himself in time. It wasn't absolution he was after, he reminded himself. He was here because he owed her something, that was all. If it hadn't been for him, she wouldn't be mixed up in this nightmare. Getting her out safely was just a debt he owed. Like the debt he'd owed Russ....

He eased himself to his feet, breath hissing as his entire body protested. There wasn't an inch of him that didn't feel bruised and torn, and he silently cursed his own carelessness. There had once been a time when they would never have caught him. But that had been a long time ago, and all those war-honed instincts had dulled with age and lack of use.

He'd sharpened killer instincts of another kind over the past fourteen or so years, but the skills that kept him alive in the boardroom and stock market wouldn't keep him alive out here. He had to go deeper to find those other, older abilities, to unearth things he had buried within himself long ago and had prayed never to use again. To find the Shadow Warrior he'd once been.

"You were the only man I ever loved."

The words went through Tag like slivers of steel. He flinched, the raw pain in her voice so real it became his— shrapnel in his heart. He dropped to one knee beside her, feeling sick and hollow. "My God, Meggie," he whispered, reaching for her, "what have I done to you?"

"Don't!" She recoiled from his hand and got to her feet, not looking at him. "I don't want your sympathy." If he touched her, Megan knew, she'd cry. And she'd be damned if she'd let him see her cry.

He was still kneeling, head bowed slightly, one hand outstretched. He let it drop, still not moving, and Megan found herself gazing down at him, torn between the anger and something else, some tug of unexpected emotion she couldn't even identify. He looked so vulnerable! Like a man who'd lost it all and just didn't give a damn anymore.

Then it was gone. He uncoiled to his feet, lithe and dangerous, looking as if he'd just stepped out of the jungles of South America with a band of guerrillas at his back and a price on his head. "We'd better get moving." His eyes brushed hers, expressionless, then moved on to scan the tree line. "I figure they've been on our trail for a couple of hours by now—five men, maybe six. They'll split up into two, maybe three teams, fanning out to pick up our trail."

He shaded his eyes, staring out over the treetops. "He's got a slick up there rigged with twin sixties, and a dozen or so mercs just in off some action down in Central America, still all worked up and itching for blood.'' He gave his head a shake, then realized Megan was staring at him in bewilderment. He smiled. ''A helicopter with M60 machine guns mounted in each door.''

''And the mercs are . . . mercenaries?''

He nodded. ''Ex-Special Forces, most of them.''

He shifted, eclipsing the sun. His shadow fell across her and Megan shivered. ''How do you know so much about them?'' she whispered. ''How can you know what they're . . . thinking?''

His eyes met hers again, still expressionless. ''I'm one of them,'' he said quietly. ''Or I used to be. A long time ago.'' He was looking beyond her again, his face cold and hard, and Megan had the sudden feeling he wasn't looking at anything in this time or place, was seeing things she didn't want to think about. Then he shook himself free of it and turned away, starting to walk down the grassy hillside into the next valley.

The muscles in Megan's legs started to protest almost at once, but she ignored them and kept walking. The dead grass was long and tangled, booby-trapped with hidden gulleys cut by spring runoff, loose rocks and thistles with thorns like razors. Tag moved through it seemingly effortlessly, stepping over barricades of brambles that Megan had to fight her way through or around, instinctively avoiding the loose rocks and grass-covered holes that seemed to trip her at every step.

Tag stopped at the bottom of the long slope and looked around to see how Megan was doing. She was nowhere in sight and he froze for an instant, his heart in his throat, until he spotted her about two-thirds of the way down the hillside, angling toward him. She was moving slowly, stumbling now and again in exhaustion, and he swore under his breath.

Damn it, maybe he should have risked taking the Jeep. The odds had been a hundred to one of their getting through Lucas's men, but what the hell were the odds of making it on foot? Megan was practically finished—he'd been pushing hard all afternoon, too preoccupied to realize she'd been falling farther and farther behind.

Watching her, he had to smile in admiration. She was something else! So exhausted she could hardly stand, she still managed to put one foot doggedly in front of the other, covering mile after mile of rugged terrain without a whimper of complaint.

But how much longer could she keep it up? Lucas and his men were in fighting trim, crack soldiers who could hump fifty pounds of equipment and weapons over terrain a hundred times worse than this without even breathing hard. And they were, as Lucas used to say, strongly motivated. Until now, he and Megan had just been another operation to them. But that fracas up at the lodge had changed everything. It was personal now. And mean.

Something brushed his cheek, and Tag glanced at the sky uneasily as another flake of snow followed the first. The clouds were lower now, sullen and heavy, and he suddenly realized that the temperature had dropped sharply in just the last half hour. He winced. The last thing he wanted was to get caught out in the open if it really started coming down.

Megan stopped beside him, breathing heavily. He looked down at her. "How are you holding up?"

"Don't worry about me." She said it flatly, her eyes defiant as they met his briefly. "I'll make it."

There was no mistaking her meaning, but Tag decided to ignore it. Sooner or later the shock of seeing him again was going to wear off and there was going to be hell to pay, but this wasn't the time. Or the place.

"I've got my gear stashed in a cave a couple of miles upstream." He nodded toward the creek that was wending its way along the valley floor. It was deep and swift here, its blue crystalline surface roiled with eddies and streaks of foam where submerged boulders and other flood debris disturbed its powerful, headlong rush.

"Let's move." He turned and started upstream. Every instinct he had was screaming at him to pick up the pace, but he ignored them. He just couldn't risk it. If Megan gave out he was going to have to carry her, and that would slow him down even more. Better to keep moving at a slow, steady pace that would conserve what little energy she had left. Just in case...

The next mile and a half was relatively easy walking and they covered it in better time than Tag had hoped. The snow didn't seem to be amounting to much, either. There were times when it would almost clear and a few rays of watery sunshine would actually break through; then it would grow gray and dim again and a squall of snow would hit them, thick as a blanket.

"Wait..."

Megan's voice stopped Tag in his tracks. He turned to find her standing a few feet away, staring intently back the way they'd come. He was beside her in an instant, the M16 braced between his arm and body, safety off. He thumbed it to automatic fire and stepped around her, shielding her with his body.

"I...thought I heard something." She was poised like a deer catching scent, every line of her body taut. A few brittle flakes of snow tumbled by, but nothing else moved. Megan shook her head. "I guess it was nothing. It's so quiet...."

Too quiet. The kind of quiet that preceded a hell of a storm, as though the whole valley and everything in it had battened down tight. The mountains had disappeared behind dirty gray clouds and the only thing that moved was the wind, picking up now, clattering the bare branches of a nearby poplar like dried bones.

A little chill wound its way down Tag's spine. Lucas was out there somewhere. And at least two other men from the original Shadow Company. Men who knew how to move like their namesakes—but these shadows killed like men.

He shrugged his shoulder muscles to loosen them and glanced around uneasily. It was too open here, too vulnerable to a double- or even triple-pronged attack. He hoped to outrun them, but if it came to a firefight, he wanted to be dug in deep with plenty of cover, and solid rock at his back. "Let's get moving," he growled, shepherding Megan toward the water. "This is where we cross. The trees on the other side give us good cover all the way."

"Cross?" Megan gave the creek an apprehensive glance. It had widened to maybe sixty feet here, the water so clear she could see the bottom as though looking through glass. It didn't seem to be that deep, but the current was very fast, foaming and tossing spray over half-drowned rocks. "You're kidding, right?"

"It's not as bad as it looks."

"Like heck it's not," she retorted emphatically. "It's wet, it's cold and it's moving like a freight train! I don't swim, remember? I don't even like deep *baths*."

"I remember." He grinned suddenly, that off-center, teasing grin that had been the first thing she'd loved about him.

And for an instant she was there again, sitting on the edge of the pool on the *Paradise Orchid*'s promenade deck, daring to trail her feet in the warm water while she watched Michael swim. He'd cut across the pool under water and had exploded to the surface right in front of her, water cascading from his sleek, muscled body. He'd shaken his head and the air around them had been rainbowed, and he'd reached up and slipped his arms around her and pulled her into the water with him before she'd even had time to protest. She'd submerged and come up sputtering, and he'd been both contrite and amused, wrapped his arms around her tightly and had told her to relax, that he'd never let her go.

She'd completely forgotten her fear of water in that instant, aware only of what seemed like an acre of wet, naked male skin, the muscled thigh that had slipped between hers in the most outrageously intimate way, the power in the arms locked around her. Her bathing suit, a prim one-piece that had seemed sedate enough on dry land, suddenly didn't feel adequate at all as he held her against him. She could distinctly feel the roughness of the hair on his chest against her breasts, and even more distinctly felt her own nipples pebble in response to that erotic touch.

There was another response as unmistakable, his this time, but he'd simply laughed softly and given her a quick hug. "Witch," he whispered against her ear, his warm breath making her toes curl. "You've done me in!" Then he'd lifted her onto the side of the pool, and turned and dived away with a powerful kick, surfacing feet away and giving her a private, warm smile that was like sharing a secret.

And much later that night, under the Southern Cross with the perfume of frangipani in the air, he'd drawn her into his arms and had kissed her for the very first time.

The memory lasted no more than a split second, but it unnerved Megan completely. She backed away, shaking her head. "Uh-uh. No way."

"Megan," he chided gently, "do you think I'd go to all the trouble to get you this far just to let you drown? Trust me." He caught her hand and stepped off the low bank into the water. "Come on, angel. There's nothing to it."

Megan didn't know if she took that first step or if Tag just tugged her gently in, but a moment later she was up to her knees in what felt like liquid ice and it was too late to argue. His hand was strong and warm around hers, reassuring in its solidarity, and Megan found herself following him trustingly as he made his sure-footed way through the swift water.

It was so cold it literally made her breathless and it boiled around her legs, pulling at her greedily, swirling and glittering. It made her feel dizzy and off balance, and she had the sudden sensation that it was alive, waiting for her to take a misstep on the treacherous bottom so it could tear her feet out from under her and swallow her.

Hypnotized by the swiftly moving water, she didn't see the deceptively steep drop into the central channel until too late. Her footing dissolved and suddenly she was in well over her knees, thrown off balance as the powerful current tore at her.

"Tag...!" She gave a muffled gasp and threw her free hand out, trying to catch herself.

But he was there, throwing his arm around her waist to catch her even as she started to go down. She clutched at his jacket as he steadied her and she felt the familiar strength of his arm lock around her, looked up to find the even more familiar planes of his face and mouth mere inches from hers. He seemed to go very still, and in that moment Megan forgot to breathe, forgot the icy water numbing her feet and legs, forgot everything but the raw hunger in the green-flecked eyes burning into hers.

They were Michael's eyes, yet not Michael's—his had looked at her with want, not need, had gently coaxed, not simmered with something dark and primitive. They were compelling eyes, both erotic and dangerous, and she became vitally aware in that moment of the latent power in the arm circling her waist, the chill of steel where the big rifle he was holding pressed against her back, the flex and shift of his thigh as he braced his legs against the current. A flurry of snow swirled around them, curtaining off the rest of the world, and Megan watched their breaths smoke in the chill air, mingling and rising as one.

She didn't know which of them heard it first. The faint sound had been hovering at the edge of her consciousness for some time, but it was only when Tag threw his head up and stared at the sky that she realized what it was. She turned clumsily in the circle of his arms and looked behind her. The valley had all but vanished behind a light curtain of swirling snow, the tall trees eerie and ghostlike along the bank, and the tumbling gunmetal water racing around them was the only movement.

And then it was there, huge and black, materializing out of the snow like something from her worst nightmare: a big military helicopter, coming in fast at treetop level. Huge pinwheels of turbulent air and snow corkscrewed behind it as it roared over them, the pulsating thunder of its big rotors making the air shake, and for a moment Megan actually thought it had gone by without spotting them.

Tag wheeled around, shouting something she couldn't hear. She nearly lost her footing in the swift water, staggered around just in time to see the big chopper tuck its nose down and pivot sharply. Then it was coming in again, so low its rotors beat the water into froth around them, and Megan could clearly see Tiger Jack crouched in the open door, and watched stupidly as he swung the machine gun toward her.

Something slammed into her from behind and she was thrown forward so violently she didn't even have time to scream before she was under water. She sucked in a breath, swallowing water, and flailed wildly as the world turned to icy blackness. The current sucked at her and she gave another convulsive gasp, choking on water and sand. Then something grasped the back of her collar and lifted her bodily to her feet.

Tag shoved her so forcefully toward the near bank that she took three stumbling strides before she fell again, gagging and coughing. Something huge and deadly hovered overhead, filling the sky with its maniacal roar, and she faintly heard Tag shouting at her to run, but could do no more than claw herself onto her hands and knees in the shallow water and gasp for air.

Gunfire chattered above her, so close it made her flinch, and it was only when Tag had reached down and grabbed her by the upper arm to drag her upright again that she realized it was him firing. She managed to stagger to her feet and then they were running for shore, stumbling and tripping through the shallow water as the roar of the helicopter filled the sky above them.

Megan didn't know if she tripped or if Tag pushed her, but she went sprawling facedown in the grass as a dark shadow glided across them. She curled up into a ball and covered her ears with her hands, stunned with noise and fear—she could hear Tag swearing and the clatter of gun-fire. Then the darkness and the noise drew back again; she heard Tag give a gasp of ragged laughter and dared to open her eyes.

The helicopter was hovering on the far side of the stream, and it took Megan a moment to realize something was wrong with it. Leaking oil-black smoke, it labored to lift, then turned ponderously and rattled away, leaving a smear of smoke against the sky.

"Are you all right?"

It was Tag's voice, rough with shock, and she looked around stupidly to see him down on one knee beside her, his face drawn and white. "I—I think so. Nothing hurts, any-way. Am I bleeding somewhere?" She looked down uncer-tainly, wondering why he seemed so worried.

"No." He gave a harsh gasp of laughter and smoothed her soaking hair back from her face. "I thought I'd lost you, Meggie girl." He managed another laugh, as rough and shaken as the first, and he cradled her against his shoulder. "I thought I'd lost you for good that time."

Megan nodded, suddenly so tired she felt numbed. His jacket was rough against her cheek and she turned her face so it was in the curve of his throat, breathing in the musky warmth radiating from him. She thought she felt the cool touch of his lips on her cheek, the touch of his breath on her ear. Then he let his hands slip from her and eased himself to his feet.

Wearily, staggering slightly, she stood up. "They're going to be back, aren't they?"

Tag nodded, feeling his heartbeat slowly settling back to normal. He lifted the M16 and released the spent maga-zine, then took another out of his pocket and slapped it home.

"I didn't do more than ding the engine housing. They'll have it patched and be airborne in less than an hour. But it's the others we have to worry about now. The chopper found us by accident—it was just dumb luck he broke through that snow cloud practically on top of us—but they'd have been on the radio with our position before they even got turned around."

Megan gave him a frightened glance. She was trembling slightly and he frowned as he looked down at her. "The cave where I hid my gear is about a half mile from here."

"Sh-shouldn't we keep moving?" Another shiver racked her. It was snowing again, steadily this time, and a fine dusting of it glittered on the stiff grass. "If we stop, they'll find us."

"Maybe," Tag said tightly. He nodded skyward. "But if this snow starts coming down like I think it's going to, it'll cover our tracks."

"But—"

"You've got to get out of those wet clothes before you freeze to death," he said bluntly. Megan looked down at herself dully, suddenly aware that she was soaked to the skin. She shivered again, more violently this time. "You need rest, food. You're running on pure adrenaline right now, but that won't last forever. And I didn't—"

"I know, I know." Megan turned wearily and started walking toward the hills, nearly stumbling with exhaustion. "You didn't risk your neck rescuing me just so I could freeze to death." He fell into step beside her, but it was too much of an effort to even turn her head to look at him. "So you keep reminding me. Although if you're waiting for me to thank you, you're going to wait a long time. I figure you owe me."

"I didn't come up here for your thanks," he growled. He strode ahead of her abruptly, lengthening his stride. "I got you into this mess, I'll get you out. It's that simple."

It wasn't until he'd actually said the words that Megan realized, oddly enough, that they weren't the ones she'd wanted to hear.

Yet it had been that simple. A debt owed, a debt paid. She of all people should appreciate the tidiness of it. After all, she dealt with *debit* and *credit* columns every day, balancing one against the other until, in the end, nothing at all was left.

Maybe it was the ugly, bare-bones civility of it that bothered her. Maybe at some level she'd managed to convince herself that it all had some heroic, deeper purpose....

It made her feel emptier and colder than she already was, and it wasn't until she stumbled blindly and fell that she even realized she was crying.

The small cave that Tag had used as a base camp was set high in an outcropping of rock that jutted out from the flank of the mountain like a spur, jagged and inhospitable. The opening was just a crack in the rock, all but hidden by a gnarled old pine that grew sideways out of the mountain, groping for the sun, and unless you knew it was there, you'd never notice it. Or even if you noticed it, you'd simply take it for a narrow fissure, never dreaming it opened up onto a small, dry cave.

Which was why Megan wasn't having anything to do with it, Tag realized. She stood shivering in the shadow of the old tree, peering mistrustfully into the crack, then she shook her head and stepped back. "I'm not crawling in there."

"Damn it, Megan," Tag said through clenched teeth, "just *do* it. There's nothing to be afraid of. It's just a cave!"

"And what if something's already in there? A—a bear?"

"Oh, for—!" He swallowed the rest and braced the M16 against the tree, then dropped to his hands and knees and eased himself into the fissure. It was a tight fit, made even tighter for the parts of him that didn't bend too well, thanks to Lucas's men. He swore under his breath as he wriggled the last foot or two, his bruised ribs protesting every inch of the way, then he was through.

The cave was small and dry, barely high enough for him to sit upright but deep enough so he could stretch out full-length if he did it carefully. The floor was carpeted with dried leaves and pine needles that had blown in over the years, and when he'd first explored it he'd found tufts of feathers and a drift of rabbit fur, soft as thistledown. But whatever predator had brought them there was either long dead or had moved to other quarters, leaving a snug little hideaway that couldn't have been more perfect if he'd designed it himself.

His small cache of supplies was where he'd left it, dry and undisturbed. He pulled the flashlight out of his pack and turned it on, shielding it with the sleeping bag until there was just a soft glow that would reassure Megan without lighting up the entire countryside. Then he wriggled back out the way he'd come, and eased himself stiffly to his feet.

Megan was still standing there, hunched up and shivering, and he nodded toward the fissure. "Your turn, angel." He left her to think about it for a moment, walking a few steps away and then turning to look critically at the cliff face. From out here the light was all but invisible and he nodded with satisfaction.

His ploy with the flashlight worked. Reassured by the warm glow and more confident now that she could see what she was crawling into, Megan finally inched her way into the fissure. Tag took one long, sweeping look down the valley for signs of their pursuers, then followed her.

Megan was sitting with her arms wrapped around her knees, eyes closed, shivering so badly he could hear her teeth chatter. Her face was pale in the dim light, her thick lashes and dark hair glittering with flakes of melting snow, and when he put the back of his hand against her cheek she didn't even move.

Tag swore quietly. Her skin was like ice. Not just a surface cold from wind and snow, but the kind of deep, deadly cold that cut right to the bone. He kneeled in front of her and started unlacing her boots. "Get that jacket off, Meg," he said with quiet urgency. "And everything else, too."

He pulled the boots off, spilling water, and slipped the soaked wool socks off. Her wet feet and ankles were as cold as stone and he started rubbing them, chafing the icy skin, kneading the muscles in her calves to stop them from cramping. To his relief she showed no sign of frostbite, and her toes curled strongly when he ran his fingernail down the sole of her foot. No lasting damage, thank God. She'd be all right. If he could keep her from slipping deeper and deeper into the deadly sleep of hypothermia, down into the false warmth that would kill her as certainly as Lucas.

She still had her eyes closed and he leaned forward and gave her a sharp shake. "Wake up, Megan! You have to get these things off." She opened her eyes slowly, looking at him without comprehension, and Tag felt a jolt of fear. He gave her another shake, harder than the first. "I said wake up, damn it! Keep your eyes open. And help me get these things off."

He unbuttoned the heavy army jacket and started tugging it off, but Megan muttered something in protest and tried to shove his hands away. "Tired," she whispered, her eyes starting to slide closed again. "Jus' wanna sleep."

"I know you want to sleep," Tag told her tersely, "but you're not going to, understand? Fall asleep, and you might not wake up." He pulled her forward and wrenched the jacket off roughly, eliciting a mumble of complaint.

"S-stop it!" She knocked his hands away from the buttons on her blouse and clutched it closed, trying to wriggle away from him. Her voice was thick and furry with exhaustion. "What are you doing! Leave me alone!"

"Quit fighting," Tag growled impatiently. "Damn it, Megan, there's a time and place for modesty, but this isn't it! We were married, remember?"

He said it deliberately, trying to jar her into anger, but she either hadn't heard him or simply didn't care. She kept plucking at his hands and twisting this way and that, as determined to keep her clothes on as he was to get them off.

Ignoring her flailing hands, he untied the belt from around her middle and started tugging the oversized pants over her hips. He managed to get them to her thighs before one of her fists caught him a glancing blow on his already bruised cheekbone and the rest of his patience evaporated.

He grabbed her shoulders and gave her a fierce shake. "Stop it!"

His voice cracked off stone, loud and angry enough to make Megan flinch. He released her and she rocked back, her eyes wide and filled with sudden fear. Tag swore under his breath, ignored the urge to wrap his arms around her and comfort her. Jaw set, he got the rest of her clothes off, leaving her cotton bra and panties on as much for his sake as hers, and then briskly rubbed her down with a dry T-shirt from his pack, trying to keep his mind strictly on business.

But it wasn't that easy. Her damp skin glowed like satin in the dim light and memories he'd tried to forget kept flooding over him, filling his mind with the remembered softness of her, the warmth. He gritted his teeth, holding the other more intimate memories firmly at bay as he toweled her back, the satiny sweep of her hip and stomach, her thighs, his hands businesslike and impersonal.

She'd quit fighting by then, and sat crouched on her knees with her head down and arms wrapped around her as he gave her back and shoulders another brisk rubdown. He toweled her hair as dry as possible, then unrolled the light, down-filled sleeping bag and drew it around her. "It'll be dark in another hour. As soon as you've warmed up a bit, we'll head out—we're sitting ducks up here. And I don't like the look of that sky. We could be in for a bad storm, and I want to get down off this mountain before it hits or we might not make it off at all."

Megan hadn't even moved, her slender body racked by shiver after shiver. It was a good sign, proof her body was fighting off the cold. He tugged the sleeping bag more tightly around her, feeling her tremble, but it was only when he heard her give a deep, unsteady sob that he realized she was crying.

"Megan?" He put his fingers under her chin and lifted her face. Her cheeks were glazed with tears. "Meggie...?"

She turned her face away. "I c-can't," she said in a sobbed whisper. "I can't go on!"

"It's all right, sweetheart," he said quietly. "You'll feel better after you've rested up a bit and had something to eat."

"Please," she sobbed. "I can't. I've been k-kidnapped and drugged and chased and sh-shot at and nearly drowned and I just can't take any more!" She broke down. "I'm so c-cold. S-so cold!"

"Don't quit on me now, sweetheart," he whispered, slipping his arms around her and cradling her against him. "Hang in there, Meg. You're doing fine."

She was stiff and unyielding in his arms, fighting his touch, his comfort. But he hung on to her grimly, rubbing her back and shoulders through the sleeping bag, and finally he could feel the tension start to break. Slowly, bit by tiny bit, she started to relax against him.

He was crouched beside her at an awkward angle, the aching muscles in his back and legs reminding him all too clearly of the abuse they'd already been through, and he finally just sat down and pulled her gently into his lap. Leaning back against the rock, he stretched his legs out, feeling the weariness wash over him like a leaden wave, knowing he was going to pay dearly for even this few minutes' rest.

He pulled his heavy jacket and shirt open and drew Megan inside, then wrapped the sleeping bag around them both, tucking it tightly around her bare legs and feet. She murmured something sleepily and snuggled against his naked chest like a kitten as his body heat soaked into her, and he sighed deeply and tightened his arms around her. Her hair smelled of snow and mountain air and he rested his cheek against it, then lowered his face into the curve of her neck.

"It's okay now, Meg," he whispered against her ear. He kissed the side of her throat, letting his lips linger on her cold, damp skin, warming her with his breath. "Everything's going to be okay, Meggie. I won't let them hurt you,

I promise. I won't ever let anything hurt you again.'' She shivered, but lightly this time, and he could hear her breathing deepen and steady as she slid swiftly into sleep.

Chapter 5

Tag swore wearily and relaxed back against the cave wall, every bone in his own body screaming for rest. Instinct told him they had to keep moving, that the longer they stayed up here with no supplies and little shelter, well within the radius of Lucas's search teams, the stronger the likelihood they wouldn't get out alive.

Always keep moving, that whispery voice from the past reminded him. *Never stay in one place long enough to let them draw a bead on you....*

But what were their chances if he *did* push on tonight? Megan's reserves of strength were just about gone. She needed rest and food, and chances were the only way he was going to get her off this mountain tonight was to carry her. It was a miracle she'd stayed on her feet this long, considering what she'd been through. Hell, he was just about at the end himself and he hadn't spent the last five days in a drugged stupor, being terrorized by strangers.

As it always did when he thought of Megan's ordeal, a bolt of anger shot through him. He struggled to fight it down. Anger could kill as certainly as ordinary stupidity—Lucas had taught him *that*, too.

Tag smiled faintly into the darkness, listening to Megan's deep relaxed breathing as she slept, safe, in the circle of his arms. There may have been one thing that Lucas had overlooked, though. This wasn't just about life and death anymore. Bringing Megan into it had made the stakes a little more personal, a little more deadly. He had twice the reasons to stay alive now; twice the determination to bring Lucas down. Perhaps, in the end, revenge was the most powerful motivator of all.

He dozed on and off, his dreams strange and oddly erotic, and awoke at least twice aroused and uncomfortable. The last time he awakened it was with a jolt, his heart pounding, the dregs of a muddled nightmare still floating through his mind. He shook it off impatiently, cursing his own carelessness at having fallen asleep. The slit of pale gray at the cave entrance had darkened and he could tell by the way his breath crystallized in the still air that the temperature had dropped again. The wind had picked up, too. He could hear it out there, whining around the cave entrance.

He should get up and take a look. But the prospect was less than tempting. It was damned cold out there, and he was comfortable right where he was, wrapped in the sleeping bag and close to Megan's growing warmth.

She was still sleeping deeply, curled up in his lap, head tucked under his chin. She'd slipped her arms around him and was holding him tightly, probably not even aware of what she was doing, and Tag could feel the light, rhythmic beat of her heart against his.

He could feel her breasts, too, small and tidy but eminently feminine, like everything about her. Her hipbone was pressed almost painfully against his and she'd wriggled around so her round little bottom was cupped perfectly in his lap, something his body, if not his mind, had been aware of for some time, and which had undoubtedly resulted in some of the more graphic overtones to his dreams.

He tried to keep from noticing certain other things, but it was pretty difficult. The feel of her skin, for instance—as soft as brushed velvet. The long sweep of her bare back. It was incredible how well he knew her trim body, considering how little time he'd had with her. Three weeks in all, although he'd never seen her naked, had never made love to her, until that last night. Yet it was as though his hands and body had memorized every lovely curve and indentation of her, as though sometime during the long and wondrous night she'd imprinted herself upon the essence of his soul. She even *fit* against him perfectly, light enough to be comfortable yet heavy enough for him to be very much aware of her being there.

Maybe a little *too* aware. His body, already whetted from the dreams, responded eloquently, and he winced and swore under his breath as Megan shifted in her sleep, unwittingly provoking an already volatile situation.

Damn it, what was going on here? Not the physical response; a man would have to be a veritable saint *not* to respond to a lapful of all-but-naked woman. But what about all those other feelings that seeing her again had set into turmoil—the feelings he'd convinced himself would never surface again? He'd tried his damnedest all day to pretend they weren't there, but there was a limit to how much pretending a man could do.

The best thing, the *safest* thing, was to just ignore them. To do otherwise was inviting serious trouble, and not only from the possibility of stepping in front of a bullet when his attention drifted at the wrong moment. There was Megan to consider. She hated his guts, not surprisingly, and it was better if he just left it that way. Hurting her once had been unavoidable. Hurting her a second time would be unconscionable.

And yet . . .

No! He wasn't going to start playing *that* game, by God. *And yet* never did anything but get a man into trouble. Second-guessing was for amateurs.

Megan stirred again, murmuring something in her sleep, and Tag tucked the edge of the sleeping bag snugly under her chin. She looked very serene, the perpetual little frown between her brows all but gone, the exhaustion and fear erased. Her skin was like warm silk and he couldn't stop himself from caressing her cheek lightly with the back of his hand. She may have smiled, although it was hard to tell in the shadows. But Tag felt something pull wire-taut within him, a peculiar sensation that almost felt like wistfulness.

Which was crazy. And yet...

He sighed, giving his head a despairing shake at his own whimsy. "What am I going to do with you, sweet Meggie," he breathed. "What in hell am I going to do with you?"

Finally he couldn't put it off any longer. He eased himself out from under Megan and got to his feet, wrapping the down-filled bag around her tightly and leaving her asleep.

It was bad outside. Worse than he'd anticipated. The whole world had disappeared in dirty gray clouds and wind-whipped pellets of snow that stung like hail. It was already starting to build up and it crunched like broken glass under his boots as he walked the perimeter of his small outpost, breath puffing in the icy air. The wind keened along the rock face, erasing his footprints even as he made them, and he could hear the big pines above him creak and moan.

He swore quietly, shrugging his shoulders more deeply into his heavy jacket. If there was a big storm front moving in behind this, they were in serious trouble. Maybe the weather was going to be the deciding factor between staying or moving on, and not Lucas at all. Shivering, he turned his back on the snow-glazed landscape and wriggled his way back into the cave.

Megan was awake. She was sitting up with the sleeping bag pulled tightly around her like a buffalo robe, her eyes wide with fright.

"Sorry, didn't mean to scare you." He unslung the M16 and set it aside. "I thought you were asleep."

"I thought you'd gone," she whispered, her knuckles white where she was clutching the sleeping bag. "When I woke up and you weren't here, I thought you'd . . . left me behind."

That annoyed him for some reason. He pulled his pack toward him and started rummaging through it angrily. "What the hell do you take me for," he growled. "I told you I came up here to get you out, didn't I?"

Hostility replaced the fear in her eyes. She pulled the sleeping bag tighter and glowered at him. "You took my clothes off."

Tag gave her a sharp look, then realized that she'd been so exhausted she simply didn't remember what had happened during those few minutes before she'd fallen asleep in his arms. Which was probably just as well. "I kept my eyes closed," he drawled.

Her reply was uncharacteristically profane, and he looked at her impatiently. "Look, Megan, give me a break, okay? For one thing, I was trying to keep you from freezing to death—you'll see me in hell before thanking me, I know, but there it is. And for another, I *am* your husband. Or was, at any rate. I've undressed you before."

Even in the dim light from the half-obscured torch, he could see the blush flame across her cheeks. Again, it annoyed him for absolutely no reason he could pin down. "I don't get my kicks from molesting half-conscious women," he said testily. "I stripped you down and I wrapped you in that sleeping bag, and apart from that I kept my hands to myself."

Ignoring her, he lit the tiny primus stove and dug around in the pack until he found the box of C rations, then opened a tin of peaches for himself and one of powdered chocolate for Megan.

Megan hadn't realized how hungry she was until Tag handed her the steaming mug of hot chocolate. She accepted it gratefully and took a deep swallow. The chocolate was rich and sweet and hot, and was probably the most delicious thing she'd ever tasted. "Good," she murmured, licking a chocolaty mustache off her upper lip. She could feel its heat seeping right through her, and for the first time in days she felt almost safe.

"Just C rats. Probably been around since Vimy Ridge, but it's hot and your body needs the sugar." He frowned as he watched her take another deep swallow. "How long has it been since you had anything to eat?"

She shrugged, cradling the mug against her for its warmth. "Last night, maybe. I ... I seem to remember eating something. But it's fuzzy...."

He said something under his breath, his eyes glittering with deep anger, then handed her the other open tin. Megan's eyes widened with delight. The peach slices floated in a thick syrup and she drank it right out of the tin, then struggled to fish one of the slices out with her fingers. Tag wordlessly handed her the big survival knife and Megan deftly speared a slice and ate it, too hungry to care about table manners.

It was only when she'd worked her way through most of the peaches that she realized the picture she must be making, sitting cross-legged in a cave, eating C rations off a knife the size of a machete. She paused, then smiled in spite of herself and handed both the knife and the tin to Tag. "If you'd warned me we were dining out," she dared, "I'd have packed the silver."

To her relief, Tag's mouth twitched slightly. Then, as grudgingly as she'd done, he smiled. "This is the last time we book a budget vacation through *that* travel agent."

The gasp of laughter escaped in spite of Megan's best efforts to swallow it. She shivered and pulled the sleeping bag up to her ears. "Well, at least the air-conditioning works."

"Next year, Paris," he quipped.

They both laughed, and in that long, shared moment, Megan distinctly felt the unacknowledged tension between them loosen slightly. For an instant Taggart Welles and the fox-faced man and even the horrors of the past few hours disappeared, and it was just her and Michael again, laughing over some silly, shared thing. His eyes caught hers and she could have sworn he was thinking the very same thought, could almost smell the honeyed scent of frangipani in the air.

Then it was gone. She looked down, suddenly flustered for some reason, and Tag shifted restlessly beside her as though he, too, had been caught by surprise by whatever had happened. The wind moaned at the cave entrance, plucking at the rock like something wanting in, and she shivered. "Is it as bad out there as it sounds?"

"Yeah." He looked at her. "How do you feel?"

"I'm all right." She let her gaze slip, and stared at a tiny gray feather lying on the debris carpeting the cave floor. "I seem to remember coming a bit unglued earlier. Crying and . . . carrying on. I'm not usually the hysterical type. I'm sorry."

"You weren't hysterical," he said quietly. "You were tired and cold and scared, and I was pushing you too hard. You've got more endurance and guts than most men I know."

She glanced up at him uncertainly, surprised to see by the expression on his face that he meant it. She smiled faintly. "I don't *feel* very gutsy. I feel scared to death." Then she looked at the feather again, unable to meet his eyes. "What I said out there, about not thanking you. That wasn't . . . right."

"Meggie, you don't have to say—"

"I do," she said simply, looking up to meet his eyes. "If you hadn't gotten me out of there, they'd have killed me."

"You're not out of it yet," he reminded her with a crooked smile. "Between the weather and Lucas, the odds aren't good that we'll even make it off this mountain."

She nodded, knowing he wasn't trying to frighten her, but was simply stating the truth. Another little shiver darted through her but she ignored it, and found her gaze drawn to his profile as irresistibly as a moth drawn to candlelight.

"There was a man there," she said softly, "who knew you. Tall, with a narrow, foxy face. Is that the Lucas you keep mentioning?"

He nodded, his eyes suddenly narrowed and cold. "Jack Lucas."

"Was any of it true...the things he told me about you? About the CIA, the...the murders?"

For a moment or two she didn't think he was going to answer. In a way, she was almost relieved. There were probably some things she didn't really want to know.

"Lucas was my C.O. for most of my first tour in Nam. And part of my second. Shadow Company. Special Forces. We were the best of the best, each one of us handpicked and trained by Jack Lucas himself. They called us the Killer Elite. And gave us every dirty job that came along...." He frowned slightly and drew a spiral on the ground with the tip of the knife.

The shadows gave his face a lean, dangerous look that made the back of her neck prickle, and Megan sat very quietly in the warm fold of the sleeping bag, watching him wordlessly.

Then he gave himself a little shake, as though casting off the past, and looked up at her, his eyes infinitely weary. "Some things happened on my last tour—things I had a hard time dealing with. I transferred out of Shadow Company, finished my tour with another unit, came home, and tried to put it all behind me. I kept in touch with some of the guys for a while, but it was different back in the real world. We all had our own lives, and one by one we just drifted away from each other."

He drew one knee up and draped his arm over it, tapping the tip of the knife blade gently on the toe of his boot. "There was only one guy I stayed in contact with—a note at Christmas, an occasional phone call if he was passing through Houston, a postcard now and again. We'd been through some pretty heavy stuff together in Nam and although we didn't spend much time together it was nice knowing that someone was out there who understood, that if things got real bad and you needed to talk...."

Again he lapsed into a thoughtful silence. Megan picked the tiny feather up and smoothed it in her palm, waiting.

"Russ was into shortcuts, into deals. He was always on the track of the really big one, half a step away from the winner he always knew was his if he could just get things together. He called me a couple of times with the opportunity of the century—some of it was probably legit, but he was walking pretty close to the edge sometimes, too. The last time he called, about two years ago, he told me that he'd finally lucked into something that was going to make him richer than he'd ever dreamed."

"And he wanted to cut you in," Megan said softly.

Tag nodded, smiling faintly. "He was calling from Bangkok with, as he put it, 'the opportunity of a lifetime.' He said he'd been contacted by some of the old Shadow Company and that they were into something big. When I tried to pin him down with names and details, he clammed up, just said it was payback time. That we'd watered half of Southeast Asia with American blood and that it was time for us to reap the harvest—I can't remember his exact words, but that's near enough."

He glanced up at Megan. "I wasn't surprised. War brings out the entrepreneurial spirit in some people, and Vietnam wasn't any different. There were a thousand scams going on. The place was ripe for the picking if you were into quick cash, and a lot of guys came home rich. Some stayed there after the war was over, too, into drugs, women, weapons, contraband—you name it, someone's making a buck off it."

He looked away again, the frown back. "I told him 'thanks but no thanks.' He laughed and said he'd drop around next time he was in town and tell me how much money I'd lost by not coming in with them when I had the chance. Then, about eighteen months ago, I got a letter from him. It was postmarked Hong Kong and had taken seven weeks to reach me." He reached into an inner pocket and drew out a slip of folded paper, looked at it for a long moment before handing it to her silently.

It was grimy with fingerprints and what looked like smears of blood, and had been folded and refolded so often the paper was starting to tear. Gently, she opened it. It was a piece of stationery from a Hong Kong hotel and on it, hurriedly scrawled in pencil and so faded she could hardly decipher them, were four sentences.

They're going to kill me unless I get out. You told me in Nam if I ever needed help, you'd be there for me— well, buddy, I need it now. It goes higher and wider than I could have dreamed, and you're the only one I trust.

Megan folded the paper carefully and handed it back to him. "Did you go after him?"

"I was in Hong Kong two days later," Tag said quietly. "But Russ had vanished. So I started digging around, trying to pick up his trail, chasing leads all over half of Southeast Asia. It was pretty obvious after only a few days that Russ had been playing ball with some real tough characters. The deeper I dug, the worse it got. Smuggling, drugs, illegal arms sales—everywhere I turned, his name kept popping up.

"Then, in Bangkok, a guy by the name of Frank Elliott contacted me. He said he was part of an international task force on crime, coordinated jointly through the DEA and CIA. He'd been following Russ, and when I turned up he naturally started following me. It didn't take him long to realize I wasn't involved, that I was just looking for an old friend. And that's when he decided to recruit me."

"Recruit?"

Tag's smile was humorless. "Russ's 'opportunity of a lifetime' was a treasure-hoard of gold bullion, historical artifacts, priceless art pieces and just about anything else you can name that had been 'acquired' by a small group of U.S.

servicemen during the final months of the war in Vietnam.''

" 'Acquired' meaning stolen.''

"Looted. By them directly, or by hired bandits—the mountains in Cambodia, Thailand and Laos are thick with them. Drug lords mostly, but they're flexible. Most of this stuff was Laotian and Cambodian, including a huge collection of stuff taken out of Angkor Wat. But they'd also looted half the temples and palaces in Burma and Thailand, and had even gotten their hands on a collection of T'ang Dynasty porcelains and jade smuggled out of China during Chiang Kai-shek's purge.''

"Good grief,'' Megan whispered. "You're talking about the national treasures of most of Southeast Asia!''

"A good part of it. The plan was to wait a few years, then bring it into the States a bit at a time. The intervening years were to be spent putting together a list of international collectors and dealers who were interested in what they had to offer, no questions asked.''

"Payback,'' Megan murmured.

"Exactly. When things started to fall apart during the last year in Nam, a lot of guys decided that it was time to start looking out for Number One. We weren't winning the war, so if you were going to get shot at, you might as well make it worth your while. And when you're in a part of the world where twelve-year-old girls are selling themselves on the street for a bowl of rice and a bit of rat meat, it isn't hard for an enterprising soldier to find someone willing to sell a piece of priceless Cambodian temple art for five bucks and a package of cigarettes.''

"My God,'' Megan sighed, "greed never changes, does it? But how could they put together a treasure trove like that without someone finding out? You can't just walk in and loot a country blind without *someone* noticing.''

Tag gave a snort. "By that time, U.S. withdrawal was a foregone conclusion. The communists were knocking on the back door, and South Vietnamese government officials and army officers by the hundreds were scrambling to get out of the country before it fell. And they were willing to sell their own grandmothers' gold teeth to buy their way out. It wasn't hard for a government official to bribe his counterpart in Thailand or Laos or wherever—hell, in most cases the governments that were supposedly protecting their countries from being looted blind were the very ones doing the looting. Ancestral honor doesn't hold a candle to a Swiss safety-deposit box full of Krugerrands.''

Megan nodded despondently.

''A couple of years ago the guys behind the scheme decided they'd been sitting on their pot of gold long enough and it was time to cash in. Everything had been in place for years, so when the time came to put things into motion it ran like clockwork. It didn't take this international task force on crime that Elliott worked with long to figure out something was going on. Pieces of museum-quality Oriental art were turning up here and there, and word was out that someone was moving large quantities of gold bullion. The task force went nuts trying to figure out who was behind it, but had no luck. Until Russ got involved and started shooting his mouth off. Elliott told me he'd been getting close to breaking the case wide open when Russ suddenly disappeared—and I stumbled into the situation.''

''If Russ was such a security risk, how did he get involved in the first place?''

Tag smiled. ''Simple. He'd known about it from scratch. In Nam, he'd known about every dodge and game in town. Instead of forcing his hand right then—and risking going out on patrol some night and not coming back—he sat on the information. Two years ago, when word got out that something big was going down, he heard about it and made his move, demanding to be cut in.''

Megan suppressed a shiver. ''And they killed him.''

Tag's face went still and cold. ''Yeah,'' he said after a moment, his voice harsh. ''Although I didn't know that for sure back then. Elliott figured there was the possibility that

Russ had gotten away and was in hiding. That's why he wanted me—like Russ, I knew most of the men involved. Including the guy heading it up.''

Megan looked up. ''Lucas.''

''Lucas,'' he said in that icy, remote voice. ''Elliott said he wanted me to infiltrate the group, that someone on the inside feeding him information would wrap things up that much sooner. He gave me this long song and dance about having the opportunity to find out what had happened to Russ and serving my country at the same time. It all sounded very heroic and noble, but I didn't give a damn about any of it except finding Russ and, if possible, getting him out of Southeast Asia in one piece.''

''So you agreed to help Elliott.''

''He told me I'd have no problem getting in, that Lucas knew me, trusted me. After all, I'd been one of his chosen few once.'' Tag's voice was bitter. ''I wasn't so sure. There had been no love lost between Lucas and me toward the end, and when I finally transferred out of Shadow Company he'd made it perfectly plain it was my loss, not his. But I was worried about Russ. The guy had asked for it, but he'd saved my life in Nam. Twice. I figured if there was a chance in a million he was still alive, I owed it to him to do everything possible to help him. So . . . I made a deal.''

He was staring at the ground and Megan waited for him to go on, wondering where all this was leading. How in heaven's name had a man's sense of obligation to an old friend resulted in his marrying a stranger on a south-seas cruise, or in her being kidnapped and nearly murdered? She shivered lightly and pulled the sleeping bag more tightly around her shoulders.

''I agreed to help Elliott if he could guarantee that when he closed the trap on Lucas, he'd let Russ off easy.''

''And he agreed?'' asked Megan in surprise.

''Without even blinking.''

''And Lucas?''

"Greeted me like a long lost brother." The knife thudded deeply into the dirt beside Tag's right foot. "He just happened to be in Bangkok that week, checking on things. It wasn't hard to find out what hotel he was staying at and book myself in. We both *happened* to be in the hotel bar my first night there and we had a drink together to toast old times. I mentioned I'd come over to scout out the import-export opportunities. He asked me if I was interested in making a lot of money, I said I didn't know a man who wasn't . . . and the next thing I knew I was coordinating shipments of tenth-century Cambodian artifacts out of Laos into Amsterdam and New York."

Megan frowned. "You make it sound awfully easy."

"Too easy. One of the things Lucas taught us in Nam was that a man's survival instincts will pick up danger even if his eyes and ears tell him it's safe. I can't explain how, but I could always tell if a trail was mined or a hootch was booby-trapped or a ville that *looked* quiet enough was actually a VC ambush. And right from the instant Lucas shook my hand in that hotel bar, my instincts were screaming at me to get the hell out before whatever happened to Russ happened to me."

"But you didn't."

He shook his head, smiling faintly. "I was damned if I was pulling out before I'd found out what had happened to Russ."

"And Elliott? Did he know you suspected trouble?"

"I told him." The smile turned grim. "First-time jitters, he called it. Told me every good agent gets them." He glanced up at Megan. "I didn't like it, but I agreed to stay in for another week. Long enough for him to mobilize a full-scale bust. Two days later, by complete accident, I stumbled onto what Lucas was really doing."

"Gold bullion and stolen art weren't enough?"

"The gold bullion and stolen art were sidelines. Five or six million a year, maybe. Chump change. It had just been a way to provide seed money to set up the main operation.

These guys didn't ransack whole countries and spend fifteen years setting up this kind of an organization just to peddle bootleg jewelry and temple baubles, Meg. They're running China White." He smiled faintly at her blank look. "The White Horse, angel. Pure, high-grade heroin."

It shouldn't have surprised her, of course. You didn't have to be part of the drug scene to know about the Golden Triangle, that dangerous, wild region high on the Mekong River where Laos, Burma and Thailand meet. The mountain people up there had been tending terraced fields of scarlet opium poppies for centuries.

She nodded slowly. "So Elliott and the others were able to bust the operation. Except that Lucas got away and is now after you. Which doesn't explain why—"

"Elliott didn't do anything," he said softly. "Because Elliott was one of them."

Megan, her mouth half-open, simply stared at him.

"He's CIA, all right. But he's working for Lucas, planted in the crime task force to advise Lucas of their every move. And to keep the task force from stumbling too close to Lucas's operation." He sighed deeply and leaned against the cave wall, rubbing his left shoulder. "Russ had gotten in 'way over his head with this bunch. They'd played him along for awhile, but when he got to be more trouble than he was worth, they killed him. When I came blundering in, they weren't sure if I was DEA or CIA—or just plain stupid. They decided to play me along like they had Russ, until they figured out what kind of a risk I was. I'd been right about Lucas—he hadn't trusted me any more than I'd trusted him. Both of us had smelled trouble a mile off."

"But you got away before they could do anything."

"I didn't get away." Tag closed his eyes, then drew in a deep breath and looked at Megan again, haggard and tired. "I was obviously too much of a threat to ignore, but they didn't dare kill me, either. Not without knowing what kind of muscle I was working for and who might come looking for me if I just disappeared. So they did the next best thing.

Elliott set up a meeting between me—his new operative—and three members of the task force: one was another CIA man, the second was with some British agency, the third was a Canadian RCMP officer on loan from some special investigative branch in Vancouver. Ten minutes after the meeting started, six men burst in with machine guns and took everyone out.''

Megan felt herself pale. ''How did you—''

''Dumb, blind luck. I got lost, can you believe it?'' He gave a hoarse bark of laughter that held more horror than humor. ''I spent twenty minutes wandering around downtown Bangkok, and by the time I got to the meeting place it was all over. I must have been shell-shocked or something, because it never hit me that I'd been set up. The first thing I did was call Elliott.'' He gave another snort of humorless laughter. ''He must have nearly had a coronary when he heard my voice. But he didn't waste any time.

''Ten minutes after the news had hit the wires, word was out that I'd been responsible. That I'd been bought off and had set the ambush up, had maybe even been in on the kill. And ten minutes after *that*,'' he added softly, ''every intelligence agency, drug-enforcement organization and police force in the free world was after me. Taggart Welles had suddenly become the most wanted man alive.''

''My God,'' Megan whispered. ''And that's when you turned up at the cruise dock in Singapore. As Michael Walker.''

He may have winced slightly. ''I'd managed to get that far in one piece, no thanks to Elliott,'' he said in a low, hoarse voice. ''I'd dyed my hair and changed my eye color with contact lenses and bought a new passport in Manila, but I knew it was just a matter of time before someone spotted me. My only chance was to get back to the States and try to clear my name.

''I was planning on jumping a freighter when I saw the cruise-ship listings in the paper one day—and I realized it would be a hell of a lot easier to get back to the States as a passenger aboard a luxury cruise ship than as a stowaway on some freighter. It wasn't hard to fake what I needed to get on board. And what fraudulent papers didn't cover, old-fashioned bribery did. Once I was on board, no one questioned me.''

"So the Honolulu police were right all along," Megan said softly. It occurred to her, very idly, that she should be feeling something. Anger, probably. Anger would have been nice. At least it would have warmed her. But there was absolutely nothing there. No anger, no hatred, no pain. Just an empty, cold place that almost felt like hopelessness.

"I've been on the run for the past year," Tag said quietly, "playing cat and mouse with Lucas and every cop and federal agent in the country. I can't turn myself in because it's my word against Elliott's, and I don't have a shred of proof in my favor."

"But surely there's *someone* you can go to," Megan said with a shiver. "This is the United States, not some little Latin American country run by a military junta. We don't have secret police who can whisk you off the street and into jail without a trial or—" She stopped dead at Tag's expression.

Chapter 6

It's not just Elliott and Lucas," Tag said quietly. "I stumbled into something big, Meg. Really big."

"Big?" Megan swallowed.

"It goes right up to some of the highest levels of government in the country—people with key roles in intelligence, national security, drug enforcement, foreign relations, even the people who formulate policy. Together they run one of the biggest heroin operations in the world—and they're doing it right out of high-level government offices in Washington."

"That's ... preposterous." Megan simply stared at him, wanting to jump to her feet and tell him she didn't believe a word of it. But something stopped her. Something in his eyes, perhaps, or in the haggard lines of his face. "My God," she whispered, "it *is* the truth, isn't it?"

"As soon as I got back to the States, I discovered what I should have already guessed—that the operation is a lot bigger than a bunch of Shadow Company renegades smuggling gold and dope. I'd figured all it would take to get things straightened out were a couple of phone calls to old friends in high places who owed me favors. But all those calls did was tell me that I was in deeper trouble than I'd ever dreamed. My little escapade in Bangkok shook up some very powerful people, Meg. People who are worried about what kind of trouble I can stir up. And those very powerful people want me dead."

"Good lord," Megan whispered.

"It gets worse," Tag said grimly. "I contacted a friend of mine a few months ago, ex-Special Forces now working in some hush-hush job in Washington. He and Lucas crossed horns a couple of times in Nam and Rick packs some heavy-ordnance hate for the guy. I don't know many details, but I do know Rick left a leg and six of his best buddies in a rice paddy somewhere in the Delta and he holds Lucas personally responsible.

"When I told Rick what was going on, he got that look he used to get just before a night patrol—the kind of look a wolf gets when it scents a rabbit. He told me to take cover and stay there, then he went to work. It took him months, but he finally started making progress. I doubt anyone else could have done it—he had security clearances to God himself for one thing, and unlimited access to the Pentagon computer and links through it to every intelligence-bureau datafile on the globe. And he's like a pit bull; once he smells blood, he's in for the kill and nothing on earth will discourage him.

"He picked up the scent through the CIA, tracing backward from the information Elliott had filed on me after the Bangkok mess. And what he finally found scared even him—a whole sublevel of secret computer files and communications, linking all the people involved and protected by unbreakable codes. Or almost unbreakable. It's like a second level of government operating invisibly within the infrastructure of the real one, with its own staff, facilities, communications, even its own financial network. They launder the huge amount of drug money coming in by 'hiding' it in the government computers as foreign investments or loan payoffs, then 'spending' it on fraudulent budgets and government contracts—a billion here, a billion there. Hell, these days, who'd notice?''

Megan swallowed. ''And they know you know.''

Tag's eyes held hers. ''Yeah. Rick and I had already decided that there had to be one key figure in all this—someone very high up in the government who was running the whole show. It also meant we didn't know who we could trust; *anybody* could be part of it. We didn't dare try to go public until we had the evidence nailed down tight, but once Rick broke their codes and got inside the network, we knew it was just a matter of time before he triggered some kind of warning flag and they knew someone was on to them.''

''He also figured they'd be able to track down whoever had breached their security—tracing his footprints through the computer the same way he'd traced theirs—so he didn't have any time to waste. He managed to uncover one name—a code name. References were made again and again to someone called The Black Dragon.''

''The Black Dragon?'' Megan looked at him sharply, some half-remembered thing teasing her. She'd dreamed of dragons...black dragons with shining emerald eyes....

''Meg?''

She blinked, realized he was looking at her oddly, and shook her head. ''Sorry. It's nothing. Just a...a nightmare I had. Do you know who this Black Dragon is?''

''At first we figured it was one of their Asian contacts. Then we decided it was someone here in the States, maybe a connection with the Chinese drug network. But the deeper Rick dug, the more convinced he was that the Black Dragon was the man we were looking for—the key guy running the whole operation. Two weeks ago he called me and told me he was practically there, that he was just cross-checking one more thing to make sure he was right. We arranged to meet two days later, and he said he'd have everything we needed to bring the whole thing down like a house of cards.''

He stopped, his face grim. "They were waiting for us. It was just luck neither of us walked into the trap. Rick saw it first and warned me, and the two of us took off in opposite directions. I haven't been able to contact Rick since."

Megan's heart gave a thump. "You don't think he's . . ."

"Dead?" Tag's smile was grim. "I don't know. If he is, the cops kept it pretty quiet. Then again, if the Black Dragon's as high up as I think he is, that's possible—he'd have put his CIA goons on it and told the local heat to back off."

"And the information Rick said he had?" she asked quietly.

Tag shrugged. "If he's alive, he still has it. If he's dead, it's possible the Black Dragon's people have it now."

"And with it, any hope you have of clearing your name," she whispered. She reached for him, but he was too far away for her to do more than touch her fingertips to his. He glanced up, seemingly startled by her gesture, and on an impulse, Megan moved closer to him. She put her hand out again. Her fingers almost brushed his bruised cheek before she caught herself and she let her hand fall to his arm instead, filled with a fierce, tender urge to comfort him, yet confused by her own erratic emotions.

"What are you going to do now?"

It was distracting, how close she was sitting. The sleeping bag was bunched up against his hip and Tag swore he could feel the pressure of her thigh inside it, but told himself he was imagining things. Her serious little face was distractingly near, too, the anguish on it so real it was as though she were actually feeling *his* pain. It surprised him so much that for an instant he forgot what she'd asked.

He'd told her the truth because he figured she deserved it, not because of any illusions he had about her forgiving him. Grudging understanding had been the best he'd hoped for; what he saw on her face was something else altogether, something he couldn't quite pin down. . . .

Then he remembered she'd asked him something, and he gave himself a shake. "Get you the hell out of here and

somewhere safe, first. Then find out what happened to
Rick. I was trying to track him down when I got word Lucas had snatched you.''

Megan frowned slightly. ''Lucas was talking about
some . . . files. Files you have that he wants. Would that be
the information Rick had?''

Tag looked at her sharply. ''Are you sure?''

''Positive.'' She shivered slightly. ''He talked in front of
me as though I wasn't even there. He gave orders that you
weren't to be killed until he had a chance to find out where
they are.''

''That's interesting.'' Tag's mind went spinning off in a
hundred directions, none of them particularly useful. ''It's
probably the information Rick said he'd have for me, all
right. But does that mean Rick is dead, or just in hiding,
or . . . ?'' He shook his head, frowning.

''I feel as if I've fallen into someone else's nightmare,''
Megan whispered. ''At least with your own you get to wake
up, but with this . . .'' She shivered again.

Tag didn't even realize he'd planned to touch her until his
fingers brushed her hair. She looked up, slightly startled,
and he drew his hand back with an odd reluctance, glad that
at least she didn't flinch as though his touch was repulsive.
And that she didn't look at him with undisguised fear anymore, either. It shouldn't have mattered, of course, but for
some strange reason he found it did.

''Do you have any antiseptic?''

He blinked, annoyed to find that his attention had wandered again. When he saw her hand move, he reared back,
throwing his arm up instinctively and catching her wrist before the blow could land, realizing, an instant later, that
she'd only intended to touch his bruised cheek. She was
staring at him in shock and he managed a dry smile, releasing her wrist. ''Sorry. Reflex.''

To his utter surprise, she smiled back. It was very faint
and slightly uncertain, but it *was*, undoubtedly, a smile. ''I
didn't realize you considered me one of the enemy.''

It surprised him even more to find himself capable of laughter. "You pack quite a wallop, angel." Grinning, he rubbed his jaw. "Between you and Lucas's men, I may wind up eating through a straw for the next week."

"I'd been saving up for nearly a year," she said with a trace of humor in her voice. Then she frowned, her gaze drifting to his right temple. "That's a bad cut," she said quietly. "It could do with a half dozen stitches, but if you've got some adhesive tape, I'll do the best I can."

Tag touched his temple gingerly. It was swollen and painful, and his hair was stiff with dried blood. He winced, shaking his head. "No adhesive tape, but I appreciate the thought."

"Some rescue this is," she muttered. "No transportation, no food, no fire, no first-aid kit."

"I kind of figured," he drawled, "that either we'd *di di* clean, or we'd get killed." He had to laugh at her expression. "*Di di* is Vietnamese for get moving or clear out or run like hell. Either way, adhesive tape isn't a priority item. Extra magazines for *this*—" he tapped the M16 with his toe "—is."

She nodded, a worried little frown settling between her eyebrows, and she nestled down into the sleeping bag as though suddenly chilled. "What are our chances of getting out of this alive?" she asked quietly. "And don't sugarcoat it. I hate men who pat me on the shoulder and tell me not to worry my pretty little head about things."

He met her gaze evenly. "Odds are against us. The weather might work in our favor, or it might kill us. We may get away from Lucas and walk into a CIA trap, or get picked up by some local cop who recognizes me—either way, we probably won't last long, not with the Black Dragon's people everywhere. For that matter, we might freeze to death right here. Somebody will find our bones and write a doctoral thesis on us. Or a romance novel."

She gave him a peevish sidelong look, pulling the sleeping bag tighter. "You could have sugarcoated it a *little*."

"Hey..." He leaned toward her and turned the edge of the bag up around her ears. "I told you I was going to get you out of this, Meg, and I mean it. And to hell with the odds."

She didn't say anything, simply sat there looking up at him with a peculiar expression in her eyes. They were the color of dark chocolate, those eyes, and they never wavered from his, even when his hands released the sleeping bag and moved upward to touch the warmth of her cheeks.

Her face was as dirty as a child's, a streak of grime across her forehead where she'd wiped away a trickle of sweat, a smear of dried blood on her chin from a deep thorn scratch, the smudges on her cheeks tear-tracked. Her usually glossy hair was matted with milkweed seeds and foxtails, and he felt something pull achingly tight within him. She hated being dirty or rumpled, was as fastidious as a cat about herself and her surroundings.

"Poor, sweet Meggie," he whispered. "What have I done to you, angel? How in the hell did I convince myself that you wouldn't be hurt in all this?"

Her lips were like satin against his, and he moved his mouth to capture them more fully. He had actually cupped her cheek in one hand and had started to slip the other around her shoulders before he realized what he was doing.

"Damn it, no!" He recoiled with a soft oath and turned away, teeth gritted. "I swore I wasn't going to do that." Not again, he added silently. I'm not putting either of us through all that again. It had been hard enough leaving her once. It had been like ripping a part of himself away and leaving it behind, and there had been a time or two in the past year when it had occurred to him that he'd received two Purple Hearts for less painful wounds.

"Tag?" Her voice was a whisper, the touch of her fingertips on his cheeks more sensed than felt. "Tag, I—"

He was starting to turn toward the unexpected gentleness of her voice when he heard the first shout. He had rolled to his knees and grabbed the M16 while the answering shout was still hanging in the air. He turned to extinguish the flashlight but Megan was there before him. She flung herself across it, smothering the light in the folds of the sleeping bag until she could fumble for the switch.

He inched nearer to the cave entrance, swearing ferociously under his breath. Damn it to hell, how careless could a man get! He might as well have hung out a sign or sent up fireworks or . . .

He caught the anger after a moment and took a deep, calming breath as the adrenaline hit him, feeling every one of a dozen animal senses within him come vibrantly alert. His hearing sharpened so acutely he could distinctly hear Megan swallow somewhere in the darkness, and he strained to listen for footfalls outside or the sound of a rifle bolt snicking into place.

Everything was silent. His skin crawled and he had to fight to stay where he was, knowing instinctively that their best hope lay in staying hidden. But some other part of him kept screaming that they were trapped like fish in a barrel, that one good spray of automatic-weapon fire through that narrow opening would finish them once and for all. Or a grenade. He swallowed, wiping a trickle of sweat from his cheek with his arm. All one of them had to do was spot the fissure in the rock and toss a grenade in. . . .

He could hear Megan's fast, shallow breathing and reached out through the darkness toward her. She recoiled with a swallowed scream when his fingers brushed her cheek, then her fingers meshed with his and he drew her in behind him, tucking her safely down against the rock at his back. As gestures went, it wasn't much. It wouldn't keep her alive if Lucas's men found them in here. But if she was going to die, at least the last thing she'd feel was another human being's body warmth against her.

Footsteps crunched in snow just outside the cave entrance and Tag stiffened. There was a crackle of static, then a tinny voice saying something Tag couldn't catch. They were in radio contact with someone; the helicopter, maybe. Or Lucas himself.

"Damn, it's cold out here!" It was Tiger Jack's voice, so near that Tag felt Megan flinch. There was the sound of someone stamping cold feet and blowing into cupped hands. "Snow's blowing too hard to hold tracks, but if they came this way, they either went straight up this cliff face or they're heading south along the draw. And unless Welles and the broad sprouted wings while we weren't lookin', my money's on the draw. Anybody else have any luck?"

"Not a damned thing," the other voice growled. "Orders are to pull back."

"You kiddin' me? We can get 'em if we just keep going! There's no way the woman can keep up this pace much longer, and Welles is pretty banged up. I say we—"

"*Orders* are we return to base. Lucas says that storm front is coming in fast, and he wants us to head back—wind and visibility are so bad he grounded the chopper twenty minutes ago. In another half hour that blizzard's going to hit, and I don't intend to be still standing here arguing with you when it does."

"And Welles? You mean we're just lettin' him go?"

"The blizzard will finish what we started," his companion snapped. How long do you think they'll last out here?"

"He's got through tighter spots than this," Tiger Jack grumbled. "The guy was Shadow Company, remember? Just like *we're* Shadow Company. And Shadow Warriors don't quit on account of snow!"

"You want to tell Lucas he's wrong?" There was silence, then a derisive snort. "Okay, then. Let's go."

Footsteps crunched again, getting fainter and fainter until they vanished altogether. Tag realized he was holding his breath and he eased it between his teeth.

"Do...do you think it's a trap?"

Tag wet his lips, eyes narrowed. The possibility had occurred to him, too. But why go to the trouble of an elaborate charade to lure them out when a smoke grenade or a signal flare tossed into the cave would do the trick more effectively?

He waited another ten endless minutes, then gingerly eased himself out of the cave, half-expecting to feel cold steel the instant his head emerged from the rock face. But there was nothing outside except a few wind-blurred footprints in the snow where the two men had stood in the lee of the cliff. The sky was the color of lead.

He swore softly, looking at that sky. Then he wriggled back into the cave. He found the flashlight beside his pack and turned it on, not even bothering to shield the brilliant glow. "We're in trouble." Megan's eyes locked with his, wide and questioning. "It's getting bad out there. We've got to get moving, fast."

"Moving?" Megan heard the tension in her voice.

"There's a ski chalet about six miles down the valley. I found it when I was trying to find Lucas's place. We're going to make a run for it."

"Six miles is a long way in bad weather."

"We can't stay here, Meg," Tag said with quiet urgency. "Not without proper clothing and shelter. If I knew for certain it would be just one more day, I'd risk it. But there's no telling how bad that storm's going to be. Or how long it's going to last. All I do know is that if the reports are bad enough to spook Jack Lucas into calling his men in, it's enough to scare the *hell* out of me."

Megan nodded, her heart sinking. "Then I guess I should get dressed," she said calmly. She reached for the pile of icy, wet clothes that Tag had tossed aside.

"Wait." He shrugged out of his heavy jacket and unbuttoned the wool shirt he was wearing underneath. "Put this on first. It's a little bloody, but it's dry. Then put the other shirt over it, and the jacket over the whole lot and button it up tight. Once you start walking, the wet shirt and jacket will keep your body heat in and you'll be good and warm."

Again, Megan simply nodded. The shirt was torn and bloodstained, but it was deliciously warm and dry and she pulled it into the voluminous folds of the sleeping bag with her and wriggled into it gratefully. Almost at once, she was aware of the warm, musky scent of him wrapping around her and she suddenly found herself thinking of things she hadn't thought of in a long, long while: the way his hair smelled in the sunshine, the feel of his cheek against hers in the late afternoon before he shaved for dinner, the damp little curls around the back of his neck after a hard set of tennis. . . .

She gave her head an impatient shake. Oh, no, you don't, she told herself firmly. Not this time. Granted, some of the things he'd told her today explained a lot. And he *had* risked his neck to come up here and get her away from Lucas. But he'd said it himself—he owed her. There were some things that just couldn't be explained away by desperate necessity. And only so much she was prepared to forgive.

"Ready?"

He was on one knee by the cave entrance, leaning casually on the big rifle as he waited for her, and Megan shivered abruptly. Over the past few hours she'd been lulled by the familiar, quiet voice, had found it very easy to imagine that it was Michael there in the shadows across from her. But, suddenly, all that changed. He looked very big and very dangerous in the semidarkness, his face hard with shadows, his eyes unreadable. It was like hearing a familiar voice and looking up to see a stranger where you'd expected an old friend, and a little thrill of shock ran through her before she could stop it.

"Yes," she whispered, wishing she could see his eyes clearly and at the same time glad she couldn't. "I—I guess so."

The storm hit them nearly an hour later, booming down the long eastern slopes of the mountains like a locomotive. It was dark by then, and the powerful beam of Tag's light was unable to pierce the swirling maelstrom for more than a couple of feet in any direction.

The wind was the worst, battering at them, driving sting-ing sheets of snow into their eyes and mouths, stealing the air right out of their lungs. The snow was piling up by now and Megan floundered through it blindly, falling over hid-den rocks and deadfalls, swearing breathlessly as she stum-bled through deep drifts.

How Tag could possibly know where he was going, Me-gan had no idea, and after a while she didn't even care. She just kept following him like an automaton, exhausted and half-frozen, simply concentrating on taking the next step, battling her way through the next drift. She didn't even re-alize he'd stopped until she plowed into his broad back, nearly falling as she tried to keep her footing in the deep snow. Tag reached out and caught her by the arm, and it was only then that she realized the seemingly solid wall of snow in front of them *was* solid. She blinked, decided she wasn't seeing things after all, and grinned a little stupidly.

Tag tried the door of the cabin, not surprised to find it locked. "Stay here. There's a window on the far side—I'll crawl in and unlock the door from the inside."

"You mean break in?"

"Don't hassle me, Megan," he said wearily. "I'm cold and I'm tired and I'm in no mood for a lecture. We'll light a fire, use what we need, and clean the place up before we leave. If it'll help your conscience, leave the owner a note explaining that we got caught in a storm and thanking him for his hospitality."

He didn't bother adding that he'd been counting on find-ing the place empty. If the owners had been up here enjoy-ing a last weekend of skiing, it could have been awkward. The fewer people who knew what direction they were tak-ing, the better. And he hadn't relished the thought of trying to explain just what he and Megan were doing up here in the first place, bruised and bloodied and outfitted like com-mandos.

He made his way around to the back and deftly knocked out a window with his elbow. Reaching inside, he unlatched it, then levered the window up and slipped inside. Lowering himself to the floor, he swept the beam of the flashlight around swiftly. It was one large room, a small kitchen to one side and a big bed on the other, with plenty of comfortable chairs and tables scattered around, and what would be, in daylight, a breathtaking view of the valley and mountains.

It was also silent and still, and he gave a satisfied nod. They could hole up here in relative comfort until the storm blew itself out, and by the time Lucas and his men dug themselves out and got the hunt under way again, he and Megan would be long gone.

He unlocked the door and pulled it open, then reached out and unceremoniously hauled Megan into the cabin. A flurry of wind and swirling snow came with her and he slammed the door shut on it, then brushed a minor avalanche of snow out of the folds of her jacket and pants and hair.

"Should be a lamp around here some—aha!" He lifted the camp lantern down off the hook by the door, pumped it up and lit it. Adjusting the flame, he set it on a big pine table. "I've proved I can make light. Let's see how I do making fire." He shot Megan a reassuring smile. "There's a mountain of firewood outside, and that thing looks like it means business." He nodded toward the huge black-and-chrome wood stove sitting imposingly against one wall of the kitchen.

"Do we dare light a fire?" Megan asked through her chattering teeth. "Won't the smoke give us away?"

"Not in this weather. And Lucas isn't stupid—he knows this storm has got us holed up somewhere. He's in no hurry."

It wasn't long before Tag had a crackling fire going, and in a surprisingly short while the worst of the chill was starting to lift. Megan stood as close to the stove as she could without actually setting herself on fire. The snow on her clothing and hair melted and she was soon surrounded by a puddle of water, too tired to even take her jacket or boots off.

She gave a squeak of protest when a thick towel dropped over her head and Tag started rubbing her wet hair vigorously. "I know you're getting tired of hearing this," he said, "but I want you out of those clothes."

"You men are all alike," she mumbled through the towel. "Show a girl a good time, and before the evening's out you're trying to get her naked."

Tag gave a long, lazy laugh. He pulled the towel back so he could look down at her, his gaze moving slowly from feature to feature as though it was the first time that day he really *had* looked at her. "You're incredible, Meggie Kirkwood," he murmured. "I think that's what I missed the most about you. The way you could always make me laugh...."

And I missed your laugh, Megan found herself thinking. The hazel eyes that used to be emerald were so near she could see flecks of gold and green in them and she decided she liked them better that way. They were warmer than Michael's eyes, gentler. She'd always liked hazel eyes....

It was odd, Tag found himself thinking, but there were moments when it was like being back on the *Paradise Orchid* with her, when all the horrors of the intervening year vanished and it was as though they'd never been apart. He caught himself thinking seriously about trying to kiss her. Would she let him, or would she rear back and try to scratch his eyes out at the first touch of his mouth?

Odds were about fifty-fifty either way. She *seemed* calm enough, but he knew from experience that she was like an iceberg, with ninety percent of what she was feeling and thinking hidden safely away. For half an instant, remembering the taste of her, he almost decided it was worth the risk. Then he caught the impulse and reined it in sharply, smiling at himself and his own impossible fantasies.

He dropped the towel around her shoulders and turned away before he did something he'd undoubtedly regret, wondering as he walked across the room why every time he got close to her, common sense went out the window. "I found a robe in one of the closets," he said over his shoulder. "Why don't you get out of those wet clothes while I go out and look around."

If anything, the storm was even worse. It didn't seem possible that any living thing could survive that howling chaos of wind and snow, but Tag reminded himself that he hadn't lasted this long by being careless. Odds were a million to one that Lucas wouldn't send anyone out until the storm eased, but it was the one-in-a-million chance that sent him out into it himself.

He secured the area as best he could with what he had, fumbling with the trip wires and booby-traps with half-frozen fingers. Finally, convinced he'd done all he could, he stumbled back to the cabin. There was nothing out here that would stop a determined intruder, but the smoke grenades and alarms would alert him in plenty of time if someone *did* come near. He'd contemplated using real explosives, but there was too great a chance of some innocent civilian stumbling across one of them. He had no qualms about stopping Lucas's men with whatever force it took, but he had enough things on his conscience as it was to keep him awake nights without adding murder.

In spite of having assured herself that he *would* come back, Megan was still relieved when the door slammed open a few minutes later and Tag stumbled in on a gust of howling wind and snow. He locked the door securely behind him, then took off his heavy jacket and shook it, creating a miniature blizzard.

His cheeks were ruddied, his hair a tangled mat of melting snow and he shook his head as he kicked off his boots. "Man, it is turning *mean* out there! I'll bet the temperature's dropped ten degrees just since we've been here." He leaned the M16 against the wall and dropped his pack beside it. "How are you doing? Getting warmed up?"

Megan nodded, bundled to the ears in the heavy sapphire-blue velour robe he'd found for her. "I was going to put the kettle on." A shiver racked her and she clenched her teeth to keep them from chattering. "But that pump doesn't work." She nodded toward a small hand pump mounted beside the sink."

Tag just smiled. "They probably drained it to keep the pipes from freezing. It just needs priming." He looked at her more closely. "You okay?"

Megan nodded again. "I feel fine. But I can't seem to stop shivering!" As though to emphasize the words, another fierce shudder ran through her.

Tag gave a quiet laugh and put a large, warm hand on her shoulder, gently kneading the taut muscles. "You've been running on scared all day—it had to catch up to you sooner or later. Come on over here and sit down."

She followed docilely as he led her across the room to a big easy chair and gave her a gentle shove toward it. She collapsed into its cushioned depths with a sigh and closed her eyes. Tag was back a minute or two later and he wrapped a puffy quilt around her, setting her feet on a wide hassock and tucking the quilt securely around them. Then he pulled the heavy tweed vertical blinds across the picture window, shutting out the night.

"Here. Drink some of this." She opened her eyes with an effort. Tag held out a whiskey glass with a scant inch of amber liquor in it. "The owners of this fine establishment have left us a well-stocked liquor cabinet. I'm sure they won't mind if we use some of their brandy, purely for medicinal purposes."

Megan thought of thanking him, but it seemed like too much of an effort. She managed a nod, then took a tiny sip of the brandy. It was as mellow as candlelight, warming her all the way down, and she snuggled more deeply into the quilt and robe and just let the waves of exhaustion lap over her, not even bothering to fight the shivers. Now and again she took another little sip, feeling it kindle a deep heat that spread slowly through her until even her fingers and toes tingled.

She must have slept, because when she opened her eyes again there was a fire crackling in the small potbellied stove that squatted on its ceramic hearth beside her and the brandy glass was sitting on a nearby table, almost empty. She sat up sleepily and looked around.

Tag had lit another lamp and the small cabin glowed cozily in the flickering golden light. He was in the kitchen, and he turned around then and smiled when he saw her. "Just in time, angel. You nearly slept through supper."

He carried a tray over and set it on the coffee table, and Megan suddenly realized she was ravenous. He'd found three or four varieties of cheese and nearly twice that of party crackers, as well as a tin of smoked oysters and a jar of what looked like caviar. She looked up at him in astonishment and he laughed.

"We lucked out when we found this place. Our hosts have left enough supplies to feed a small army." He handed her a steaming mug. "This soup's from a dry mix, but it's good."

Megan took a cautious swallow of the hot soup, not surprised to find it every bit as good as he'd promised. She helped herself to a plate of cheese and crackers and balanced it on her knee, then leaned back with the soup mug cupped between her hands. "This is all so...bizarre. A few hours ago some guy in a helicopter was shooting at me, and now I'm sitting in a snug little cabin drinking brandy and eating cheese as though I've just come in from an afternoon of skiing. None of it feels real. Not Lucas, not the helicopter, not...any of it."

"It'll feel real enough tomorrow, angel," Tag said dryly. "All those muscles you used today clambering around those mountains are going to stiffen up and you'll be lucky if you can crawl out of bed."

"Is he going to find us?"

"Lucas?" Tag shook his head. "He's not crazy enough to be out in this storm. We're safe for a little while."

Megan nodded, somehow not even surprised to discover she believed him. Common sense said she should have been terrified, yet there seemed to be some other part of her that sensed it was safe here, protected from the storm and Lucas and any other horrors the night might hold.

Because of . . . Taggart.

Odd, she'd almost stopped thinking of him as Michael now. Megan looked at him again, letting her gaze trace the hard, strong outline of his profile. His jaw was dark with bruises and she could see it was swollen, then realized that the skin around his left eye was puffy and mottled as well. He was eating very slowly, as though it hurt to chew, and she saw the way he winced every time he lifted his arm too quickly, how he was favoring his left side. She put the mug aside and slipped out of the quilt, not saying anything as she walked into the kitchen.

It took her a few minutes to find everything. Tag looked up quizzically when she came back with the second tray and set it on the table beside him. "You've been taking care of me all day, Taggart," she said quietly. "I think it's time I spent a few minutes returning the favor." She dropped the towels across the arm of his chair, then stood back. "Now, as you've been telling me at every opportunity today, I want you out of those clothes."

Chapter 7

He looked almost comically startled for a moment, then he threw his head back and gave a long, lazy laugh and started unbuttoning his shirt. "When a beautiful woman tells me to take my clothes off, I'm not going to argue with her. Even though I have a feeling this is going to hurt me a hell of a lot more than it's going to hurt you."

Megan gave a soft exclamation as he slipped the shirt off with a grimace of pain and she saw the extent of the damage Tiger Jack and Jacoby had inflicted. His abdomen and ribs were one huge mass of bruising, with two or three darker fist-shaped blotches the color of eggplant extending around to his kidneys. His back had been pummeled and his right shoulder was badly scraped where the shirtsleeve had torn away, as though he'd fallen hard against something.

Megan rinsed the wash cloth in the basin of hot water she'd brought in and started gently washing his back. He was leaner and harder than he'd been a year ago, his body stripped down to fighting trim, and he radiated an elemental, almost predatory maleness. It took no effort at all to imagine him prowling the jungle under a shadowed moon with the glint of steel in his hand, and she subdued a little shiver.

He shrugged his shoulders as though loosening the muscles across them, then leaned forward and rested his forearms on his thighs, relaxing with a noisy sigh. "God, that feels good," he murmured. "You've got hands like an angel, Meggie. You touch all the right places in all the right ways."

"You're a mess back here," she said quietly, running the cloth over the livid bruising. "You didn't get banged up like this from a few random punches, Tag—they deliberately beat the daylights out of you, didn't they?"

Tag winced as she touched a particularly tender spot on his rib cage. "Payback," he growled. "I put them all through a lot of aggravation over the past year."

"They didn't break anything, did they?" She ran her hands lightly down his ribs.

"No," he replied through his teeth, "although it wasn't for lack of trying. That Tiger Jack's got a punch like the kick of a mule."

"And a head to match," Megan muttered. "Don't tell me you actually fought in Vietnam with that guy."

"He's part of the group Lucas put together after I left Shadow Company. Hanson and a few of the others, too. They're all real bad news, Tiger Jack most of all. It's like someone forgot to tell him the war's over. He still thinks he's back in the Nam."

"This is almost personal between you and Lucas, isn't it?" she asked quietly. "It's as though he's not after you just to stop you from exposing their drug operation, but for some private revenge, too."

"Yeah, I guess in a way it is." He flinched as she started carefully cleaning the scrape on his shoulder. "Shadow Company wasn't just a team of soldiers to Lucas, we were *his*."

"Hold on," Megan told him. "This might smart a bit...."

Tag drew his breath between his teeth with a hiss. "Damn it to hell, woman, what is that stuff? Battery acid?"

"Alcohol. Quit wriggling around so I can put this ointment on it."

He peered at the tube suspiciously. "What's that?"

"For heaven's sake, stop being such a baby! It's just a little scrape."

"Then why," he asked through gritted teeth, "does it feel like you're amputating my arm?"

"You were telling me about Lucas," she said mildly, dabbing the scrape with the ointment.

Tag braced himself, then relaxed with a grunt when he realized it wasn't going to sting. "Nothing was black and white over there, that was the problem. A lot of the time we were in places we weren't officially supposed to be, like Cambodia or Laos, operating completely on our own. We'd be in the bush for weeks at a stretch, out of radio contact, and a lot of the time we just had to make up the rules as we went along."

Megan rinsed the cloth again and started cleaning the cuts and abrasions on his face. She wiped at the crusted blood on his lower lip gently.

"Am I ruined for life?"

"What?" She looked up, startled to find his eyes so close. They held hers, warm and amused. "Am I ever going to be able to kiss properly again, or—?"

"I'm sure it's fine," she said hastily, suddenly flustered.

He started to say something, then obviously thought better of it and subsided, his eyes holding a wicked glitter. He probed the split in his lip with his tongue, smiling. "I was going to suggest that we—" He stopped again, the smile widening. "Well, maybe not."

It was maddening, having her this close and not daring to do anything about it. That lush little mouth of hers just begged to be kissed. He had a sudden insane urge to say to hell with propriety and to hell with common sense, and take her in his arms then and there. It took no effort at all to imagine tugging her into his lap so she was astride him. He would bury his face in the sweet valley between her breasts, run his hands up the curve of her back, down and around her taut little bottom. Then he'd feel her poised above him, before she gently, gently eased herself down, over, around, swallowing him up in one long silken...

The erotic image vanished in a sunburst of pain and he flinched, swearing. She gazed at him with concerned innocence, but he couldn't help wondering if there wasn't just the faintest hint of a smile on her mouth as she went back to cleansing the deep cut on his forehead where Tiger Jack's rifle butt had caught him. "Where was I?"

"You said you made your own rules when you were out on patrol. I gather you didn't like Lucas's rule book?"

"Lucas was always a renegade, that's what made him so good. But that last year, he was taking us into places we had no business being, doing things I just couldn't stomach anymore. We had a couple of dustups over orders he gave that I ignored, and pretty soon the tension in the unit was so bad it was affecting everyone.

"It was just a matter of time before the trouble between Lucas and me started getting people killed, so I transferred out. A week later, Lucas was up on the carpet for allegedly ordering his men to wipe out an entire village—old men, kids, women, babies, livestock...if it moved, they killed it. Lucas swore it was a VC stronghold, but the question was raised whether 'excessive force' had been used." Tag's voice was bitter.

"I got called in to make a report, based on the time I'd spent with Lucas. By that time I was so fed up that I let loose with both barrels—but after the dust settled, nothing much came of it. Lucas got sent back into the field with a slap on the wrist and a warning to modify his methods. I might as well have saved my breath!"

Megan was staring at him in horror.

"Lucas didn't appreciate my gesture. By the time I showed up in my new unit, word was out that there was a bounty on my head—*beaucoup* dollars. One story put it as high as fifty grand."

"A bounty?" Megan's voice rose with shock.

He grinned fleetingly. "I never did know if the story was true or not—there were a hundred rumors a day making the rounds. That could have been just one more." He let the smile go. "But he was capable of it. I'd broken my code of honor with him, turned against one of my own. I think if he'd figured I was a real threat to him or Shadow Company, he'd have had me killed without a qualm. Except he'd have done it himself. More honor in it that way. More... irony."

Megan nodded slowly, starting to dab ointment on the cut. "Somehow I have no trouble believing that. He has the coldest eyes I've ever seen in my life." She shivered slightly. "No wonder the Black Dragon sent him after you." She worked in thoughtful silence for a moment or two, some half-formed memory flirting around the outskirts of her mind. It was a tantalizing image of something... something coiled and scaled, like a snake. She could almost see it in her mind, remembered glittering green eyes... not Michael's eyes, something else. Something...

It hit her so hard she sat down on the hassock with a thump, staring at Tag in shock. "My God! The Black Dragon was *there!* With Lucas, I mean. With me."

Tag looked at her intently. "What are you talking about, Megan? What do you mean, he was there?"

"I was drugged and nothing made much sense, but I remember somebody being there who seemed very... important. I don't know how I know that, I just do. And there was dragon—a black dragon! It had black scales and a red tongue and green, glittery eyes. And it's so clear! Like a picture or a... a tattoo, maybe. Why would I remember something like that if I hadn't seen it?"

Tag was as taut as a steel spring. "Meggie, try to remember everything you can. Did you see his face? Or a name—did you hear a name? Anything, Meggie—try!"

Megan pressed her fingertips against her temples, trying to capture that elusive image, to coax it nearer. With her eyes closed she could see the dragon clearly, coiled malevolently in front of her. There were other memories, too, ghost-flickers of images, voices, fading before they were fully formed. But like skittish elves, they vanished the moment she tried to grasp them. She gave up finally and shook her head, opening her eyes. "I'm sorry. All I can remember is that horrible dragon." She shuddered. "And being afraid. I can remember that. Being deathly afraid."

"It's okay, Meggie," he said softly. "I'm not going to let anything happen to you, I promise."

She smiled faintly. "Oddly enough, I believe you. Somehow you'd look right at home on a horse, all decked out in armor with a sword and a lance, charging full tilt at dragons."

Tag had to laugh. "Must have something to do with the black-and-blue marks all over my body."

"No," she said very seriously. "It's something in your eyes when you talk about Lucas. Something...hard. It's the kind of look that makes me very glad I'm not your enemy." The kind of look, she added silently, that I caught glimpses of a year ago and didn't understand. She went back to tending the cut, drawing it closed with adhesive tape, then covering it with a piece of gauze. "Well, that's the best I can do. It isn't very elegant, but it'll keep it clean. How does it feel?"

Tag touched the dressing lightly, and nodded. "Feels good, considering he nearly split my skull open."

She tossed the blood-smeared cloth into the basin of water. "I need clean water. While I'm doing that, how would you like to take your pants off?"

Tag looked up at her with a slow, beguiling smile. "That's the most promising offer I've had in I can't remember how long."

Megan gave him a look of long-suffering tolerance as she picked up the tray. "All I'm interested in is that gash on your leg, dragon slayer."

Tag grinned and stood up, hands going to the buckle on his narrow belt. Megan turned away and walked into the kitchen, his quiet laugh following her, and she realized she was blushing. Damn him, how did he do that! She should be immune to that good-natured teasing of his; should be immune to everything about him, as a matter of fact. She'd spent the last year hating him as passionately as she'd once loved him, and here they were sitting by a snapping wood fire, chatting like old friends.

Of course, she reminded herself as she filled the basin with clean hot water, why should she be surprised at this bizarre turn of events? He was handsome, he was charming, he was easy to be with—all the things he'd been a year ago, with an added aura of raw danger that only added to his appeal. It had taken her all of five minutes to fall headlong in love with him on the *Paradise Orchid*; who knew what tricks her heart was up to this time?

"Just watch yourself, Megan Kirkwood," she muttered under her breath. "Professional dragon slayers do *not* fall in love with mousey little accountants from Des Moines, Iowa. So for heaven's sake don't make a fool of yourself *this* time!"

When she walked back to where Tag was sitting, she was a little unnerved to see that he'd taken her at her word. He was naked but for his briefs, the discarded jeans lying modestly across his lap. Reminding herself of her resolve, she set the tray down and became very businesslike, pointedly keeping her gaze away from his. The cut on his upper thigh was jagged and deep, and it was obvious by the way it had been bleeding that all the hard walking today hadn't done it any good.

Megan frowned as she kneeled beside him. "How did this happen?"

"Knife," he said simply.

"Much higher, and he'd have gotten an artery."

"Much higher, and that's not all he'd have gotten."

She started washing away the smears of dried blood, trying to be as gentle as possible. "I think I can pull the edges together and tape them—that way it will heal more quickly, and you won't have such a bad scar."

"Scars can have their benefits," he said dryly. "Women usually find them fascinating. And one right there would be quite a conversation starter, don't you think?"

"I think," Megan said pointedly, "that if you and a woman are in a situation where she can see this scar, you're well beyond *needing* a conversation starter."

He chuckled. "You have a point there."

Megan finished cleansing the wound as best she could, then she soaked a piece of gauze in alcohol and glanced up at Tag. "Hang on—this is going to hurt."

She could see Tag's knuckles whiten where he was gripping the jeans. His breath hissed, but he sat very still until she'd finished. "Hang on a minute—I'm not through yet."

She hurried into the kitchen, and when she came back and laid the safety razor on the tray beside him, Tag stiffened. "Now wait a minute! What the hell are you going to do with *that*?"

She smiled. "I hate to get personal, but you've got hairy legs. The adhesive tape won't stick, so I'm going to shave around the cut." She kneeled between his legs again and worked up a lather of soap around the cut, then glanced up at him as she picked up the razor. "I wouldn't move too quickly while I'm doing this, if I were you."

"You don't have hand tremors or anything, do you?" he asked nervously as he eyed the razor nearing his inner thigh.

"Not often," she replied sweetly. Ignoring Tag's eloquent oath, she carefully shaved around the cut, wiped the skin clean with more alcohol, and closed the ragged wound with narrow strips of adhesive tape. She nodded in satisfaction at her handiwork, then smeared antiseptic ointment on a gauze pad and laid it across the cut, securing it by wrapping gauze tape around his thigh. She adjusted it a bit, then started smoothing the edges.

"Megan, for the love of God!" Tag reached down suddenly and caught her wrist. "Give me a break, will you?"

"I'm sorry! Is it too tight or—"

"No, it isn't too tight," he said hoarsely. "The bandage is fine. My leg is fine." He eased her hand well away from his thigh and released it. "The rest of me isn't ... so fine."

Megan put her hand on his leg and could have sworn she felt him flinch. "Are you all right? Do you want to lie down? I could help you if you—"

"Megan," he said through gritted teeth, "I do not want to lie down."

"But what—?"

"Meggie, sweetheart ..." He gave a rough, tight laugh, his knuckles still white where he was gripping the jeans across his lap. "I may be bruised and cut up and sore as hell, but I'm still a man. And you, my love, are very much a woman. And when you touch me like that, *where* you were touching me, it sets up certain ... reactions. Physical reactions. Reactions I don't have a lot of control over. Do you ... understand what I'm saying?"

Megan suddenly, definitely, understood what he was saying. A hot, crimson blush poured across her cheeks and she got to her feet hastily, fumbling with gauze and adhesive tape, dropping the scissors, nearly spilling the basin of water.

"Meggie," Tag said with a gentle laugh, "calm down. It's a little embarrassing, but it's not mortal. Things like this happen—it's a normal, healthy response to a very attractive woman and some pretty intimate circumstances, that's all. I know it's been a long time, and I know the situation is a little awkward, but I hate to think you're still shy with me."

To her astonishment, Megan was able to smile. "I guess," she said carefully, "that it's a good sign . . . all things considered."

"A very good sign," Tag assured her with a low laugh. "Now, why don't you go and make yourself a pot of tea while I cool off a bit. I seem to recall you like tea before bed."

He said it innocently enough, but Megan felt the second blush sweep across her cheeks on the tail of the first and she shoved all her first-aid supplies onto the tray and hurried into the kitchen.

She could still see the expression on his face when she'd called down to have a pot of tea brought to the suite on the night of their wedding. She'd done it out of sheer nervousness, following her normal evening routine simply because she didn't know what else to do. Although, if she remembered correctly, Tag had taken her into his arms not long after the steward had brought the tea, and it had grown cold while they'd gotten preoccupied with other infinitely more interesting things.

Tag was still smiling to himself when he went outside a few minutes later to take one last look around. There were no two ways about it—Megan Kirkwood was one hell of a woman!

For the first time in weeks he felt there might be a hope of getting through this, and it was all her doing. One look into those chocolate-brown eyes of hers, and he found himself believing that anything was possible, that he could slay any dragon.

He grinned, giving his perimeter alarms a final check. No dragon was going to get through *this* tonight, that was for sure. He glanced over his shoulder and could make out a tiny square of light glowing through the darkness and swirling snow, and he grinned again. It was like a beacon, guiding him back to warmth and safety, and he felt a little jolt of anticipation, suddenly impatient to get back.

Which wasn't the way it was supposed to be, he brooded as he waded through the last drift. No complications this time, wasn't that what he'd promised himself? No complications, and no long empty nights gazing at the ceiling wondering where things had gone wrong.

Megan was asleep when he got back, curled up in one of the easy chairs with her feet tucked under her and a half-full mug of tea still in one hand. He shook his head as he gazed down at her, wondering what it was about her that always made him feel twenty years younger and ready to howl at the moon.

There were clean sheets and blankets wrapped in protective plastic in the closet. He made up the bed, then filled the two hot water bottles he'd found and tucked them between the sheets to warm them. Megan was still sleeping soundly when he went back to her, and although she mumbled something and frowned when he eased the mug out of her fingers, she didn't waken. He slipped his arms under her and carried her across to the bed, then eased her out of the robe and between the sheets, glad she'd left her underthings on. God knows, they were distracting enough, the soft white cotton drawing his gaze to her full breasts, down to the shadowed V of her thighs.

He tucked the blankets and quilt around her shoulders and then, on a whim, bent down and kissed her. "Sleep well, angel," he whispered. "And don't worry about those dragons. I'll be right here, lance at the ready."

It was a few minutes later that he heard her cry out. She was thrashing around as though caught in the throes of a bad dream. He made his way between the chair and the table and started across to the bed.

"Tag!" Her voice was a cry of terror and loss, and she sat straight up, clutching the sheets tightly against her.

"Meggie?"

She stared up at him blankly for a moment, then closed her eyes and gave an unsteady little laugh. "I—I must have been dreaming."

"Are you okay?"

She nodded, still looking shaken. "Yes, I'm fine. I thought...well, it doesn't matter." She looked up. "Is it still storming?"

"Worse than ever. How about a hot brandy to help you sleep?"

"No, thanks, I'm all right." She looked up at him a little uneasily. "You're not going to sneak out in the middle of the night or anything, are you? I mean, I'm not going to wake up in the morning and find you've...gone?"

Her voice was so quiet that it took Tag a minute to realize what she'd said. She was staring up at him apprehensively, still clutching the blankets against her chest, her eyes dark and worried.

"Damn it, Meggie, of course I'm not going to sneak out in the middle of the night! What the hell do you think—" But there was no need to ask the rest. He sat on the edge of the bed and gripped her shoulders firmly, looking down into her eyes. "Is that what scared you just now? Is that what you were dreaming about, that you woke up and found yourself alone?"

She didn't say anything. But she didn't have to. Her eyes said it all. God in heaven, what hell had he put her through? How many times had she dreamed of waking and finding she'd been deserted? "Listen to me, Meggie. I'm not going to walk out on you, understand? Not tonight, not any night. Like it or not, you're stuck with me until this is over. *Trust* me."

She nodded finally, although he could still see the faint doubt in her eyes. It frustrated the hell out of him, yet there was nothing he could do about it. Trust was something you earned, not something you bought with words and good intentions. He'd already betrayed that trust once; it would be a long time before she gave it to him again. If she ever did.

"Are you sure you don't want something? Tea?"

She smiled faintly, shaking her head, and lay back against the pillow. "Maybe you could leave one of the lamps on...."

"I'd intended to." He tucked the sheet under her chin. The bed rocked as he stood up. "I'll be here all night, I promise. If you want anything, just sing out."

She nodded and closed her eyes, then suddenly looked at him again. "Where are you sleeping?"

He nodded toward the far end of the room. "I've pulled two of the chairs together. Don't worry about me."

He was halfway back to his makeshift bed when he heard the bed sheets rustle. She was sitting up again, looking at him with a frown. "That's crazy," she said quietly. "You couldn't possibly sleep like that—even if you weren't one gigantic bruise from head to foot."

He grinned at her. "I could always toss you out of bed and take it myself."

"Or you could sleep here with me," she said very seriously.

Tag's stomach pulled tight. He swallowed. "Meggie..."

"I meant just *sleep*," she said firmly. "And I'm serious, Tag. There's no reason why you shouldn't. We're both adults, give or take a lapse or two. You know me well enough to know *I'm* not going to molest *you*, and if I didn't trust you I wouldn't have suggested it. And besides," she added with the trace of a smile, "I've seen the shape you're in. I don't think you're going to be any threat to a lady's virtue for quite a while, dragon slayer."

Tag had to smile. "You *do* remember what happened a little while ago, don't you?" he urged gently. "All systems are checked for 'go', angel."

"Tag," she reminded him patiently, "you're exhausted. You're not going to get any rest bedding down on a couple of chairs. And I..." She shrugged, letting her gaze slip from his. "If you want the truth, I'd feel better with you here. I know it's silly, considering I spend every night of my life alone, but..." She looked up at him almost pleadingly. "I just want to feel somebody warm and alive beside me tonight. To know there's somebody... *there*."

Tag felt his resolve crumble. He took a deep breath, wondering if she had any idea at all of what she was asking him for. To lie there and hear her breathing beside him, to feel the warmth of her body, to remember that one, wondrous night when— He caught the thought and shoved it brutally aside. "Okay, angel. You've got it. One warm body, used but in good working condition, yours for the asking. Just give me a few minutes to check things, okay?" Megan smiled, a little shyly this time, and wriggled back down under the blankets.

She was nearly asleep when he'd finally wasted more time than he could possibly justify. He stood before the bed and contemplated leaving his shirt and jeans on, then decided the shirt could come off but he'd keep the jeans on, finally swore under his breath and took them both off. He folded the corner of the blankets back, then smiled broadly when he realized she'd smoothed the top sheet under the pillow on that side, a broad hint that he was supposed to sleep on the sheet and not under it with her.

He slipped under the blankets and she turned her head to look at him. "No funny business, remember," she said sleepily.

"No funny business," he assured her. "Go to sleep, angel." She mumbled something drowsily, already doing just that, and he stifled a sigh and lay staring at the ceiling. It was, he decided, going to be a very long night.

Chapter 8

She was in a cave and something was pacing back and forth outside, something huge and dark and evil. It clawed at the rock, wanting in, and she sat frozen, wanting to scream but unable to make a sound as, stone by tiny stone, it started tearing its way inside....

Megan awoke with a start, her heart racing. The wind was screaming around the windows like the thing in her dream, banging at the panes, and she could hear the silken whisper of snow against the glass. She sat up, feeling very groggy and stiff but infinitely better than she had yesterday. The cabin was very quiet, although she could hear faint music coming from somewhere. Across the room, the blinds on the big front windows had been partly opened, revealing a bright, swirling landscape of wind-lashed snow.

Tag was sitting in one of the easy chairs, long legs stretched across a hassock, a book in his lap. He looked up as she walked toward him, and smiled. ''Well, well, Sleeping Beauty. I was beginning to think you were out for the count.''

Yes, become a Silhouette subscriber and the celebration goes on forever.

To begin with we'll send you:

4 new Silhouette Intimate Moments® novels — FREE

a lovely 20k gold electroplated chain—FREE

an exciting mystery bonus—FREE

And that's not all! Special extras— Three more reasons to celebrate.

4. **FREE Home Delivery!** That's right! We'll send you 4 FREE books, and you'll be under no obligation to purchase any in the future. You may keep the books and return the accompanying statement marked cancel.

If we don't hear from you, about a month later we'll send you four additional novels to read and enjoy. If you decide to keep them, you'll pay the low members only discount price of just $2.74* each — that's 21 cents less than the cover price — AND there's no extra charge for delivery! There are no hidden extras! You may cancel at any time! But as long as you wish to continue, every month we'll send you four more books, which you can purchase or return at our cost, cancelling your subscription.

5. **Free Monthly Newsletter!** It's the indispensable insiders' look at our most popular writers and their upcoming novels. Now you can have a behind-the-scenes look at the fascinating world of Silhouette! It's an added bonus you'll look forward to every month!

6. **More Surprise Gifts!** Because our home subscribers are our most valued readers, we'll be sending you additional free gifts from time to time — as a token of our appreciation.

FREE! 20k GOLD ELECTROPLATED CHAIN!
You'll love this 20k gold electroplated chain! The necklace is finely crafted with 160 double-soldered links, and is electroplate finished in genuine 20k gold. It's nearly 1/8″ wide, fully 20″ long — and has the look and feel of the real thing. "Glamorous" is the perfect word for it, and it can be yours FREE in this amazing Silhouette celebration!

SILHOUETTE INTIMATE MOMENTS®

FREE OFFER CARD

4 FREE BOOKS

20k GOLD ELECTROPLATED CHAIN—FREE

FREE MYSTERY BONUS

PLACE YOUR BALLOON STICKER HERE!

FREE HOME DELIVERY

FREE FACT-FILLED NEWSLETTER

MORE SURPRISE GIFTS THROUGHOUT THE YEAR—FREE

YES! Please send me my four Silhouette Intimate Moments ® novels **FREE**, along with my 20k Electroplated Gold Chain and my free mystery gift, as explained on the opposite page. I understand that accepting these books and gifts places me under no obligation ever to buy any books. I may cancel at any time for any reason, and the free books and gifts will be mine to keep!

240 CIS YAET (U-S-IM-02/90)

NAME
(PLEASE PRINT)

ADDRESS   APT.

CITY   STATE

ZIP

SILHOUETTE "NO RISK GUARANTEE"
• There's no obligation to buy — the free books and gifts remain yours to keep.
• You receive books before they're available in stores.
• You may end your subscription at any time — just by letting us know.

FILL OUT THIS POSTPAID CARD AND MAIL TODAY!

Postage will be paid by addressee

BUSINESS REPLY CARD
FIRST CLASS   PERMIT NO. 717   BUFFALO, N.Y.

SILHOUETTE BOOKS®

901 Fuhrmann Blvd.,
P.O. Box 1867
Buffalo, N.Y. 14240-9952

NO POSTAGE
NECESSARY
IF MAILED
IN THE
UNITED STATES

"What time is it?"

"Nearly two in the afternoon—you slept for about twelve hours straight. Feel any better?"

"Twelve hours!" She combed her hair back with her fingers and walked across to the windows. "My legs are stiff, but I feel great. It's worse, isn't it? The storm, I mean."

"Worst storm in twenty-five years, according to the news reports." Tag nodded toward the small battery radio he'd found. "The whole state has shut down—roads closed, power lines down, whole towns cut off. The Governor's talking about bringing in the National Guard to help transport food, fuel and other supplies into outlying areas."

She smiled faintly. "Are we an outlying area?"

"Honey, we're not even on the map."

The snow was flying almost horizontally, and she could make out huge drifts rising around the cabin like dunes. "We're going to be here until July," she muttered.

"Well, look on the bright side—if we can't get out, Lucas and his boys can't get in."

"Except they have a helicopter. And God knows what else." She shivered slightly, listening to the wind keen.

"Megan, you can drive yourself crazy wondering what they're going to do next. One thing Lucas taught me was not to waste energy worrying. Save your strength, stay alert and take it as it comes. As long as this storm keeps up, we're safe here."

Megan nodded, only half-convinced, trying to take some comfort in the fact that Tag looked as though he didn't have a worry in the world. A good night's sleep had erased the gray, haggard look he'd had, and although his jaw and left eye were still bruised and swollen, he looked fit and rested. He'd found a pair of deep-blue jogging pants and a heavy, white turtleneck sweater somewhere, and he looked like a ski instructor resting up after a bad tumble down the slopes.

"Hungry? I had caviar and hot chocolate for breakfast, but if that doesn't catch your fancy, I can hunt up something else."

"What I'd *love* is a shower!" She ran her hands through her hair again, wrinkling her nose expressively. "It's been days since I washed my hair or had a bath."

Tag grinned and stood up. "Actually, I have a surprise for you, angel. But you have to cover your eyes."

"Tag..."

"You'll love it," he told her with a laugh. "Trust me. Come on—cover your eyes."

"This is ridiculous!" But she heaved a sigh of resignation and put her hands over her eyes.

"Don't turn around until I tell you."

"Hurry up!"

"What's the rush?" he called from the other side of the room. "You're not going anywhere for a day or two."

She could hear a scuffling noise, then a loud bang, and a muttered curse or two. It sounded as though he were dragging a trunk across the floor, then there was a hollow clang, like someone thumping an empty rain barrel. "Can I look now?"

"No... give me another minute." There were more dragging sounds. "Okay, that'll do it. Come on over and have a look."

Megan wheeled around and headed for the kitchen, stopping dead with astonishment when she saw what he'd brought in. "Where on earth...?" Her eyes widened and she walked slowly toward the large galvanized bathtub. "Oh, my God, I don't believe it! Tag, you are undoubtedly the sweetest, most wonderful man in the entire world. No, make that the entire *universe!*"

He grinned, obviously pleased by her reaction. "There's plenty of hot water in the stove reservoir, and I found you some shampoo and soap."

"It's the most beautiful thing I've ever seen!" Megan ran her hands along the edge of the tub. "Taggart, as far as heroes go, you're the absolute all-time best. Dragon slaying is nothing compared with this!"

"I'll rig up a curtain to give you some privacy, and you can splash away to your heart's content."

He was smiling down at her and Megan felt her heart give a little unexpected tug of pure affection. It was exactly the kind of thing that Michael would have done, simply yet touchingly sweet, the kind of thing a man does for a woman he cares about. Yet it was the last thing in the world she would have expected from this tall, cold-eyed man. A gesture almost as unexpected as all the others: the moments of gentleness, the patience even when there was no time for patience, the flashes of good-natured teasing when laughter was exactly what she needed to hold fear at bay. It all added up to something other than what was obvious, and it confused her. Her meticulous accountant's mind didn't like puzzles, and that's exactly what Taggart Welles was!

"Tag..." Megan caught his arm and looked up at him seriously. "Thank you."

"No problem," he said quietly. His eyes held hers for what seemed like a small eternity. Then, slowly, they dropped toward her lips and Megan knew he was going to kiss her, knew with the same certainty that she was going to let him. And it didn't even surprise her....

It seemed to surprise him, though. He frowned slightly and paused with his lips mere inches from hers, then drew back slowly, his breath whistling between his teeth. "I'll...get those sheets," he said hoarsely.

The spell broke and Megan turned away with a nod, not daring to trust her voice. Oh, God, what was going on, she asked herself desperately. She couldn't possibly still feel anything for him after what he'd done to her. No woman could be that foolish, no heart that vulnerable.

She felt caught in an emotional tailspin and it took her a few moments to regain her composure. She was very glad that Tag was busily occupied stringing nylon cord between two of the open beams. After a couple of false starts and an adjustment or two, he rigged a makeshift room-divider of flowered bed sheets that screened the tub and stove from the rest of the cabin. Then he started scooping steaming water out of the reservoir on the big wood stove while Megan waited impatiently.

"Okay," he finally said, "it's all yours."

Megan moved toward the tub greedily, her arms laden with shampoo and soap. "Go away," she told him bluntly, dabbling her hand in the water to test it. "Perfect!" She straightened to find him still standing there. "Go. *Go*."

He went.

It was, Megan decided, the closest thing to heaven she'd ever experienced. The water was hot and the tub was deep, and she sank down until nothing but her head and the tips of her knees were exposed. Five days of imprisonment and a day of panicked flight, exhaustion and terror vanished in one long, delicious immersion. She scrubbed herself furiously from head to foot until her skin glowed, and by the time she finished shampooing her hair for the last time the water was starting to get markedly cool.

"You reasonably decent?"

Tag's voice came from just around the makeshift curtain and Megan looked up suspiciously. "Why?"

"The second part of the surprise."

"You mean there's more?"

"Absolutely." He leaned around the edge of the sheet and Megan hastily submerged herself beneath the soapy water. "I found this when I was digging around looking for something to put on this morning." He stepped around the curtain and held up a pair of turquoise slacks and a matching cable-knit sweater that had probably cost its rightful owner a small fortune in one of the better women's boutiques.

He tossed them on the wooden chair Megan had moved beside the tub to hold her toiletries, and grinned down at her, his eyes glinting with devilry. "And, as the pièce de résistance . . ." He produced a pair of blue lace bikini briefs with a flourish and held them up. "Now I'm just using guesswork here, you realize, but I figure these should fit just about perfectly."

"Taggart Welles!" Megan tried not to laugh but found it impossible not to. "Did you find those in somebody's closet, or did they come out of that hand-dandy pack you brought with you, tucked between the Uzi and the hand grenades? I suppose that's another thing Lucas taught you. Sort of a grown-up version of the Boy Scout motto about always being prepared?"

Tag gave a lazy laugh. "They either belong to our hostess, or our host has some hormonal problems he should have looked at."

"Well, I appreciate the gesture," Megan told him dryly, "but I am *not* wearing some other woman's lingerie! Eating her caviar, sleeping in her bed and wearing her bathrobe are bad enough."

"They're new. The price tag's still on them, see?" He held it up. "You can write her a check for them." He hung the tiny bit of lace on the back of the chair. "I looked for the top half, but no luck."

"Thank you," Megan repeated with a wry smile. "I'm not going to model them for you, though, so you can leave now."

He feigned a look of disappointment, then strolled away with a laugh. Megan tried to wipe the smile off her own mouth, but couldn't do it. She finally just gave up and left it there as she stood up and stepped out of the tub, wrapping herself in one of the big bath towels Tag had thoughtfully provided.

There was no doubt about it, he was the most beguiling rogue she'd ever met. If he had deliberately set out to steal her heart again, he was doing a darned good job, yet she couldn't for the life of her think why he'd bother. Ego? Arrogance? Cruelty? Somehow none of them fit. Maybe he was just one of those men who pursues women simply from habit, addicted to the chase and burdened by neither conscience nor guilt.

The world was full of them, or so her mother had always said. In fact, her mother had always suggested that any man who so much as looked at her must be after something. "Good heavens, Megan, you don't really think he's interested in you for your looks, do you?" She'd give that warbling laugh, as though the thought was preposterous. "He's after something, mark my words. Why, Peggy would have seen through him in a flash. Pretty Peggy wouldn't have wasted a moment on a man like that."

Well, heartbreaker or not, Taggart Welles was the only hope she had right now. He'd gotten the daylights beaten out of him to save her; the least she could do was offer a day or two of trust in return.

She held up the blue briefs, then on a whim removed the price tag and slipped them on. They fit perfectly. Only proving, she supposed, that Tag noticed a lot more than he let on. She breathed a silent apology to the woman whose clothes she was borrowing, then pulled on the slacks and top. As much as she hated the liberties she was taking with a stranger's home, she couldn't stomach putting on dirty clothing after her first bath in six days.

Tag looked up from the book he was reading as she came around the bed-sheet curtain, his eyes running over her with disconcerting thoroughness. "Looks good. Perfect fit, too."

"They're a little tight across the—well, back here," Megan said doubtfully, eyeing her faint reflection in the window.

"Not enough so you'd notice," Tag murmured, the look of frank, male approval on his face suggesting that he had, in fact noticed only too well. "Besides, no one's going to see but me."

Somehow, Megan didn't find that nearly as comforting as he probably meant it to be.

All in all, Tag found himself thinking a few hours later, they both seemed to be handling the situation pretty well. Megan was taking being snowed in with the man who had deserted her the day after marrying her, with grace and a good deal of dignity. More of both, probably, than he deserved.

Mind you, he was vitally aware of all the unasked questions that hung in the air every time she looked at him, and he'd come close a time or two to broaching them himself. But always, at the last instant, he'd catch himself. Maybe these things had their own pace, he decided. She didn't seem in any hurry to confront him about what had happened a year ago. Maybe she needed to absorb things one step at a time, and when she was ready to talk about it, she'd let him know.

That, he thought with a flash of grim humor, or he'd wake up one morning to find himself unmanned by his own survival knife. In fact, the thought had crossed his mind the previous night when she'd come at him with that damned razor!

"Supper's ready."

Megan's quiet voice brought Tag out of his musing. He tossed the book aside and joined her at the big round table, giving a low whistle as he looked at the spread she'd set out. He helped himself to a smoked oyster and a cracker, eyeing the selection of savory spreads, cheeses and party crackers. "How the heck did you put all this together in an hour?"

"I've got talents you haven't even begun to discover," she advised him, setting a steaming casserole in the middle of the table. "Doctor Auld and his wife obviously enjoy the good life when they're up here. That pantry's stocked like a cruise liner."

At the word *cruise*, Tag shot her a searching look. But either she'd used the analogy without thinking, or it was a one-shot jibe. "*Doctor* Auld?" he asked, taking the easy way out.

"I found a phone bill with their name and address on it. I want to send them a check for everything we've used when this is over. I figure it's the least we can do."

"Sounds fair enough." He gave an appreciative sniff as Megan ladled a thick chowder into his bowl. It was loaded with tomatoes and spices and plump clams, and smelled too good to be true. "Where did you learn to cook like this?"

Megan sat across from him, her smile taking on a faintly bitter edge. "My mother believed the most important assets a woman can have are a pretty face and a good figure. Failing that, she'd better know how to cook." Tag arched an eyebrow, and Megan's smile widened. "She wasn't antifeminist, she was just a realist. Beautiful women have a natural edge; the rest of us have to work at creating one."

"And you don't think you're beautiful," he said casually.

"Peggy was beautiful."

"That wasn't an answer."

"I've never given it a lot of thought." She was starting to look annoyed. "Would you like some of this?"

He reached across and helped himself to a wedge of cheese and a handful of crackers. "So tell me about Peggy."

"You know about Peggy. I told you about her when we... before."

"You told me you had a younger sister who died a few years ago. But that's all I know."

"There's nothing else *to* know." Her voice was clipped, almost angry. "Peggy was seventeen when she was killed in a car accident. It was after a party, they'd been drinking... the usual horror story."

"You must have been pretty upset," he said mildly.

"Of course I was upset! She was my sister."

"And that's when you moved back in with your mother."

"That's right." She stood up abruptly and walked into the kitchen. "She got... sick. After Peggy died. So I left college to look after her."

"That must have been rough." Tag watched her thoughtfully. "Having to drop out of college, I mean, and move back in with your mother. You must have been very close to her."

"She was my mother." The words were as crisp as new snow and she shot him a look that said, clearly, back off.

"And your father died when you were...?"

"I was fourteen when my father died, all right?" She grabbed a stack of dirty dishes from the counter. "And I'm not really in the mood to be interrogated."

She turned, strode across to the sink and dumped the dishes into it with a crash that made Tag wince. He swallowed a sigh and got to his feet, wincing again as his bruised ribs complained. Megan put the plug in the sink and splashed some detergent over the dishes, then worked the pump angrily until it relinquished a gush of icy water. She gave it another couple of furious strokes, then leaned across to pick up the big kettle bubbling softly on the stove.

"Better not touch that without one of—"

"Ouch! Damn it!" She snatched her hand back from the metal handle, shaking her fingers furiously.

"—these," Tag finished saying, handing her the pot holder. He nudged her gently out of the way and picked up the kettle, then poured boiling water into the sink. "And that wasn't an interrogation, Meg," he said quietly, returning the kettle to the stove. "I was just interested, that's all."

Megan started washing the dishes, not saying anything.

Tag leaned back against the counter beside her. "Angel, we could be snowed in for days. It's not going to be very pleasant if we're not talking."

"It's not my idea of pleasant even if we *are*!" She scrubbed furiously at a plate. Then, abruptly, she let go of it and stood there for a silent moment, staring into the soapy water. She sighed deeply and shoved her hair off her forehead with her arm. "That was a stupid thing to say. I don't imagine being stuck up here with me is your idea of a great time, either."

"Oh, I don't know." He smiled at her, feeling the prospect was not at all unpleasant. "I can think of worse things."

She gave a short laugh. "Yeah, well, so can I—getting shot at by helicopters, to name one." Then her smile faded and she looked down at the dishes again. "I didn't mean to

take your head off,'' she said softly. "It's just that I...well,
I guess I'm still working a lot of things out. Emotional
things.''

He reached down and lifted her hands from the water.
"How about coming back and finishing your supper?'' He
handed her a towel. "We can talk about whatever *you* want
to talk about, okay? Except the weather,'' he added with a
wince as a blast of wind made the windows rattle. "That's
out of bounds.''

She smiled faintly and dried her hands, then followed him
back to the table and sat down. She took a sip of the chowder, staring thoughtfully into the bowl. "My mother told me
once that when she found out she was pregnant with me, she
tried to give herself an abortion.'' If she heard Tag's startled oath, she didn't let on. "She and father weren't married then, and she didn't *want* to be married. She planned
to be 'discovered', and become the next Marilyn Monroe.''

She looked down at the chowder for a long time, then
gave her head a shake. "Anyway, she botched the abortion
and married my father a few weeks later. She had a hard
pregnancy, a long labor, and then nearly died during the
delivery.'' She smiled fleetingly. "Needless to say, when I
finally arrived, I wasn't high on her list of favorite people.
And to top it off, I was apparently a miserable baby—col-
icky and croupy, crying all the time. She finally told my Dad
that either they got someone in to look after me, or she was
leaving.''

Tag found it difficult to keep his mouth shut, knowing if
he voiced his opinion of her mother it would precipitate a
chill inside the cabin even worse than the one outside. He
decided to occupy himself with the chowder, proud of his
self-control.

"I was three when Peggy was born. Mother sailed through
her pregnancy that time, giving birth to the quintessentially
perfect baby. Peggy didn't cry, Peggy didn't throw up her
strained peas, Peggy didn't do anything but lie there being
angelic.'' She smiled faintly. "I don't remember much of

this, naturally—just what I've been told a thousand times. But I do remember my life changing. It was when the *don'ts* started: don't play in the house or you'll wake Peggy, don't throw your toys or you might hit Peggy, don't pester your mother while she's feeding Peggy.''

Tag glanced at her, but she was staring past him to the storm outside. ''It didn't help that she was beautiful, too. When I was born, I was a fat little red lump with a mop of black hair—Mother always said I looked like a Gypsy. But Peggy had blond hair and huge blue eyes...the nurses called her the Kirkwood Cherub, and fought over who got to hold her.''

''And where was your father while this was going on?''

His voice must have been a little too well controlled, because she gave him a quizzical look. ''Poor Dad was trying to cope with a rambunctious three-year-old—me—and run his own business at the same time. The nanny left not long after Mother got home with Peggy—they had a row over something, and Mother fired her on the spot.'' She stared out at the storm again, then blinked and turned her attention back to Tag. ''Dad more or less raised me by himself, I guess. Mother was too busy taking care of Peggy to have much time left over for me.''

''And as you both got older, you and Peggy never got closer.''

''I was as much to blame as she was, I guess. I resented all the time and attention she got from Mother, not to mention the piano lessons, the dance lessons, the art lessons. And she was jealous of the relationship I had with Dad. I suppose, like most firstborns, I saw her as an interloper...suddenly I had to share everything, even my father. If Peggy wanted my toys, she took them. If I protested, I was selfish; if I helped myself to her toys, I was greedy. If she hit me, it was because I must have done something to her first; if I hit her back, I was a bully.'' She smiled. ''It was a classic no-win situation. The harder I tried, the harder it backfired on me. If I gave her one of my dolls, she wanted

them all—and when I'd try to get some of them back, she'd
start screaming and I'd catch heck for not sharing."

And I'll bet dollars to doughnuts, Tag thought, that
Pretty Peggy Kirkwood learned how to work the system *real*
early. "And your dad couldn't see what was going on?"

"Oh, he knew Mother was spoiling Peggy rotten, but
there wasn't a lot he could do. He compensated by buying
me little things and spending as much time with me as he
could. But after he died..." She shrugged, toying with the
chowder. "I dreamed of the day I could leave for college, of
getting my business degree and finally having a life of my
own somewhere as far from Des Moines and Peggy as I
could get."

"But there wasn't enough money for college after your
dad died," Tag said quietly.

She'd forgotten she'd told him about that. "Not college
and acting classes for Peggy. So I went to a local business
school instead, and continued to live at home."

"And saved your money, planning to go to college and
pick up your degree. Until Peggy died and your mother got
sick."

Megan smiled faintly. "The summer Peggy died, I was
working for a local accounting firm and still living at home.
But I was going to attend college that fall, and move into a
tiny apartment I'd found near the campus. I'd fallen head
over heels in love with one of the partners at the firm where
I was working. He took me out a couple of times, and I was
really starting to think life was working out."

She frowned slightly, turning her head to gaze out the
window. "The doorbell rang one evening and I answered it.
It was Ian. We didn't have a date planned or anything, but
I figured he'd just come over on the spur of the moment. I
was so busy making a fool of myself over him I didn't even
realize how nervous he was. Until Peggy came downstairs all
dressed up, and I realized Ian wasn't there to see me at all."

"Nice guy," Tag muttered, stabbing a smoked oyster with his fork and fantasizing for a malicious moment that it was Ian the Accountant's heart.

"I went absolutely crazy. I made a big scene at the door and when Peggy said she didn't even know Ian and I had been dating, I called her a liar and ran upstairs. I remember watching the car pull away and hoping it crashed so Peggy would be out of my life once and for all."

"And then it did."

Megan nodded. "I was sick when the police came with the news." She smiled raggedly. "Boy, talk about a guilt trip! And the worst part was, I found out much later that Peggy honestly didn't know I was interested in Ian."

"And then your mother got sick."

"Yes. I left home and started college as I'd planned, but then she got worse. She . . . well, she couldn't cope on her own. She'd pinned all her dreams on Peggy, and when Peg died Mother just came a little unraveled. I finally had to quit college and move back home, and I spent the next five years convinced that Peggy was *still* ruining my life, even after she was dead. All Mother talked about day in and day out was Peggy—and what a poor substitute I was."

She was staring down into the bowl as though she'd forgotten he was there, and Tag found himself watching her thoughtfully. So that was it. He'd never been able to get to the bottom of why Megan couldn't seem to recognize the striking beauty that had caught his eye the moment he'd seen her. Hers was a subtle, exotic look, her dark sparkling eyes tilted and mysterious like a cat's beneath her thick bangs, her golden skin flawless, the perfect oval of her face framed by a chin-length cap of glossy brown hair. She had a dimple in her chin and a matching one in her left cheek when she smiled, and there was something about her that caught a man's eye and held it.

Like right now. He blinked, realizing she was looking at him quizzically. "Personally," he said with a slow grin, "I prefer brunettes over blue-eyed blondes any day of the week.''

She looked across at him, her eyes wide with surprise and some other, less definable emotion. Then she smiled, that sweet, shy smile that never failed to make his breath catch just slightly on the rare times she used it, and she glanced away, a faint blush grazing her cheeks.

Megan stood in front of the floor-to-ceiling windows and stared out into whirling whiteness. The wind screamed unceasingly, its voice rising and falling, and she could feel the cabin shudder under its onslaught, each furious gust like the blow of a fist against the solid log frame. It was like something alive, she found herself thinking. Something alive and hungry that wanted them, its howls of frustration rising ever louder as the cabin withstood its efforts to snap the logs apart and reach inside....

Something touched her shoulder, startling her so badly she recoiled with an involuntary gasp, nearly knocking the mug out of Tag's hand. Steaming coffee slopped over the rim and he swore, juggling the mug. ''A 'no thanks' would have sufficed,'' he growled, shaking coffee from his hand.

''Sorry.'' Megan took the mug.

''I'll live,'' Tag muttered, retreating to one of the easy chairs. ''Relax, Megan. He's either gone back to Seattle to wait out the storm, or he's snowed in just like we are. Nothing's moving out there tonight. Trust me.''

Megan nodded and she wandered across to the little wood stove between the windows, too restless to sit down. ''I keep thinking about work. This is our busiest time—the end of the fiscal year, with taxes due and everything. They'll be wondering where I am, why I haven't even called....''

Especially Adam, Megan reminded herself. Poor, sweet Adam, who'd known that something had happened to her on the cruise a year ago but had never pried. He'd seemed content simply to be there for her in case she needed someone to talk to or a shoulder to cry on.

Howard would be less charitable. A prim, fastidious bachelor of forty-nine, Howard was of the opinion that women were pleasant enough to have around, but one couldn't depend on them. Women were prone to falling in love, getting pregnant, quitting their jobs to go backpacking through Nepal or who knew what else. Her disappearance would receive a knowing I-told-you-so smile, and a reminder to his younger brother that in future they would hire only *male* accountants, preferably those with wives, babies and new mortgages to keep them motivated.

"Are you still working with...what was it? Aber, Crombie and Fitch? Except there's no Aber and no Fitch, only a bunch of Crombies, but they can't change the name because—"

"Abington, Cambie and Finch," Megan reminded him dryly, "except William Abington's been dead for fifteen years and Rupert Finch retired, so it's just Howard and Adam Cambie. And they haven't changed the name because it's been Abington, Cambie and Finch for three generations, and most of the older clients think the world is changing too much as it is, thank you very much."

Tag laughed. "And how long do you have to work for the brothers Cambie before you get your name on the door? Or is that honor reserved for the dead and retired?"

She should have been annoyed at his irreverence, but it was almost impossible not to laugh. "It won't be in Howard's lifetime. He's sweet, but a little stodgy. He's not convinced some of his older clients are ready for a woman accountant yet, so he lets everyone think I'm one of the secretaries."

"A tad old-fashioned, brother Howard."

"A tad," Megan had to agree with a soft laugh. "But I'm pretty old-fashioned myself in a lot of ways, so it works out."

"Yes, I...had noticed."

Tag's eyes held hers, warm with memories, and Megan felt herself start to blush. She could still remember stammering the truth that night as she'd slipped between the sheets and into his waiting arms. How he had almost, but not quite, hidden his surprise at discovering the shy almost-twenty-seven-year-old woman he'd married was still a virgin.

Megan frowned very slightly and turned back to look out the window. There'd been something about that night that had never quite made sense. Two things, actually. The first had been Michael's—Taggart's—gentle and loving concern when she'd admitted never having made love before. "We can wait, Meggie," he'd whispered. "It's been a long, long day, angel, and I don't want to rush you. We have plenty of time...."

She'd been touched by his thoughtfulness, had been so tired and nervous that she'd very nearly accepted the graceful excuse he'd provided to postpone their first night of lovemaking. But she hadn't. And no matter how hard she tried to convince herself otherwise, the truth was that she hadn't been seduced that night. Michael Walker had made love to her because *she'd* wanted it.

That it hadn't been planned had become even more obvious a few minutes later, when it became apparent that he'd come to her unprepared. It had been Michael who had gently inquired if she were using any form of contraception, Michael who had handled a potentially embarrassing situation with grace and good humor, who had interrupted their lovemaking to slip out of bed, dress and go down to the ship's pharmacy. And it had been Michael who, with patience and tenderness and skill, had shown her things and taken her places that night that she'd never even dreamed were possible.

Neither action had been that of a coldhearted, ruthless con man. No more than the patience he'd shown with her these past two days, the unexpected moments of gentleness that seemed to surprise him as much as they surprised her. It was as though there were two Taggart Welleses: the hard-eyed, dangerous one—the Shadow Warrior who carried cold steel and still stalked shadowed jungles in his mind; and the other Taggart, the teasing, caring man who had come aboard the *Paradise Orchid* a year ago and stolen her heart.

"What about you?" she asked suddenly, turning to look at him. "You've been on the run for over a year now. What about your job? Your family? Do you ever think about what they're doing, how they're coping with your disappearance?"

"All the time," he said quietly. "But you can't let it eat you up, Megan. You've got to shut down all those feelings, and shut them down hard. The minute you let your emotions take over, you're dead. You'll do something stupid, jeopardizing not only yourself but the very people you care about."

Like you jeopardized yourself to rescue me from Lucas? she wanted to ask. But there was no point; she already knew the answer she'd get. He talked of paying back debts as though he'd invented the notion, as though caring was a weakness that needed justification. But maybe, for a Shadow Warrior, it was....

"Is that what you did in Honolulu?" she asked instead, not even knowing she was going to say it aloud until she heard the words. "Was that how you were able to just walk away, as though none of it had even happened?"

Chapter 9

Tag winced. He let his gaze slide from hers and leaned forward, resting his elbows on his knees and staring down into his coffee cup, tipping it this way and that. "I wondered when you were going to get around to asking."

"I figure I deserve an answer," she said quietly.

"Yeah." His voice ragged. "I just wish to hell I had one to give you, angel."

A sliver of anger darted through Megan. "If you think it's going to be that easy, you're dead wrong." She set the mug down with a bang. "Damn it, you owe me at least this much! I waited at that dock until nearly midnight, half out of my mind with terror. I booked into the hotel, sure you'd show up with some perfectly reasonable explanation. And when you didn't, I called every hospital in the city, every hotel, every cab company, praying someone could tell me what had happened to you.

"My money started running out by the third day, so I changed hotels, afraid to come back to the mainland in case you were hurt or in trouble and needed me. I spent the next week walking up and down every street in Honolulu, eighteen hours a day, trying to find someone who'd seen you, who had some clue. And I cried, Taggart. I cried and tried to tell myself it was all a mistake, that you hadn't just used me like the police kept saying. That it hadn't all been lies!''

Her voice broke and Megan wheeled away, staring out the window at nothing. She blinked back tears, refusing to give in to them. She'd cried enough, damn it. She shouldn't have any tears left after the past year.

''Meggie...'' Tag let his voice trail away, not even knowing what he'd wanted to say. He put the mug on the table beside him and stood up. ''Meg,'' he said quietly as he walked over to where she was standing, ''all I have are explanations, not excuses. I don't know if there are excuses.''

She didn't say anything, but he could see her shoulders stiffen slightly. ''I didn't plan what happened between us. I'd come aboard intending to just disappear by blending into the crowd. I'd thought I would stick tour brochures in my pocket and hang a couple Nikons around my neck and wander around buying cheap souvenirs, play Joe Tourist in Paradise. Then Janie Rodgers introduced me to you and...'' He drew in a deep breath and released it slowly, wondering why it was so important to get the words right.

When you looked at it head on, it would probably be smarter to just leave it the hell alone. Let her think what she wanted to think. He'd done what he'd done because there hadn't been a choice, because it had been him against nearly impossible odds and when it comes down that close to the line a man does whatever needs to be done to stay alive. No excuses. No apologies. No looking back.

Except...she was right. It wasn't that easy. Tag looked at Megan's still, pale profile, as delicate as porcelain. He'd known better. And the guilt he'd been carrying around for the better part of a year had been righteously earned.

''Meg, when I left the ship that morning, I intended to come back. I was going to take you up to the hotel suite and tell you everything—who I was, the mess I'd gotten you into, the works. And I was going to leave the next move up to you. If you didn't want any part of me, I figured we'd get the marriage annulled then and there. And if you'd wanted to stick with me, well, I figured we'd come up with some plan to keep you safe while I sorted things out.''

Megan made no sign she'd even heard him. She could have been carved from stone, standing there staring out into the furious night.

''But when I got down to the dock, I saw what I thought were two of Lucas's men waiting for me. As it turned out, they weren't but in the time it took me to figure that out, I also started to realize just what I'd done to you. I'd dragged you into a life-or-death situation without even warning you what was going on. And worse than that, I'd put you into serious danger. I knew if Lucas ever traced me to you, he wouldn't think twice about using you as bait to draw me out.''

He stepped nearer to her, tracing the curve of her cheek with his eyes. ''Meg, I know you don't understand this, but I turned and walked away because I thought it was the fairest thing to do. Because—''

''Fair?'' It was no more than a whisper, and she turned her head to look straight at him. ''You thought it was *fair* to just walk out of my life as though I'd never existed? To leave me standing on that dock with a day-old wedding ring and a broken heart?'' Her voice broke and she swallowed, her angry gaze never wavering from his. ''I wasn't just a rental car that you could abandon by the roadside once it got you safely to your destination, damn it. I was your *wife!*''

He reached for her. ''Meggie . . .''

''I loved you!'' She spun away from his outstretched hand with a sob.

''I know.'' His voice was rough and he ached with a deep, chilling despair. ''God, Meggie, don't you think I know that? But somehow I let myself believe that you'd get over it in a few weeks. By then you'd know I'd used a false name when I married you, and I figured you'd get an annulment and that . . . would be the end of it.

"The end of it?" She gave a sob of laughter. "You think you can just annul love, Taggart? That you can just turn it off painlessly like turning off a light switch?"

"I was trying to protect you, Megan," he said quietly. "The last thing in the world I wanted to do was hurt you."

"My God, I don't know whether to laugh or cry!" She managed another rough laugh, scooping her hair back from her face with both hands. "Why couldn't you have just *trusted* me, Tag? Why didn't you at least give me a chance?"

"Meg . . ." He gazed into her eyes, then turned away with a soft oath. "Hell, what's the use! I can't explain it to myself, why pretend I can explain it to you?"

He knew she was standing there watching him, filled with anger and confusion, needing answers he just didn't have. He stepped to the window, standing, as she had done, looking out into the night. There was nothing to see but sheets of snow, whipping this way and that between the tall trees. It was drifting against the window and he could hear it whispering against the glass like tiny claws, as the wind howled in the darkness like something wild and hungry.

Dreams, that's what it had all been about. There was something about her that had made it easy for him to believe in dreams again. To open up those parts of himself kept locked up and hidden so long and so well that he himself had forgotten they were there.

And it had scared him.

Because dreams could be deadly. Lucas had taught him that. Dreams made a man think about tomorrow, and a man who anticipates tomorrow is liable to be too cautious today. And while caution and leisurely contemplation of dreams might be fine if you're in a staff room a hundred klicks from the front, it can kill you on a dark jungle night when death is only a footstep away. . . .

* * *

It was a little after midnight when Megan awoke. She stared at the big windup alarm clock on the bedside table and frowned, then rolled onto her back, wide awake and restless. The cabin was quiet except for the wind and the soft crackle of the kitchen fire. One of the lamps was still on, the flame turned so low it filled the room with more shadow than light, and in the dim, butter-gold glow, she could see Tag's dark head resting against the back of the sofa. He'd fallen asleep there, probably, too weary to get a pillow and blanket from the closet and too proud—or wary—to slip into the bed beside her.

She sighed. They hadn't traded more than a dozen words all evening, both of them stiff and polite, each careful not to meet the other's eyes. That was the problem with being snowbound in a one-room cabin, she thought with a flash of humor. There were no dramatic exits to be made, no doors to slam—you just had to sit within feet of each other and listen to the wind, thinking of all the things you'd like to say but didn't dare.

Although what it was she wanted to say, *should* be saying, she didn't quite know yet. She felt caught in an emotional whirlpool, unable to tell right from wrong anymore, torn between her own pain and Tag's. Even the anger was becoming more and more difficult to hang on to.

She sat up, contemplating lighting the lamp and trying to finish the mystery novel she'd started that afternoon. Except she knew she'd have no better luck with it tonight than she'd had earlier, her mind wandering after just a paragraph or two. Her gaze was drawn to Tag's tousled head again and again, and finally she kicked the covers off and reached for her borrowed robe, then slid out of bed. Gathering up the extra pillow and a blanket from the closet shelf, she padded across to the sitting area.

Tag looked up curiously as she came around the end of the sofa. He was sitting in a comfortable slouch with his head cradled against the back cushion, long legs on the hassock, crossed at the ankle. A whiskey glass rested on his thigh, maybe a quarter full, and an open bottle of bourbon sat on the table at his elbow.

Megan suddenly felt awkward. "I, uh, didn't mean to disturb you." She gestured with the blanket and pillow. "I thought you'd fallen asleep...."

He smiled faintly. "Nope. Just sitting here thinking. Would you like a drink?" He nodded toward the bottle. Megan shook her head and Tag chuckled. "Smart move. The good doctor may know his caviar, but he's a lousy judge of bourbon." He sat up slightly and set the glass aside, then screwed the cap back on the bottle firmly, giving Megan a wry smile. "Which is probably just as well. I got it out planning to get stinking drunk."

Megan frowned, hearing what sounded like raw pain in his voice. "Are you all right?"

"Nothing's hurting, if that's what you mean." His mouth twisted in what might have been a rough smile. "Physically, anyway."

It should have pleased her, Megan thought. Damn it, he owed her a bit of pain! But the satisfaction was strangely hollow. It started to fade before it was even fully formed, leaving her feeling weary and sad. She nodded and started to turn away.

Tag looked up. "Don't go, Meg," he said quietly. "Not on my account, I mean. I'm cold sober and wide awake and it's warm here by the fire, so if you feel like staying...."

It wasn't quite an invitation, Megan decided. But it was, undeniably, an offer of companionship on a cold night when sleep was elusive and dawn an eternity away. And suddenly she realized that she wanted very much to stay. She nodded again, not daring to say something that might break the fragile peace, and dropped the pillow onto the floor. She sat on it and drew her bare feet into the folds of the heavy robe, then draped the blanket lightly around her shoulders.

He'd changed out of the jogging pants and back into his jeans, and the lower legs were wet with melted snow. She glanced up at him. "Any sign the storm is letting up?"

"Weather report said it's supposed to break late tomorrow or the next day, but by the look of it out there tonight, I wouldn't bank on it."

She put her hand over the dressing on his thigh where it peeked out of the rip in his jeans. It was warm to her touch, but not unhealthily so. "I meant to change that dressing and check the cut for infection," she said quietly. "How does it feel?"

"Stiff as hell, but it's healing clean." He smiled down at her, his eyes toast-warm in the dim light. "You do good work."

Megan had to smile. "Thank you, but if you don't mind, I'd rather not have to do any more of it. So if you could keep the bullet holes, stab wounds and general wear and tear to a minimum for the rest of this escapade, I'd really appreciate it."

"I'll do my damndest," he promised with a chuckle.

A log snapped in the small wood heater beside them, a warm comfortable sound, and Megan leaned back against the sofa and relaxed. The silence grew, but it was a companionable silence this time, the tension between them seemingly gone for now. Outside, the wind's howl reached a crescendo, and she shivered. "Do you do this sort of thing often?" she asked suddenly.

"What sort of thing?"

"Whatever it is you do. All this cloak-and-dagger stuff." She turned her head to look up at him. "You never have explained what it is you do. If," she added with a faint smile, "you *can* tell me. If you're a double agent or a hit man or something, perhaps I'm better off not knowing."

"A *hit man?*" He gave a long, lazy laugh. Still smiling, he eased his long legs off the hassock and dropped his feet to the floor, leaning forward to rest his elbows on his knees. "Meggie, I'm just a businessman. Or was, before I got mixed up with Elliott and Lucas and the rest. Oil, mostly, although we started branching out in the last few years. It wasn't huge as empires go, but it was *my* empire.'' He was silent for a moment, and she could see a muscle in his jaw ripple. ''But I guess that's all done with now.''

''But surely that means you have the resources to get all this sorted out—money, contacts.''

''They confiscated everything I own, Meggie,'' he said gently. ''Company assets, records, files, bank accounts—the works. For evidence, supposedly. Remember, these people are government. They can do just about anything and get away with it. Who's going to argue with the CIA? And as for contacts, well . . .'' He smiled dryly. ''Even the whiff of CIA has people running for cover. I doubt there's a person out there who'd risk even taking a phone call from Taggart Welles these days, let alone offering to help.'' The smile turned bitter. ''Besides, I was pretty successful. And a lot of people like to see a high-flyer brought down. Even if I get my name cleared, I'm finished. There'll always be people who'll figure I must have been guilty of *something*.''

''What are you going to do?'' she asked softly. ''When this is all over, I mean.''

He shrugged, looking at his hands. ''Start over again, I guess. I haven't really given the future much thought—there didn't seem to be much point to it, all things considered. I've just been concentrating on getting through one day at a time.''

Megan put her hand tentatively on his arm. ''I can't even begin to imagine what it's been like for you.''

He smiled. ''You'd be surprised how easy it is to disappear in this country. I keep moving, never staying in one place longer than a couple of weeks, doing odd jobs to support myself—hell, I've done more honest labor in these past eighteen months than in the past eighteen years!'' He smiled fleetingly. ''As long as I don't do anything to draw attention to myself, it's easy.''

"Easy," Megan echoed with a shiver. "How in God's name do you keep going? Never trusting anyone, jumping at every strange sound, looking over your shoulder all the time...."

"You." He said it very softly, turning his head to look at her. His eyes captured hers, held them. "You're what's kept me going, Meggie."

She was so taken by surprise that she simply stared at him, faintly aware that her heart had skipped a beat. He smiled faintly and ran the back of his hand down her cheek. His knuckles were rough, fight-scarred, but his touch was incredibly gentle and she felt her heart give another odd little tremor.

"I used to pretend you were waiting for me, Meggie," he murmured. "Then when this mess was over, I'd go to Des Moines and get you, and we'd buy a house and have kids and do all the things married people do. I used to think about where we'd live, what kind of a house we'd build, even the color we'd paint the walls."

Tag tipped her face up, his gaze moving slowly over her face, feature by feature. "All I'd have to do was close my eyes and you were there with me, Meg. I could hear your voice, your laugh. Could smell your perfume. Remembered what it was like kissing you—the taste of you, the feel of your skin...."

It was the most natural thing in the world to lift her mouth for his kiss. His lips settled over hers with familiar ease and then there was the first teasing touch of his tongue, gliding between her lips, gone before she could capture it. Then it was back again, deeper this time, moving leisurely in search of hers, and Megan gave a little sigh of pleasure and satisfaction, knowing this was exactly what she'd wanted all along.

He kissed her with deep, lazy thoroughness, not bothering to hold himself back, teasing her with memories of the intimacies they'd shared. She could feel her body start to respond, and knew by the catch in his breathing that he felt the same.

He drew his mouth slowly from hers and ran his lips across her cheek, down the side of her throat, the tantalizing caress of tongue making her toes curl. She slipped her fingers up into his hair and kissed him back, tiny little biting kisses along the angle of his jaw, under his ear. Her robe had fallen partly open and he started kissing her shoulder, and she knew even as he reached down to lift her to her feet and into his arms that if he didn't stop soon, there would be no stopping at all.

And she didn't want him to stop, Megan realized with vague surprise as Tag lifted her into his arms. She wanted him to sweep her up and across to the bed and shuck her out of her borrowed nightgown and make love to her as though his very life depended upon it. She wanted to be consumed by him, filled by him, wanted to wrap her legs around him and cry out his name, to feel that hard, driving body mesh with hers so deeply and perfectly that she would never be apart from him again.

And for a moment or two, that's exactly what she thought was going to happen. Tag eased her onto the sofa and stretched out beside her, arms locked so tightly around her she could barely breathe, and then he was kissing her with a fierce, wild hunger that set every cell in her body aflame. It was sheer madness, but she didn't care. She still loved him, it was pointless to deny it any longer, pointless to remind herself of all the reasons she shouldn't. The heart didn't listen to reason. There would be time enough for reason and cold logic in the morning, but right now there was nothing but her and . . .

"Michael!"

It was, in the end, Megan's soft cry that stopped Tag. The name of the man he'd once pretended to be cut through him like a knife, slamming him into reality so hard it took his breath away. It took more willpower than he'd ever thought he had, but he drew his mouth from hers and eased himself

away from her. Damn it, what was happening here? Whatever it was, it was coming on too fast and too soon.

They'd both gotten all tangled up in the past again, and
that wasn't the way it should be. She'd wake up in the
morning and find herself in the arms of a man she didn't
even know, and she'd hate him more than she already did.
It would be one more lie. One more promise he couldn't
keep.

He drew in a deep, unsteady breath and let his head drop
back against the cushion. "Oh, Meggie...." Gently he
started to tug her robe closed. "That probably wasn't
smart."

"Probably... not." He could hear her swallow.
"Could... you just hold me for a minute or two?" It was a
hesitant, uncertain whisper, as though she half expected him
to refuse.

Tag slipped his arms around her and cradled her tightly
against him, glad of the excuse to touch her again. It was
like throwing gasoline on fire, but he didn't care. He just
wanted to lie there with her tucked into the curve of his body
where she belonged, safe and peaceful, and pretend for a
while.

"Tag?"

"Hmmm?" Tag shifted his right leg, glad the sofa was
long enough for him to stretch out comfortably. Maybe a
little too comfortably, he thought drowsily as he felt Megan
stir against him. She was lying cradled between him and the
back of the sofa, her head on his arm, one of her hands
draped lightly across his ribs. She was warm and soft and
had that delicious woman-smell he always loved of soap and
shampoo and clean water and warm skin, and he was perfectly content to spend the rest of his life right there.

"They said you were in Des Moines," she said softly.
"At... my house. Two or three times."

Tag swallowed a sigh. "I felt responsible for you," he replied finally, telling himself it wasn't exactly a lie. "I wanted
to keep an eye on you—make sure you were safe."

"Oh." It was a thoughtful little sound.

Tag swore under his breath after a moment or two. He drew back so he could look at her. "That's a damned lie, Meg," he said quietly. "It was the excuse I used, but that's not the real reason. I went to Des Moines because I wanted to see you."

She frowned slightly, her eyes searching his. "I don't understand."

"Neither do I," he said truthfully. "It...oh, hell, I don't know!" He shook his head wearily. "When I left Honolulu, I told myself I'd done what I had to do, that you'd go home and get over me, and that would be the end of it. But I couldn't get you out of my mind, Meggie. I'd dream about you every night, about Lucas finding you, and I'd wake up in a cold sweat. Finally it got so bad I couldn't think about anything else, so I decided to go to Des Moines. I told myself that if I could see you once more—just see for myself that you really were safe—I'd be all right."

"I thought I saw you once," she whispered. "Last May."

"In that little park downtown, at noon. You were sitting beside the fountain with a friend, eating your lunch. She said something and you laughed, and when you looked up, you looked straight at me—I was standing under the trees at the far side."

"My God," she whispered, "so it *was* you! I thought I was just imagining things...one instant you were there, the next you weren't." She gave a soft laugh. "I scared Trudy half to death. I went as white as a sheet and she was sure I was going to faint and fall into the fountain and drown."

"I knew it was careless, getting that close. But when I saw you there..." He shook his head again. "It was crazy—I'd left you in Honolulu because I was afraid of putting you in danger, and here I was leading Lucas right to you! I swore that was the last time—that you were obviously well and healthy and safe. But...something kept drawing me back, Meggie."

"It's strange," she whispered, "but there were times I could have sworn you were standing right beside me. I could *feel* you there. I thought I was going crazy."

"So did I," he said with a rueful chuckle. "Three or four months would go by, then I'd have to see you again. I kept telling myself I was just doing what any decent man would do under the circumstances, that it was my responsibility to keep an eye on you. But there was more to it than that, Meggie. I'd sit in my car outside your office for hours, waiting to catch a glimpse of you. Or I'd park across from your house when you were home, back in the shadows under those big oaks across the street. If I was real lucky you'd come out to mow the lawn or work in the garden, and I'd watch you. Or sometimes at night you'd turn the lights on and I'd see you in there, and it would be all I could do to keep from going over and pounding your door down."

"I don't know," she said very carefully, "what I would have done. I wasn't thinking very...logically."

"I let myself in once," he admitted quietly. "You were at work, and I'd decided to leave you a note. Not explaining everything—I knew I'd never be able to do that—but just to tell you that I was sorry for hurting you. I figured I owed you at least that." He smiled, running a strand of her silken hair through his fingers. "I remember when I walked in, all I could smell was your perfume." He'd spent most of the day there, he recalled, breathing the air she breathed, touching the things she handled every day. "I started that note a hundred times, and never got past your name...."

"I never knew," she whispered.

"It's my fault Lucas found you," he said tightly. "If I'd stayed the hell away from you the way I'd promised myself, Megan, he never would have tracked you down. This whole damned mess is my fault."

She sighed. "And if I hadn't fallen in love with you," she said quietly, "maybe you wouldn't have had to feel responsible in the first place."

"Meg—"

"No, Tag, it's true." Lying here in the circle of his arms, it wasn't difficult to understand why she had, of course. "I was always 'the clever Kirkwood girl' when I was growing up. People would introduce me as Pretty Peggy Kirkwood's sister, as though I didn't have a name. Even in school, I was the 'brainy Kirkwood'. When we were both older, I got to be really popular with the boys—not only could I help them with their homework, but if they were really nice to me, maybe I'd put in a good word for them with Peggy. They always wanted to study at my house, because she might be there. And I used to get invited to parties a lot, too. But always on the condition I brought my younger sister along."

She had no idea why she was telling him this. She'd never told anyone about those years when she'd cried herself to sleep nearly every night, wishing for golden hair and wide, blue eyes, hating the mirror that taunted her with the truth. Hating, too, the radiant, laughing sister who'd seemed to have it all.

"It wasn't Peggy's fault that she was born beautiful, but I used to wonder why it had been her and not me. It was like being invisible. People wouldn't even see me. Especially men." She smiled faintly. "If a man did start a conversation with me, I knew it wasn't me he was interested in—he was just angling for an introduction to Peggy. In high school, a couple of them even took me out until I realized I was just being used."

"Meggie..." Tag's voice was just a whisper of sound and his arms tightened slightly as though he were trying to hold the memories at bay.

"I used to dream that someday a man would look at me the way men looked at Peggy. And then I met you and everything just seemed so perfect..." She drew in a deep breath, trying to relax the tightness across her chest. One smile, that's all it had taken. One smile, a few hot tropical nights, a kiss or two, a few intimate embraces that had sent her senses and willpower reeling...and she'd been his for the taking. "I made a horrendous fool of myself, I realized that later. But for the first time in my life I felt beautiful and alive and…wanted. And when you asked me that night to marry you, I…" She managed a rough laugh. "Well, let's just say I wasn't much of a challenge. Things couldn't have worked out better, I guess. For you."

"Damn it, Megan, marrying you wasn't part of my plan!" The words were torn out of him. Tag lifted himself onto one elbow to gaze down at her intently. "Hell, nothing that happened in those three weeks with you was planned! Sure, I noticed you on that dock in Singapore—a man would have to be blind *not* to notice you. But I did *not* deliberately set out to seduce and marry you. I may be a lot of things, Meg, and I've done a lot of things I'm not proud of, but I draw the line at something that low."

She gazed up at him in bewilderment. "Then why—?"

"I don't know!" He raked his hair back with his fingers. "I knew it was wrong. Right from the start, when I began to realize you were falling in love with me, I knew I was asking for trouble. I told myself a thousand times in that first week alone that I had to break it off before we got seriously involved. Why do you think I was so damned careful about never letting things go too far when we were alone? I wanted to make love to you so badly I was half-crazy with it, but I knew I didn't dare, that I was going to have enough on my conscience when we hit Honolulu without *that* too!"

He smoothed her hair back from her face, seeing the confusion in her eyes and feeling it tear at him. "But I just…got lost, Meggie. In you. In whatever magic it was we had. When we were together, it was as though the outside world didn't even exist. We were in some special, magical place, far away from Russ or Elliott or Lucas or the fact I had a price on my head and every government operative in the world wanted me in his gun sight. For the first time in months I was able to just let go of all that, to spend time laughing and being happy without expecting a bullet between my shoulder blades at any instant.''

He swore softly, shaking his head. ''Damn it, I knew better! But you were real, Meggie. The only thing in my life that *was* real. Everything else had gone crazy, and I guess I somehow thought if I could just hang on to you, everything would work out. I felt—'' He frowned, knowing he wasn't making any sense but needing, finally, to get it said. ''Meggie, I think—for the first time in my life—that I knew what it felt like to love someone. And I didn't want to lose that. I deluded myself into thinking that *it* was the reality, not Lucas and the rest.

''Somehow it just felt right to ask you to marry me. I told myself I'd tell you the truth before we actually went through with it, but somehow I kept putting it off. During the ceremony, I kept telling myself I'd stop in time—until I heard myself saying 'I do'. And afterward, I told myself it wouldn't go any further. That I'd done enough to you already without adding more hurt, and then you stepped out of the bathroom in that silk negligee and...'' He shook his head slowly. ''Meggie, I swear I never meant to hurt you. It's just that I felt things for you I've never felt before, found myself dreaming things I'd given up on long ago, and...'' He stopped, not even knowing what it was he was trying to say.

''None of this excuses what I did,'' he said quietly. ''It was wrong, and I did it anyway—knowing it was wrong. Maybe that's the worst thing of all. I know you're never going to be able to forgive me, Meg, but you've got to believe I never meant to hurt you.''

''Oh, Tag, I—'' Her voice broke and she reached for him, buried her face against his throat and started to sob.

He held her tightly, his own throat aching, feeling each deep, convulsive sob rip through him as they ripped through her. He could hear the wind's howl over the soft sound of weeping, and wondered which chilled him more.

Damn it, how could he ever have hurt her like this? He had loved her!

For a little while, at least. And maybe he still did. As much as he could love anyone, that is.

He'd been as capable of loving as anyone, once, he supposed. Back about a million years ago, before he'd had to learn how to shut that part of himself off in order to survive, because feeling meant caring, and caring meant hesitating that moment too long in a jungled nightmare where hesitation meant death in any of a hundred brutal ways.

But he'd cared with Meggie. Had *loved*.

He sighed deeply, listening to her sobs. He'd lost it all with her. All the training, all the well-honed instincts for survival. He'd let her draw a bead on his heart as deadly as any VC sniper, and the consequences had been damned near as disastrous.

And that last night with her—that had been the worst mistake of all. She'd been as shy as any inexperienced young bride on her wedding night, had slipped trembling yet eager into his arms, had unnerved, then astonished, then delighted herself at the wonders her own body held.

She had transported him as she herself had been transported, had taught him things about gentleness and caring and giving that he'd all but forgotten. He'd let go of everything that night, had opened those forbidden parts of himself he'd never allowed to be touched before, and had frightened himself at how easy it had been.

Maybe that's why he'd run so easily, he brooded. Maybe her safety had only been the excuse he'd used, and the real reason was the heart-prints she'd left on his soul—the awareness of that ultimate vulnerability.

And now?

Now he had to get her out of this mess before she got hurt. Had to get her free not only of Lucas and the Black Dragon, but of himself. He'd never be able to love her the way she deserved to be loved. He'd lost too much of himself for that. The only thing he'd bring her was more heart-break, and he wasn't going to do that.

She was lying quietly in his arms now, and for a moment or two he thought she'd fallen asleep. But when he looked down at her, he found her looking at him contemplatively, her expression calm in spite of the glitter of tears on her cheeks.

She reached up and touched his face with her fingertips, tracing the scar on his left cheek. "I think," she whispered, "that I knew, in my heart, that none of it had been deliberate. It never made any sense that you were so concerned that night that I might get pregnant. If I was just someone you were using, it shouldn't have mattered."

"I'd never have done that to you, Megan," he murmured. "By the time we were in bed, I'd managed to convince myself that we'd work something out when we reached Honolulu. But the future was too uncertain to risk leaving you pregnant and alone." He had to laugh. "It hadn't occurred to me to make sure I had something with me that night because I'd also convinced myself I wouldn't need it—that I had enough willpower to stay the hell out of your bed, even on our wedding night."

Megan had to laugh. "Blame Janie Rodgers. She picked that negligee out for me in Bali. I wanted something frothy and lacy and a little less—-slinky. But Janie made it very plain that frothy was out and slinky was in, so..." She shrugged.

Tag winced very slightly. "Meg, can we stop talking about that damned negligee?"

Megan ran her finger down his cheek to the corner of his mouth. His lips parted slightly and she drew her fingertip lightly across the lower one, then, very slowly, she lifted her mouth to his. He kissed her gently and she slipped her tongue between his lips, teasing him, letting him almost catch it before drawing it away. There was no mistaking the fact he was still strongly aroused, and when she put her hand on his waist and pulled him toward her, he resisted.

"Megan," he whispered, "I'm not made of stone."

"No?" she asked with a laugh, moving her hips ever so gently. "Could have fooled me."

"Megan." His voice held both laughter and warning.

Megan lay there quietly for a moment, looking at him. In the shadowed light, his face was the one she remembered. The lines around his mouth were deeper and he looked a bit older, a bit more tired, but it was the man she'd loved a year ago. The man who, for a little while, had loved her back. It now seemed impossible that she'd ever hated him, had, at times in the past two days, even feared him. She felt very calm and safe here beside him; even the storm raging outside seemed to have lost some of its ferocity.

She sat up. Tag lay there for a moment looking at her, then he did the same, swinging his feet to the floor with what sounded like a weary sigh as he raked his hair back with his hand. Megan glanced sidelong at him as he sat staring contemplatively at the dancing flames in the small stove. He was leaning forward with his forearms on his thighs, hands dangling, and the borrowed sweater had pulled tightly across his shoulders.

She ran her hand across his back. It would be easy to leave things just as they were. The worst wounds between them had been healed sometime during the past two nightmarish days; if they got out of this alive, they could at least part at peace with each other and themselves.

Was that what she wanted?

Megan frowned. Strange, how rarely she ever asked herself that question. What she *wanted* had never mattered much over the years. She simply took what was given and never contemplated asking for more. But what if what was offered simply wasn't enough...?

"Tag, there's something I should tell you." He glanced around at her curiously and Megan swallowed, wishing her heart would stop pounding. "I...didn't get the annulment."

Chapter 10

Tag didn't say anything, although he frowned slightly. Megan looked down at her hands. "When I got back to Des Moines, I was so ashamed of having been taken in by what I thought was an elaborate con, that I...well, I just wanted to forget the whole thing. I should have gone to a lawyer right away but I knew I'd have to go into all the details and I just couldn't bear the thought of admitting what a fool I'd been, even to a stranger who'd probably heard it all before."

She shrugged. "And it didn't seem that important. I knew I'd never see you again, and I wasn't planning to get married or anything. I just kept putting it off. I know it was silly, but it was as though if I ignored it, the problem would go away by itself and I wouldn't have to deal with it." *Had* that been the real reason? she wondered fleetingly. Or had it been hope, all along?

Tag straightened slowly. "Do you mean...we're still married?"

Megan could feel a blush steal across her cheeks. "Yes, I guess so. At least, I'm still legally married to Michael Walker."

"Well, I'll be damned." He sounded so sincerely surprised that Megan's blush deepened. "It never occurred to me that you wouldn't...that we..." He reached out and cradled her chin in his palm, tipping her face up so their eyes met. "So you're my wife."

"Technically."

He drew in a very deep, very careful breath. "Meggie, why are you telling me this?"

Megan swallowed, holding his gaze evenly. "I think you know why," she whispered.

"Meg..." He looked at her almost wonderingly, smoothing her hair back with his hands. "Meggie, are you saying what I think you're saying?"

"I'm saying that I want to make love with my husband," she said calmly.

His eyes searched hers, then he eased a tight breath between his teeth, shaking his head slowly. "Meg, you don't want this. I've been accused of complicity in the murder of three government agents, don't you understand that? You're on the borderline yourself—by rescuing you from Lucas, I may have put you in even worse danger from the CIA. If someone gets it into his thick head that you're not an innocent victim, that you've actually been an accomplice, you're going to be up on charges right along with me. I have nothing to offer you, Megan. Even if we get out of this mess, I don't know how—"

"Tag, I'm not asking for anything more than right now. No yesterdays or tomorrows—just *now*. Whatever happens tomorrow or the next day or next week will happen and we'll have to deal with it when it does, but at least we'll have this little bit of time together. Just us—no lies this time, no false expectations."

He leaned toward her and kissed her gently. "Meg, if I thought for a moment that you wouldn't get hurt again—"

"I'm not going to get hurt," she whispered. She brushed a cowlick of hair off his forehead, and the gesture turned into a caress. "I want this because...maybe because you make me feel beautiful, Tag. Beautiful and desirable, and that's never happened to me before. And maybe because it's cold and I'm scared and I don't know if I'm even going to be alive two days from now. I just know I'm your wife, and I want you to make love to me." She kissed him, letting her mouth linger on his. "Let's help each other through this. Let's keep each other warm."

She came to her feet, smiling as she looked down at him. Then she held out her hand. He gazed up at her and for a heartbeat of time, Megan thought he was going to shake his head. Then, wordlessly, he braided his fingers with hers and stood up. Again, she could feel herself blush, astonished by her own boldness as she silently led him toward the bed.

She turned to him in the near-darkness and looked at him shyly. His eyes were shadowed and dark, but there was no hiding the smoldering hunger in them as he gazed at her, and Megan gave a delicious little shiver of anticipation. Still not speaking, he reached out and untied the belt of the robe, then drew it apart and pushed it gently off her shoulders so it landed in a sapphire pool around her feet. Lacking proper nightclothes, she was still wearing her panties and bra, and a little shiver tingled through her as Tag's gaze caressed her.

Something tightened around his eyes and he reached for her, tugging her gently into his arms. "Meg, when this is over—"

She put her fingers across his lips. "No promises we might not be able to keep, all right? I don't want to think about tomorrow. I just want tonight. Or as many nights as we can steal for ourselves, away from the real world."

His only answer was to lower his mouth and kiss her with a deep, satisfying thoroughness. By the time he eased his mouth from hers she was dizzy and breathless, and his own breathing was unsteady as he ran his lips across her cheek and slowly down the side of her throat.

"I can't count the times I've fantasized making love to you over the past year," he murmured. "There were nights when it was the only thing that kept me sane, Meggie. Nights when the only thing that kept me from giving up was the possibility of seeing you again. I'd close my eyes and you'd be there, waiting for me."

"It's real now," Megan whispered. "I'm real, Tag. Make it real...."

His hands caressed her back, keeping the chill air at bay. "I'd come in the door and you would be standing there," he went on in that smoky, warm voice. "I'd undress you, Meggie. Slowly...so slowly. Your blouse first, that pale yellow silk one you wore on the cruise, button by button. I'd slide it over one shoulder, then the other, and I'd start kissing you...." He nuzzled her throat, then ran a trail of moist, lingering kisses across her shoulder. "You'd put your arms around me and kiss me, and I would feel your breasts against my chest and I'd reach around and unhook your bra and fill my hands with you, Meggie."

The clasp on her bra parted easily and Tag had to struggle to remain calm as he drew his hands slowly up her back, then down and slowly around, drawing the anticipation out as long as possible. He could feel her give a little start as he touched her, felt his already sensitized body come vibrantly alive. "I'd feel your nipples against my palms," he whispered, "and when I'd move my hands, they'd start to pucker and go hard and I'd hear your breath catch and feel that little shiver go through you."

"Tag..." Megan's voice was just a whisper.

"Your skin would be like silk, and I'd run my hands down your stomach, undo the button on your skirt, and it would slide to the floor and you'd be almost naked for me, Meggie." He moved his hands down to the flare of her hips, caressed her back, fingers splayed. "I'd move my hands around and underneath your panties, sliding them down."

Her bottom was round and taut and utterly perfect and Tag swallowed, cupping her in both hands, lifting her slightly. She whispered his name, as he slipped the lacy briefs slowly down her thighs. "I'd start kissing your breasts, Meg," he growled, lowering his mouth to one dark nipple. He filled his mouth with her and felt her shudder, heard her soft, indrawn moan as she arched her back and drew his head against her.

He lifted his mouth from her and straightened, taking her hands from around his neck and pulling off the heavy sweater he was wearing. He put her hands on his chest. "You'd start undressing me then," he urged her softly, his eyes locking with hers. "Shirt first...one button at a time." He stood very still as she slid the unbuttoned shirt off his shoulders. "Jeans next," he whispered. "You'd pull the zipper down slowly, Meg, and—" His breath caught when she started kissing his chest, capturing a tuft of hair between her teeth and gently tugging it as she eased the zipper down.

He slipped his arms around her and started kissing her throat, loving her satiny skin, the warm scent of her. "I'd feel your hand," he whispered hoarsely, "and I'd be so ready for you I'd be half-crazy with it. I'd be on fire, Meggie, but I'd know if you kept doing what you were doing, I'd be gone, so I would stop you before it was too late...."

He reached down and caught her wrist. She melted against him and he brought his mouth down over hers in a fierce, wild kiss. Megan tugged his jeans over his hips impatiently and he kicked them off, and in the next instant they'd spilled across the bed, naked and hungry, and she was kissing him back with all the passion and need he'd dreamed of. She was like fire and silk, as lithe and sleek as a cat in his hands, and she moved sinuously as he caressed and stroked her. Moved against him, around him, until he thought he'd lose his mind.

He ran his fingers up into her hair and cradled her head, holding her still, and he started kissing her breasts again, sucking on the full, dark nipples until she was groaning his name. "Then I'd move my hands down your stomach, Megan,'' he whispered. ''And farther down, to where you're velvet-soft and warm....'' Her hands flexed in his hair and he felt her tremble, felt the first instinctive drawing back, thigh muscles tightening against intrusion.

He kissed her again, deeply, and ran his hand lightly down her thigh, eased it gently between, not hurrying her. He could feel the muscles slowly relax and he drew his fingers up the inside of her thigh, tracing lazy circles on the silken skin until she let herself relax that final trusting distance.

''You're so ready for me, Meggie,'' he murmured against her ear. She gasped his name at the first intrusive touch and arched her back slightly, moved against his hand. ''Then I'm touching that special place, Meg, and I can feel that little shiver go through you as I stroke you, can feel you start to melt....'' Exactly as in all those erotic, lonely dreams, Megan gave a low, soft moan and moved her hips in slow, rhythmic counterpoint to the movement of his hand.

''Tag, please...'' Her eyes were closed and she moved her head restlessly from side to side, lower lip caught between her teeth as she strained against his hand.

As in his dreams, Tag eased himself over her and, as in those same dreams, Megan shifted to make it easier for him, drawing her long legs up the outside of his. He moved against her, teasing himself as much as her, and it was only then that he remembered.

It took every ounce of willpower he had not to move his hips in that last strong, downward thrust, so achingly ready for her that it was like a physical pain to move away instead. Megan gave a gasp of disappointment and Tag swore, clenching his teeth so hard his jaw throbbed.

''Tag!''

''I know,'' he whispered in agony. ''My God, Meggie, I know!'' He pulled away from her, scarcely daring to breathe. ''You're not taking anything, are you?'' He asked it almost pleadingly, already knowing the answer but hoping against hope it wasn't true. ''I mean, you didn't get this sudden urge to start taking birth-control pills a few months ago or anything, did you?''

"No." It was just a sob, half laughter and half anguish. "And I don't suppose you—?"

"No," he groaned.

"I thought you Special Forces types went into battle prepared for anything," she said with a gasp of laughter.

"Hell, this is the *last* thing I figured would happen." He managed a rough laugh. "Of course, that's what I counted on the last time, too!"

"We managed then," she whispered, reaching up and drawing his mouth down to hers, "we'll manage this time, too."

He smiled. "You're right," he murmured, starting to kiss her breasts. "There are plenty of other ways . . ."

"No," Megan whispered, tugging his head up as he started kissing her stomach. "Make love to me, Tag. I mean, *really* make love to me. It's all right."

"No, it isn't," Tag said firmly. "I'm not taking a chance on getting you pregnant, Meg. Not when I don't know what's going to happen to us. To me. I could be dead tomorrow, or in jail for the next sixty years. I've done enough to you already; I won't risk leaving you to raise a baby by yourself."

Megan smoothed the frown across his forehead with her fingertips. "All those reasons are exactly why I *want* to take that risk. I'll be twenty-eight in another week, Tag, if I live that long. And you're the only man I've ever loved in all that time. If our luck holds and we can grow old together, that would be wonderful. We can have those kids you dreamed about, and live in that fantasy house. But if something happens to you, Tag, I'll have nothing. I *want* a child. Your child. I want our time together to have meant something, can you understand that?"

"Meg—"

"Shhh." She put her finger across his lips. "Taggart, you told me yesterday that I'm strong and competent. And you're right. I've only started to realize it myself, but I *am* strong. So far, I've gone through my life simply reacting to everything that happens to me, never taking charge, never reaching out and taking what I want. But these two days have made me realize just how precious life is, Tag—I want to start *participating* in mine, not just waiting to take what I'm handed. I'm not naive enough to think raising a child as a single mother is any picnic, but if it comes to that, I know I can do it. So please, let *me* choose. Trust me this time, all right? Just trust me...."

He knew, even as he was slipping into her arms, that it was crazy. There was no way a man could justify the risk. Logic told him she didn't understand the implications of what she was saying, that she didn't realize just how much danger they were both in, how very real the possibility was that she *could* wind up raising a child alone. And yet there was something in her eyes—perhaps a calm certainty he'd never seen before—that made him waver. He resisted her downward pull for a moment or two, then, with a groan of resignation, he let himself be drawn into the welcoming cradle of her thighs.

Within a heartbeat, he was lost. Part of it may have been the wildness of the night around them and part of it exhilaration at still being alive, but suddenly neither of them was holding back a thing. Tag had intended to take his time, not wanting to hurt her, had wanted the first time for her after nearly a year to be long and sweet and gentle. But Megan simply laughed and wrapped her legs around him, whispering something so deliciously explicit in his ear that his good intentions were forgotten in one fierce downward thrust of his hips that left them both gasping for breath.

It was pointless even trying to hold himself back. Megan neither needed nor wanted the slow, gentle lovemaking he'd intended, and after a moment or two he simply let himself go. It was like being caught up in a hurricane, the forces within as wild and elemental as those driving the storm outside. And the last thing he remembered before the very universe exploded around him was Megan's voice softly calling, not Michael's name, but his. And the fleeting thought that perhaps, finally, Michael Walker had been put behind them.

It was the silence that roused Megan.

She snuggled down into a warm nest of covers, more asleep than awake, and tried to recapture her dream. But something was wrong. It was one of those niggling, bothersome little things that won't be ignored, and when she finally figured out what it was, she sat straight up with an exclamation.

The wind had stopped.

And Tag was gone. His pillow was still indented where he'd slept beside her last night, but the cabin was empty.

The M16 was gone, too. The traitorous little thought that he'd deserted her again shot through Megan before she could stop it, and she gave her head an annoyed shake and slipped out of bed. All that was behind them now. What had happened a year ago had happened to a woman who didn't even exist anymore.

Even Tag had changed, learning to open up, to trust. They'd come through the past like steel through fire, finding strength in the flame. And last night . . . last night had been healing for both of them; she knowing she hadn't simply been used and abandoned a year ago, Tag knowing she'd forgiven him. Perhaps it was no coincidence that they'd wakened this morning to a bright, renewed world, the storm's fury spent.

The storm that had been their salvation. And their cover.

Megan gave a little shiver as she walked across to the big windows. That's what had gotten Tag up and out so early. They were sitting ducks up there, now that the storm had blown itself out. Lucas would have had his search teams out the instant the weather had cleared and it was only a matter of time before they found their way to the cabin.

She pulled the blinds open. Sunlight poured into the cabin, nearly blinding her, and she squinted out at a fairytale landscape. Huge, sweeping drifts of snow rose around the cabin, polished and carved by the wind, glittering in the brilliant sun as though dusted with diamonds. The sapphire sky beyond them was so clean and bright it almost hurt to look at it.

The big pines stood motionless. Their boughs drooped under garlands of snow, and now and again as the sun warmed them, one of the branches would suddenly release its burden and the snow would come cascading down, hitting the lower branches and creating a glittering avalanche that left a rainbow of sparkling ice crystals hanging in the still air.

But Megan wasn't in the mood to appreciate the beauty of the morning. Those drifts were deep. There was no way she and Tag were going to get away on foot. Even if they had proper winter clothing, it would take days to get down to a road or a telephone. Days they didn't have.

She was still staring reflectively out the window when she heard the helicopter. It was just faint at first, the familiar *whup-whup-whup* echoing across the valley, and the sound froze her where she stood. Then she spotted it, coming in low and fast from the north, flickering in the sunlight as it skimmed the snow-tinseled tree tops.

It was like an armored dragon, she found herself thinking inanely. She lost sight of it behind the big trees bracketing the cabin, and for a moment or two the sound seemed to recede and she wondered if it had gone by. It was possible. Lucas had half a mountain range to search—what were the odds of his homing in on them this soon?

Then it was right in front of her, hovering like some gigantic insect just beyond the trees where the hillside dropped sharply to the creek. The thunder of the rotors made the windows rattle, and as it edged nearer, the backwash whipped up a blizzard of snow and made the big trees flail like rags.

How she broke the spell, Megan didn't know, but in the next instant she was on the other side of the cabin, her heart pounding so hard it nearly drowned out the roar of the helicopter. She started pulling on her clothes, knowing as she did so that she had absolutely no chance of escape. Even if she managed to elude Lucas and his men, she had the mountains to face. And they would kill her just as effectively as any bullet.

Tag's pack was lying near the door and she upended it frantically, not even knowing what she was looking for. A knife, a gun...anything! Spare magazines for the M16 spilled across the floor, followed by two round, black objects that Megan numbly realized were grenades. Grenades! She bit the laughter back savagely, recognizing the hysteria in it, and snatched one of them up. It was cold, and heavier than she expected, and she shuddered with revulsion as her fingers closed around it.

Suddenly she heard footsteps. They approached stealthily from the side of the cabin, and she crouched down and scuttled behind the kitchen counter, out of sight of the windows. The footsteps moved slowly around to the front, then someone was on the wide porch, boots crunching cautiously through the snow. The intruder paused in front of the door and Megan watched the knob in stupefied fascination, her fingers tightening on the grenade as she struggled to control her panic. Tag was out there somewhere. All she had to do was stay uncaptured and alive until Tag could spring a surprise attack and—

The door splintered open with a crash and Megan recoiled with a muffled gasp as someone plunged into the room. He hit the floor on one shoulder and rolled hard, coming up in a low, menacing crouch, weapon at the ready and aimed straight at her.

Caught in the open, she froze like a rabbit pinned by the headlights of an oncoming car. They stared at each other for what seemed like an eternity, then the intruder eased his breath out and came out of the crouch cautiously, lowering the rifle. He glanced around the room swiftly, eyes narrowed, then looked back at her. "Where's Welles?"

Megan swallowed and got slowly to her feet, not even blinking as the muzzle of the rifle lifted fractionally. "Put the gun down," she said very calmly. She held the grenade up where he could see it and hooked one finger through the metal ring dangling from the pin.

He was tall and very lean, with a narrow face and pale, watchful eyes that settled on hers with predatory speculation. "I'd be very careful with that if I were you, Miss Kirkwood."

"I said put the gun down!" For an instant, Megan didn't think her bluff was going to work. But there must have been something in her expression to back up the threat, because the intruder's eyes narrowed fractionally, then, very slowly, he bent down to lay his rifle on the floor.

He straightened just as slowly, holding his hands out from his sides. "Pull that pin, and we both go up."

"Then don't do anything to encourage me to pull it." It was her voice, all right, but Megan had difficulty believing it. She sounded like someone who knew exactly what she was doing. Someone who was tired of being bullied and threatened and knew she didn't have a thing to lose. "Now put your hands behind your head. Move!"

Again, to her complete surprise, he did as she said. She dared a quick glance out the shattered door. "How many more are out there?"

"Just the—"

"Don't even breathe, buddy." It was Tag's voice, soft and deadly, and Megan's assailant stiffened. A shadow loomed just outside the door, then Tag stepped cautiously into the room, his M16 leveled at the stranger's midsection. He took in the entire room with one swift, assessing glance, then looked at Megan. "You okay?"

Megan nodded, her mouth suddenly too dry to speak. He saw the grenade just then and his eyes widened slightly. Then he gave her a dry smile before shifting his eyes back to the stranger. "Angel, you didn't pull the ring on that or anything, did you?"

Megan looked at the grenade. "I—I don't think so."

He chuckled quietly. "Just do me a favor, sweetheart, and *don't* pull it, okay? It would be a hell of a shame to blow this place into kindling, all considered. And us with it."

Megan swallowed and, very carefully, eased her finger out of the ring. Tag held his hand out and she deposited it in his palm, then scooped her hair back with both hands and drew in a deep, unsteady breath. "I saw the helicopter come in and just grabbed what I could find."

"I'd say you had everything under control." He flashed her an approving grin, then turned back to their captive, his face going hard again.

The stranger's gray eyes were like shards of ice, and when they rested briefly on her, Megan shivered. His mouth twisted in what was probably supposed to be a smile. "Welles."

"It's been a long time, O'Dell. I thought you were dead."

"I hear you're in trouble." The mouth twisted again. "Seems to me the *last* time we met you were in trouble. Tan Son Nhut, wasn't it? Something about insubordination. Threat of a court martial."

"What are you doing here?"

The eyes held Tag's assessingly. "Rick Jarvis."

The muzzle of Tag's gun lifted slightly. "What about him?"

"He's dead."

Megan caught her breath. She could see Tag stiffen, the disbelief on his face. Then the disbelief was gone and in its place was cold, murderous rage. He stepped forward lightly on the balls of his feet, the muzzle of the rifle inches from O'Dell's chest. "How?"

O'Dell's eyes were bleak. "He set up a meeting with me to hand over the information he had. When he didn't show, I went looking for him. The Black Dragon's men must have been waiting for him to make a move."

Tag swore in a quiet monotone, and Megan put her hand on his arm. "Why didn't he just stay *out* of it! He did all he could. Why did he—"

"He was trying to protect you," O'Dell said quietly. "When his meeting with you in D.C. was intercepted, he contacted a friend of his—Griff Cantrell. I think you know him."

"Cantrell? I remember him. He's a good man."

"One of the best," O'Dell said quietly. "And one of the few people Rick felt he could trust. Rick knew Cantrell had been doing some government work for me on and off, and wanted him to come after you. He seemed to *think*—" he gave Megan a speculative and not entirely unappreciative glance "—that you needed help. Although from what I've seen, I'd say you and the lady are taking care of business just fine on your own."

"The lady is my wife," Tag advised him shortly, the word so unexpectedly comfortable on his tongue that it surprised him. He looked at O'Dell speculatively. "What's this got to do with you?"

"Cantrell's out of the business. He met a woman last time out—" again, that cool glance in Megan's direction "—and hasn't been worth a damn since. So he contacted me."

"And since you had nothing better to do, you decided to help your old friend Taggart Welles."

O'Dell's face hardened. "If it was just you, Welles, I'd let you twist in the wind. Even in Nam you were always a renegade, balking at orders you didn't like, acting on your own when it suited you. You and Cantrell were two of a kind."

"We both figured our job was to keep as many of our men alive as possible," Tag said quietly. "I never saw anything wrong with that."

O'Dell gave a snort. "What you stumbled into here is too big to ignore, unfortunately. So, like it or not, I'm out here trying to save your butt."

"How did you find us?" Megan asked suddenly. "Either you're incredibly good at your job, or you had a little help."

Tag glanced around at her in surprise, not realizing she'd been following the discussion so intently. She was leaning against the counter, arms crossed, looking very calm and relaxed, considering that only minutes before she'd had her hands full of live grenade. He wasn't surprised O'Dell had backed down. The look of pure murder on Megan's face when he'd come into the cabin would have made him pause, too. No doubt about it—the shy little accountant from Des Moines had a ribbon of pure steel running through her. And she was just starting to realize it.

"Good question," he said quietly, looking at O'Dell.

O'Dell's eyes met his, cool as stone. "The Black Dragon knew Rick was on to him—he traced Rick through the computers somehow, just like Rick thought he would. They made their move on him that day you were supposed to meet in D.C. I don't think they expected you to be there—it rattled them and they split up, which was lucky for Rick. He grabbed everything he had and took off, but not before he managed to find out about Lucas snatching your wife."

"How did he find out about that?"

"I don't know the details. I just know Rick had been keeping an eye on her. He figured she was your weak spot, that if Lucas was going to hit you, he'd go for what would hurt the most."

Tag swore quietly, raking his hand through his hair. That sounded just like Rick. He'd been as angry as hell when Tag had told him what had happened on the cruise ship, had ranted and raved about honor and fairness and common decency until the two of them had wound up nose to nose, fists clenched, a gnat's whisker from coming to blows over it. He'd been disgusted by what he saw as Tag's callous betrayal of Megan's trust; somehow it fit that he'd decided to keep a watchful eye on her without saying anything. *Oh, God, Rick... I'm sorry, old buddy. I'm so sorry I got you mixed up in this....*

"At that point," O'Dell continued, "Rick and Cantrell came to me. We knew Lucas had your wife, and that he was working out of Seattle. I traced you out here, spent a couple of days quietly looking around, then I tailed one of Lucas's men up to the lodge. I broke in to check it out—it was obvious they'd been holding your wife there. It was also obvious that you'd already been in and out. I tracked you as far as the cave, then the storm hit and I had to head for cover.

"But I knew you hadn't got out of the mountains. That meant you'd holed up somewhere, so I spent two days going over aerial photos and high-resolution survey maps of the area, trying to put myself in your place. I narrowed the possibilities to a handful of locations and as soon as the weather cleared, I took up the hunt." He smiled faintly. "You're damned good, Welles, I'll say that for you. I can see why it's taken Lucas a year and a half to get even this close."

Tag gazed at the other man contemplatively. It sounded as implausible as hell, yet he remembered stories he'd heard in Viet Nam about O'Dell. The kind of things legends were made of. "In the Nam," he said carefully, "they used to say you could track VC a hundred klicks on solid rock. That you knew which way the enemy was going to move even before he did. That you could smell things and hear things no one else could."

Again, O'Dell gave them that cool, private smile. "Instinct, Welles. I had it, you had it. Most of us who came out alive had it."

Tag gave a noncommittal grunt. "So you found us. Now what?"

"Rick sent you a copy—maybe even the originals—of everything he had so far."

"Including the identity of the Black Dragon?"

O'Dell's eyes glittered. "Possibly."

"How do you know he sent everything to Tag," Megan asked suddenly, "if he was dead when you found him?"

"When I got home, there was a message on my answering machine. He said the Black Dragon's people were closing in fast and that he couldn't risk losing the information. He said he was sending everything to you, Welles. To some location you'd both agreed on if things turned bad. He said you'd know where."

Tag raked his fingers through his hair. "Yeah." He looked around the cabin, trying to make up his mind. If Rick trusted Cantrell, and Cantrell trusted O'Dell...

He gave his head an impatient shake. There were times when you just had to go with what you had. He could stand here playing "what if" until Lucas showed up, or he could risk trusting O'Dell at least long enough to get out of these damned mountains. He slung the strap of the M16 over his shoulder and wheeled away. "Let's *di di* before Lucas turns up," he growled. "But I swear to God, O'Dell, if this is a trick I'll kill you without even thinking twice about it." He picked up his pack and slung it over his shoulder, giving the cabin a cursory look. "Megan, grab what you need and let's get out of here."

"But we can't just leave the place looking like this!" Her gesture took in the rumpled bed, a few dirty dishes by the sink, the splintered door.

"Megan, damn it, this isn't the time to worry about etiquette! You have their address—you can write them a letter."

"But—"

He more or less pushed her physically from the cabin, although he did pause long enough to wedge the broken door as firmly into place as possible before starting out after O'Dell. Megan looked only slightly mollified, but she followed him without further argument.

O'Dell was waiting impatiently at the edge of the clearing. Beyond him sat a military chopper, engine rumbling, the big blades idling lazily. His mouth twisted in that smile that wasn't quite a smile. "Just like old times, isn't it?" he shouted over the sound of the engine. "An old Shadow Warrior like you should feel right at home in a dust-off from a hot LZ!"

"Yeah," Tag said roughly. Maybe that was the worst part. He'd spent the better part of fourteen years trying to forget Viet Nam and the person he'd been over there, and now he was having to face it all again. Lucas would pay for *that*, too.

O'Dell gestured them toward the chopper impatiently, and Tag shouted at Megan to keep her head well down as the three of them made their way to the open hatch. O'Dell vaulted in lightly, then turned and held his hand down for Megan and pulled her up. Tag scrambled in right behind her and O'Dell gave the helmeted pilot a slap on the shoulder and jabbed his thumb skyward. The pilot nodded, and in the next instant the engine's pitch rose to a scream and the chopper trembled, then gently lifted off, the rotors thrashing up a tempest of snow as they skimmed the hilltops, heading west. To Seattle. And temporary safety.

Chapter 11

The helicopter set them down in a small airfield just out-side Seattle. Megan saw the car with the man standing be-side it first, and she nudged Tag and pointed to it. "Are you expecting a welcoming committee?" She had to shout to be heard over the noise.

Tag leaned across to see what she was pointing at. He seemed to go very still, and when he straightened the M16 was pointing straight at O'Dell. "What's going on?" he shouted, motioning toward the waiting car.

"Colonel Buck Childress, head of a special government operations group working with the CIA."

"And maybe the Black Dragon?" shouted Tag.

O'Dell looked at him calmly. "If this was a double cross, Welles, you wouldn't be holding that M16."

Megan glanced at Tag. His eyes were narrowed on O'Dell's as though he could read intent behind the man's words. He looked hard and dangerous in daylight, his face still bruised and cut, his cheeks shadowed by a heavy growth of dark stubble. He had the look of someone who'd been pushed to the limit once too often and was now ready to start pushing back.

He and O'Dell stared at each other, neither giving ground, and Megan subdued a little shiver.

Then, suddenly, Tag gave an abrupt nod and lowered the M16. "Let's do it," he growled, leaning over to step out of the helicopter. "Megan, stay right behind me. And O'Dell, if you burn me on this, you'll be the first one down, got it?"

Megan's back prickled as the three of them walked slowly toward the waiting car. The other man stood impassively, not looking too pleased about being there on what was obviously turning out to be a beautiful spring morning. He had a stocky build, and the calm, solid gaze of someone used to being in command. His hair was ginger, thinning on top, and he had faded blue eyes that might, under better circumstances, be almost warm. He held his gloved hand out. "Buck Childress."

Tag ignored the outstretched hand. He cradled the M16 casually, although Megan had no doubt that at the slightest suspicious move it would be up and firing.

Childress let his hand fall to his side. "From what I've been told, you stumbled onto something mighty big while you were in Thailand, Welles."

"Yeah," Tag said dryly. "You might say that."

Childress looked at Megan curiously. "And you must be Megan Kirkwood. From O'Dell's report, you've been through quite a lot these last few days."

"Yes," Megan said quietly. "I guess I have."

He nodded, his eyes holding hers with faint concern. "It's a shame you had to get mixed up in this, Miss Kirkwood. I've arranged to have you taken somewhere safe until we get this thing sorted out."

"Megan stays with me," Tag said flatly.

Childress looked slightly disconcerted by Tag's vehemence. "As you wish." He glanced at O'Dell, then back to Tag. "Welles, it's imperative we get those documents your friend sent you. If he was as near to identifying the Black

Dragon as he says he was, we've got to get that information to someone who can finish his work.''

Tag's expression was cold. "Why the hell should I trust you, Childress? Or O'Dell either, for that matter. Either one of you could be the Black Dragon."

O'Dell smiled very faintly. "You've got to trust someone sooner or later, Welles. Do you know where the information is?"

Tag nodded after a moment. "I might."

"Then tell us," Childress put in impatiently, "so we can—"

"I'll get it." Tag's voice was icy. "Alone. Tell me how I can get hold of you."

O'Dell took a card from his pocket, turned it over and wrote something on the back. He handed it to Tag. "You can reach me at that number, day or night. And I put Cantrell's number under it. Just in case you want to check with him."

Tag handed the card to Megan without looking at it. "I need transportation."

"Take that car." O'Dell nodded toward a gray four-door parked nearby. "It's a rental—the documents are in the glove box." O'Dell tossed a set of keys toward Tag, who fielded them deftly. "I'll catch a ride back with Childress."

"And money." Tag smiled grimly. "You wouldn't want me to run out of gas, would you?"

O'Dell's eyes darkened, but he pulled his wallet out of an inner pocket and opened it, drew out a handful of bills. "There's close to eight hundred dollars here. That should keep you in gas for a day or two. And it's government money, Welles. So spend it wisely, okay?"

"Like you guys do with my tax dollars?"

Something that Megan could have sworn was faint amusement shadowed O'Dell's cold eyes for a moment. "And do me a favor, Welles. Don't get Megan killed. People in this country don't care if we government-agent types kill each other, but they don't like it when we take out innocent civilians. Considering the number of recent scandals, we've had enough bad P.R. to last for a while.''

"Don't worry, O'Dell," Tag grated. "The only people I'm going to hurt are the guys who smoked Russ Hammond and Rick Jarvis. And Lucas. Lucas is *definitely* mine."

O'Dell nodded slowly. "I figure we owe you that much. Get me the information that Jarvis sent you, and I'll see to it that you get a chance to meet the people who killed him."

Megan shivered and stepped nearer to Tag. She found herself trying to imagine O'Dell, or even Childress, laughing or playing with his children, mowing his lawn, chatting over morning coffee with his wife. But she couldn't. These people didn't live in any sane, normal world. Theirs was a shadow-world of lies and deceit and double-crossing, where a man's word meant nothing, where political intrigue and corruption were the everyday way of doing things.

"You *will* be in touch." O'Dell's voice was quiet.

"I'll be in touch," Tag assured him just as quietly. "Come on, Megan. Let's get out of here."

She slipped Tag an uneasy sidelong look as they walked to the car. It was a little frightening how rapidly he'd readapted to that shadow-world. Watching him, listening to him, it was hard to believe he wasn't as comfortable with these people and the easy death they dealt as she was in Des Moines. Would he ever find his way back out into the sun again? she found herself wondering. And if he didn't, could she live in the shadows with him?

Tag pulled out in a spray of gravel and dust, leaving the two men standing there without even a backward glance. His profile was hard against the sky, mouth set, chin rigid, and his knuckles gleamed white where he was gripping the steering wheel.

"I'm sorry about Rick," Megan said softly. She put her hand on his arm. "Are you all right?"

"Yeah." His voice was rough. His eyes narrowed against the glare of the sun. "It was my fault, that's what's hard to take. I went to him because I didn't know who else could help me. He could have said no. But he turned it into some kind of damned personal crusade, and now—'' He bit it off, the muscles of his jaw rippling.

"He knew the risks," Megan said mildly.

"Damn it, it isn't that easy," he said hoarsely. "It—"

"It *is* that easy!" Her voice snapped through the car. "Rick Jarvis knew the risks involved in helping you just like you knew the risks involved when you went tearing over to Hong Kong to help Russ. Or when you came tearing up here to rescue me, for that matter. You all had your own dragons to slay—and your own reasons for getting involved. You make it sound as though you just invented guilt. Well, you didn't. The world's full of it."

Megan's outburst startled her as much as it did Tag. He gave her a quizzical look and she sighed. "Sorry. It's just that I'm an expert on guilt. I spent most of my life feeling guilty for not being as perfect as Peggy, then guilty for her death, then, when my mother got sick, I felt guilty over *that*." She gave a rueful laugh. "Sometimes I think *my* family invented guilt." She reached out for his hand and meshed her fingers in his. "Rick knew what he was doing, Tag. I know losing him like this hurts, but you can't let it eat you up. The best thing you can do for him now is just make damned sure all the work he did doesn't go to waste."

"Yeah." Tag squeezed her fingers gently. "You're right. But knowing that doesn't make sleeping at night any easier." Like knowing I walked out of your life a year ago to protect you hasn't made sleeping at night any easier, he wanted to add.

"What are we going to do now?"

Tag shook off his brooding. "Find somewhere to hole up. And try to figure out who the hell I can trust, and who I can't, before I hand that information of Rick's over."

Megan frowned. "You don't think you can trust O'Dell or Childress?"

"I don't trust anybody," he said bluntly. "And I think O'Dell is telling only half the truth about what happened to Rick. I think Rick opened up to someone he trusted, and that person lured him out into the open where the Black Dragon's men could hit him."

"O'Dell?"

"I find it hard to believe. But then again, I find most of this hard to believe. Childress, I don't know about. He was in Viet Nam, too, along with the rest of us. Real straight-arrow type, everything by the book." He shook his head. "I'll be damned if I know, angel. I just know I'm not turning my back on either of them. And I'm not letting them get their hands on you. As far as I'm concerned, it's you and me against the world."

"Terrific odds," Megan sighed. "You've got a real knack for making a lady feel safe."

Tag chuckled and lifted her hand to his lips, kissing each of her knuckles in turn. "I'm not letting anything happen to you, angel. Trust me."

"I do."

Megan smiled at him, her eyes warm with memories of last night, and Tag felt his heart give a leap. She'd given herself to him with the same utter trust he saw in her eyes now, holding nothing back, opening her heart to him with the same lack of fear with which she'd opened her body. It scared him a bit, just thinking about it. Trust was such a fragile thing. As fragile as a woman's heart. And as easily broken.

"Where are we going?"

Her quiet voice scattered his ponderous thoughts. "I don't know," he said quite truthfully. "I figure we've got a couple of hours before Lucas figures we slipped through his fingers and puts out the alert. If he's smart—and he is—he'll contact the Highway Patrol and the local police and have the whole damn state mobilized to smoke us out."

"And if O'Dell or Childress are involved, they have a description of this car, too."

"Exactly. Which is why," he added with a faint smile, "we're going to make a small detour to Crazy Jack's Auto Emporium."

Crazy Jack's Auto Emporium was exactly as she'd envisioned it, a down-at-heel used-car lot dressed up like a circus with garish flags and tinsel and a loudspeaker spewing a pretaped line of sales patter that would have shamed a carnival huckster. Crazy Jack was a thin, oily man with too-long hair and nervous eyes, and he greeted Tag like a long lost brother.

Tag had told her to stay in the car, something she was only too happy to do, and she and Crazy Jack's two big mongrel hounds eyed each other suspiciously as the two men disappeared. Tag came back about twenty minutes later, grinning triumphantly as he held up a set of keys, only to disappear again between two rows of shiny cars. Then he was back, driving a bright red Camaro that he eased up alongside O'Dell's rental. He gave her a reckless grin and gunned the engine a couple of times, seemingly pleased by the guttural snarl that came from under the hood.

"Who *is* that guy?" she asked Tag in a low voice. She helped him transfer his pack and the M16, now wrapped in his jacket, into the rumbling Camaro, then slid into the passenger seat.

"I did him a favor once," he said with a smile. He lifted his hand in a lazy salute and Jack returned it, grinning like a crazed weasel. Then Tag gunned the engine and slammed the Camaro into gear and they fishtailed out of the lot with a squeal of tires.

Megan grabbed the dashboard with one hand and secured her seat belt with the other. "And you trust him?"

"I told him I was running away with another man's wife," he said with a grin. "And I happened to mention that your husband works for the government and may turn up pretending to be CIA and not to believe a thing he says. That sort of thing appeals to Jack's sense of adventure."

"And he believed you?" Megan looked at him in astonishment.

"For a hundred bucks, Jack will believe anything you want him to." He gave a quiet laugh. "In an hour, O'Dell's car will be on its way to the nearest chop shop, and by tomorrow it'll be in fifty different pieces, headed for fifty different states."

Megan had to laugh. "Well, as part of our transformation from most-wanted to simple illicit lovers, if you stop at the next shopping center I'll buy us both some clothes." Megan looked down at the oversized man's pants and jacket she was wearing, then at Tag's camouflage jacket and torn, bloodstained jeans. "If we try to register at a motel looking like this, we'll get turned in for sure. We look like a cross between Rambo and Bonnie and Clyde!"

They finally found a small shopping area in a part of town where Megan's apparel wouldn't raise too many questions. She slipped into a large discount store with her pockets full of Spence O'Dell's government funds, and came out a long while later laden down with packages and fashionably clothed in an Irish-knit sweater, snug new jeans and a broad smile of sheer relief.

Tag raised a questioning eyebrow as she dumped them into the back seat and slid into the car beside him. "A snap," she assured him with a playful grin. "I got a couple of startled looks when I walked in, but I just told the clerks I was on my honeymoon and that my new husband and I had all our luggage stolen last night."

Tag gave a snort of laughter as he wheeled the Camaro back out into traffic. "And they believed you."

"Believed me?" Megan combed her hair back with her fingers, laughing. "They were on the verge of taking up a collection for us! It was a bit embarrassing, actually—they threw in a lacy thing that's split up to here and down to there that I wouldn't be caught *dead* in, and wouldn't even let me pay for it!"

"Really?" Tag looked suddenly interested. "Split up to where, exactly?"

"Forget it," she told him, still laughing. Although on *second* thought, she found herself musing, it might be fun to show it off tonight. The old Megan Kirkwood, the shy little accountant who still wore ankle-length flannelette nightgowns to bed, would die before even trying it on, let alone wearing it in front of a man. But that old Megan Kirkwood hadn't been around a lot lately.

She gave a decidedly un-Megan-like chuckle and Tag looked at her with such an odd expression that she had to laugh aloud. "Sorry!" She reached out and slid her fingers around his. "I know it's crazy, considering the danger we're in, but I'm kind of having fun."

"Fun?" He arched his eyebrow.

"Well, not fun exactly. It's just that I've never done anything even remotely off the wall or risky or dangerous before and I guess it's a little exhilarating—like drinking champagne for the first time." She gave him a sweeping glance. "And I'm sure you remember the results of *that* experience."

Tag grinned reminiscently. "Yeah. I had *planned* to sleep on the couch that night..."

Megan gave a peal of laughter, remembering their wedding night with vivid clarity and how, had it not been for those two fortifying glasses of champagne, things might have gone very differently.

"Speaking of which," he said quietly, "I want to make a quick stop myself. If you spot a drugstore, sing out."

"I picked up toothpaste and everything we need."

"I wasn't thinking of toothpaste," Tag said with a sidelong glance that spoke volumes.

"They...umm...had a pharmacy in that store," Megan said softly, astonished to feel herself blushing. "I bought something to...umm...well, take care of that." He looked at her in surprise and she felt her cheeks grow an even deeper pink. "I know it's a bit like shutting the barn after the horse has bolted, but you seemed so worried last night and I didn't want anything to spoil the rest of the time we have together.''

He gave her a slow, approving smile. ''Let's find that motel,'' he murmured, his eyes holding hers with a look that made her heart give a thump. ''And spend some of that time together right now.''

It was nearly an hour later when they pulled into the parking lot of a large, busy motel overlooking the highway. Megan had thought they should find someplace secluded and quiet until Tag pointed out that the safest place to hide was usually right in plain sight. But it was Megan who suggested that his clothing and bruises would draw unneeded attention, so it was his turn to fidget in the car while she went in to register.

She came out a few minutes later, grinning. ''What's the joke?'' he asked as she slid into the car.

She gave him a mischievous glance. ''You'll see. Drive around to the back. We're on the top, overlooking the pool.''

''Queen-size bed, I hope.''

But Megan just chuckled, and it was only when Tag opened the door to their unit and stepped inside that he realized what was going on. He gazed around the huge room with its king-size bed, beribboned bottle of champagne and soft, intimate lighting, and started to laugh.

''Don't blame me,'' Megan protested. ''I must have newlywed written all over me, because the minute I stepped into the office the owner's wife took the keys to their bridal suite out! Just what did you tell them when you called for a reservation from that gas station, anyway?''

''I swear the words 'newly married' never crossed my tongue,'' Tag assured her with a broad grin. ''Although I *may* have said something about wanting lots of privacy....'' He checked the label on the bottle of champagne and gave her a wink. ''Maybe they just drew their own conclusions.''

"I wonder how many couples check into the bridal suite with an M16 and a bag full of grenades," Megan muttered, wrinkling her nose with distaste as Tag eased the rifle from its makeshift case. "By the way, I bought a duffle bag for your collection of toys. I was afraid if someone caught a glimpse of that rifle—one of the housekeeping staff, for instance—she'd be calling for a SWAT team."

"Smart girl," Tag said with approval, starting to rummage through the bags. He held up a wisp of lace masquerading as a bra and nodded even more approvingly, pleased to discover a pair of matching bikini briefs further down. "Speaking of heavy armament, angel . . ."

She snatched both garments out of his hands, blushing charmingly as she started pulling shampoo and soap from another bag. "I needed lingerie and . . . well, I don't usually buy things like that, but—"

"I like it," Tag murmured, giving a low whistle as he pulled out a frilly swatch of black see-through fabric that might have been a nightie. It took absolutely no effort at all to imagine her in it, and as his mind went rambling off into all sorts of erotic directions, he smiled to himself. No doubt about it, his shy little accountant from Des Moines was starting to discover facets of herself that could wind up surprising both of them! He started to dig even deeper into the contents of the bag, curious as to what else he was going to find.

"Your things are in *this* one." The bag of lingerie was whipped out from under his nose, replaced by another that looked infinitely less inviting. "And while you're entertaining yourself, I'm going to have a bath. A very long, very hot bath. In fact, I may not come out until next week."

"God Almighty!"

Megan opened one eye drowsily. She stretched languorously and smiled at Tag through the scented steam and candlelight. He was standing in the doorway, looking around him in astonishment. "Something else, isn't it?"

"Decadent is the word you're searching for." He wan
dered in and looked curiously around the huge bathroom
It was a confection of pink marble, brass, glass and mir
rors, the long vanity cluttered with glass bottles of bath salts
and oils and baskets of seashells and decorative soaps. The
huge, round tub in which Megan was blissfully immersed
was surrounded by more jars of bath salts, tropical plants
and a multitude of colorful candles. She'd lit most of them
on a whim, and the bathroom glittered and glowed like
something out of a fairy tale.

Tag opened a decanter of bath oil and gave it a sniff, then
set it down and strolled across to the tub, unbuttoning his
shirt. "Got room in there for me, angel?"

Chapter 12

Megan smiled mischievously. "There's room in here for you, me and the local football team."

Tag grinned down at her and proceeded to pull off his shirt. "Remind me to thank the management for this before we leave."

He stripped quickly, kicking his dirty clothing aside, and padded toward the tub with a lazy, promising smile that made Megan's heart do a quick somersault. She felt herself blushing lightly, still not entirely used to the easy, relaxed way he could stroll around without a stitch on. The bruising on his torso and rib cage had turned an evil shade of blue-green, while his scraped shoulder still sported a huge, vivid purple bruise that extended right down his forearm.

He eyed himself with distaste. "Not the most beautiful sight you've ever set eyes on, am I?"

"Well, you do have sort of a...well-used look," she said dryly. "Sort of like those stone garden statues when they get all weathered and mossy."

Tag winced. "You really know how to cut a guy down to size, don't you?"

Megan laughed at his expression. "Do your ribs feel better?"

"Like they've gone ten rounds in a heavyweight championship. But they feel better than before." He sat on the wide marble ledge surrounding the tub and removed the blood-stained dressing from his thigh, wincing as he eased the adhesive tape free. Megan lifted her leg gracefully and planted one dripping foot squarely in the middle of his chest, kneading the hair with her toes. "Are those jeans I bought going to fit all right?"

Tag started massaging her foot. "Perfect. Shirts, too. You've got a good eye."

"When there's something worth looking at."

He bent his head and started kissing her toes. "Even when it's weathered and mossy?"

"In your case."

"Speaking of something worth looking at," he murmured as he started stroking her ankle and calf, "I hope you're going to model that little black see-through number for me."

"I am not," Megan said with a laugh.

The way he was looking at her made her blush again, and this time it was Tag's turn to laugh. He leaned forward, running his hands slowly up her thigh as he slipped into the water. The tub was big enough for him to stretch out full length, and he eased himself between her legs so he was lying along her body, resting his forearms on the ledge at either side of her head.

"Still my shy little Meggie," he teased, kissing her gently. "By the way, I don't think I've told you yet how proud I was of you today. When that chopper came down, I was on the other side of the clearing and couldn't get back without being spotted. By the time I realized there was only one man on the ground, he'd flanked me and was at the cabin—my heart was in my mouth when I saw the door smashed in

And there you were, holding the infamous Spence O'Dell at bay with a grenade." He laughed and rubbed his nose against hers. "You probably made history. I doubt anyone's gotten the drop on O'Dell in twenty years."

"I was scared to death!" Megan slipped her dripping arms around his neck and ran her fingers through his hair. "But I'm sick of people bullying me and threatening me and pulling guns on me. And besides, I knew you'd be there any minute—it was just a matter of catching his attention."

Tag gave a lazy laugh. "I think you managed to do that, angel. The expression on his face was almost worth the scare he gave me." He kissed the tip of her nose. "Ferocious little thing when you're backed into a corner, aren't you?"

Megan looked up at him quite seriously. "I certainly never *thought* I was. But it's odd...I *do* feel different somehow. It's as though all this stuff that's been going on has put things into perspective. I'm not sure I'm ever going to be afraid of anything again—really afraid, I mean."

"I know." He kissed her gently. "I've been watching you."

"Really?" It pleased her to think that he was so in tune with her that he could see changes she was only starting to suspect. "Actually, I think it started on the cruise." She had to laugh suddenly. "Signing up for that six-week cruise was the most daring thing I'd ever done! And the whole time I was doing it, I could hear my mother telling me I was crazy, that cruises to the South Seas were for people like Peggy, not me, that I'd have a miserable time."

"Could have fooled me," Tag murmured. "It looked to me as though you were having a great time."

"I was! For the first time in my life I was with people who'd never known Peggy—suddenly I could be *me* instead of just Peggy Kirkwood's sister. It was a little scary at first, but after a day or two I really started to enjoy it."

"It couldn't have been easy getting out from under Peggy's shadow," Tag said quietly. "Your mother had your house set up like a shrine—pictures of Peggy everywhere, the walls covered with awards she'd won in everything from tap dancing to baton twirling. Even that album on the coffee table filled with snapshots and clippings. And not a damned thing of yours anywhere.''

To her surprise, it made Megan laugh. "It's awful, isn't it? There were times since Mother died that I was going to clear all that stuff out—pack it up and put it in the attic or something. But every time I'd almost work up the nerve, I'd get this rush of guilt over all the times I'd secretly wished something awful would happen to Peggy, and I wouldn't touch a thing.''

"Doesn't sound like the Meggie Kirkwood I know—the one who can still smile after being kidnapped and shot at and chased by heroin smugglers. The one who calmly pulls out a hand grenade and makes an ex-commando with a loaded M16 cry uncle. The one," he added very softly, "who makes a man want to beat his chest and howl at the moon when he's making love to her because she makes it so damned good for him.''

"It helps," Megan whispered, "when the man she's making love with makes her feel like the most sexy, seductive, beautiful woman on the face of the earth.''

"Speaking of which..." he murmured with a slow smile.

"Speaking of which," Megan echoed with a laugh as she ran her fingers down his bristly cheek, "I bought you a little present today—it's up there on the vanity.''

Tag raised his head to look where she was pointing, groaned good-naturedly and sat up, reaching for the razor and shaving foam. "Hint taken, sweetheart." There was a small round mirror on a decorative brass stand there, too, and he set it on the edge of the tub. Then he sprayed a fragrant mound of foam into his palm and lathered his face.

"You know, it's funny," Megan mused, watching him, "but when I look back at all the years I wasted resenting Peggy for being so popular and beautiful, I realize *I* was the one causing all my problems, not Peggy. I tried so hard to be like her that I lost track of the real me. And Mother wasn't being intentionally cruel, she was just so desperate to relive her own dreams through Peggy that she didn't realize what she was doing to us—both of us.''

''I don't imagine it was any picnic for Peggy, either.'' Tag dipped the safety razor in the water and gave it a shake, then started shaving his left cheek, avoiding the cut under his eyes.

''I think she and I might have become friends if we'd had more time. She wasn't a bad kid, really.'' Megan started lathering a bar of soap. ''I think the first thing I'm going to do when I get home is have a gigantic housecleaning! I'll keep all Peg's favorite things, but most of that junk Mother kept around was stuff Peggy didn't even like. And I think I'll paint the living room,'' she added thoughtfully. ''Peach and white—I've always loved that combination. And a new carpet and drapes. And maybe some new furniture and—'' She stopped suddenly and gave a rueful laugh. ''*If* I get home, that is.''

''You'll get home, angel,'' Tag reassured her softly. He felt an unexpected emptiness, hearing her making plans for a future that obviously didn't include him.

Megan started washing his back, kneading the taut muscles across his shoulders then working her fingers down his spine, and he gave a murmur of pleasure. Her gentle hands and the heat of the water started easing the tension from him, and he forced his brooding thoughts away and let himself relax.

''I keep thinking we should be doing something,'' Megan said thoughtfully. ''I feel like we're wasting precious time sitting here while Lucas is doing...whatever he's doing.''

''Running in circles,'' Tag said with a chuckle. ''And the safest thing we can be doing right now is exactly what we *are* doing—staying well hidden and working out our plan of attack.''

Megan starting soaping his shoulders. ''It's hard to believe the Black Dragon—whoever he is—is going to so much trouble to track you down. I'd think it would be easier to simply cover his own tracks so anything you *do* show the officials won't mean a thing. If this setup is as well-organized as you say, you'd think he'd have anticipated something like this and had all sorts of blind alleys and red herrings built in to confuse anyone looking too closely.''

''He did,'' Tag said quietly. ''But he didn't anticipate someone like Rick picking up the scent—someone with the background, the security clearance, the skill and the *incentive* to gnaw away at it until he figured out what was going on.''

''Or you,'' Megan said softly. She ran her hands around Tag's chest and hugged him, planting a kiss between his wet shoulder blades. ''Maybe he forgot all about things like honor and loyalty and friendship.''

Tag gave a snort of bitter laughter. ''He didn't count on me tearing Southeast Asia apart looking for Russ, that's for sure. I must have worried the hell out of them, digging around long after I should have given up and gone home.'' He lifted his chin and started shaving his throat. ''It's partly personal now. I've caused them a lot of grief, and they want payback. And no organization is completely bulletproof. Whatever Rick dug up, it must be dangerous enough to risk mobilizing the entire country on some trumped-up charge of treason and murder to shut me up.''

Megan started running her soapy hands across his shoulders again. ''So the Black Dragon runs the operation from the inside, keeping his identity a secret, while Lucas handles all the outside business.''

''Exactly.'' Tag winced as he worked the razor carefully over the bruise on the side of his jaw. ''They're shareholders in a cartel that effectively runs the world's heroin trade. They own and control it from beginning to finish: the land the poppies are grown on, the farmers who harvest the crop and turn it into opium gum, the mule trains hauling the gum out of the mountains, the factories where the gum is turned into heroin, the trucks that haul the heroin down to the docks, the freighters that carry the stuff to Amsterdam and Marseilles and New York and a thousand other places, right down to the dealers on the street.''

''And Vancouver,'' Megan said thoughtfully.

''Undoubtedly.''

''No. I mean that's how Lucas is getting the heroin into Seattle. He brings it into Vancouver by ship, then across the border—they've got people on their payroll at Customs who wave the trucks through—and down here to Seattle.''

Tag turned his head to look at her. ''How the *hell* do you know that?''

''They had some problem with the latest shipment. The freighter had engine trouble and was late docking, and the customer at this end was getting nervous. Lucas had to fly back and forth a couple of times to straighten things out.''

Tag's astonishment turned to admiration. Damn few people in that situation would have paid any attention to what was being said around them, much less put it into context and figure out what was going on. ''What other little tidbits did you pick up?''

''Not much. They have a warehouse down on the docks here in Seattle somewhere that seems to be some central depot. And there's someone there by the name of Kim...Khem...Khiem! That's it.''

''Khiem?'' Tag's voice ricocheted off the walls.

''Do you know him?''

''I know him,'' Tag growled, eyes narrowing. ''Nguyen Tran Khiem, the Butcher of Saigon. He was with the ARVN—the South Vietnamese army—and as corrupt and dangerous as they come. Lucas and others used him as an interrogator. He used to boast that if a prisoner didn't spill everything he knew in five minutes under his 'treatment' he didn't know anything worth having.'' He glanced around at Megan. ''He's one of the reasons I quit Shadow Company. I couldn't stomach Khiem's methods—and I refused to turn prisoners over to him. He enjoys his work just a little too much for my tastes.''

Megan was silent for a moment. When she finally spoke, her voice sounded strained. "Lucas thinks Khiem can convince you to tell them everything you know."

Tag gave a snort. "I don't doubt it for a minute!" He suddenly realized Megan had gone very still and he cursed himself. Tossing the razor aside, he wiped his face dry, then turned around and took the bar of soap out of her hand. "Don't worry about me, angel. I intend to stay as far away from Khiem as possible." He slipped his arms around her and nuzzled her throat, rubbing his cheek against hers. "How's that?"

"Delicious," Megan breathed, kissing the corner of his mouth, the curve of his lower lip. The tip of her tongue touched his and he murmured in pleasure, then she settled her mouth fully over his and kissed him slowly and deeply.

An aching, syrupy warmth settled in his pelvis and his body started to respond, fired by the promising heat of her kiss. He ran his soapy hands across her shoulders and down her back, then around to gently massage her breasts, her golden skin slippery and warm. The tips of her breasts were dark and full, the nipples slowly starting to pucker as he caressed them, and Megan arched her back very slightly.

"That feels good," she whispered. Her eyes were half-closed, almost sleepy, and he felt a tiny shiver wind its way through her.

"You feel good all over," he murmured, sliding his hands down her back, around the smooth curves of her bottom. He leaned back against the side of the tub and tugged her across him so she was half lying, half sitting in his lap, her arms around his neck, her mouth under his, warm and sweet and alive. He refused to give in to the sudden urgency of his own body, and he kissed her slowly, enjoying the deliciously familiar taste of her, the way her breath caught as he caressed her wet breasts. They filled his hands, hard-tipped now, and he could hear her soft moan as he teased the nipple with his calloused thumb. She was sleek and supple in his arms, moving slightly with the buoyancy of the deep water, and his own breath caught as her body teased his.

He ran his hand slowly down her ribs and over the flare of her hip, across to her stomach, feeling the muscles there tighten slightly. She put one hand over his as though to stop him and he did as she wanted, kissing her slowly, almost leisurely. When he moved his hand again she pressed it against her, moaning softly in assent, and she gave a little indrawn gasp when he slipped it into the warm niche between her thighs, seeking, finding the special silken warmth deeper still.

Her fingers tightened around his wrist and he nuzzled her neck, her ear. "Tell me what you want," he murmured.

He could hear her swallow. "I want . . ."

"This?" he whispered, caressing her slowly.

"Yes!" She flexed her hips upward, pressing herself against him.

"More?" he teased.

"More! Oh, Tag, I want to feel you touching me. I want . . ."

"This?" Her petaled warmth parted to his deep, questing touch and she groaned softly, her thighs opening trustingly to make it easier for him, groaning again as his fingers sank into her warmth. He caressed her with his thumb and he could feel her shudder, knew by the quick, urgent movement of her hips that he'd been right about how near the edge she was even though she hadn't realized it herself.

She braced her feet against the side of the tub and arched her back, so alive and responsive that it took no effort at all to know exactly what she needed from him to take her up that long, dizzying slope. He knew even before she did when it started to crest, then gently break, catching her so unaware that she gave a soft, low cry and pressed her thighs tightly together as though to stop the uprush of pure pleasure that made her cry out again, and then again.

Hearing her, watching her arch under the compelling magic of his hand, nearly sent him over the edge then and there. He gritted his teeth and cradled her against him until the last shivery little tremors ran through her and she finally relaxed against him, panting slightly, eyes heavy-lidded.

"I don't...think," she whispered breathlessly after a moment or two, "that you're...being...entirely fair."

"To you?" he purred

"To you." She rested her head on his shoulder and closed her eyes, trying to catch her breath. "It's so...one-sided. That way."

"What way?" he teased, moving his hand up her thigh. "This way?"

"Tag!" She shivered, but couldn't stop herself from moving her hips strongly upward. "You're making me so greedy I can't stand it. I could just take and take and never give...and that's not fair at...oh, Tag!...at all."

"You're forgetting something, angel," he reminded her with a low chuckle. "When you take, I get to give—and I love giving you that kind of pleasure, Meggie. I love making it so good for you that you forget all about me and just let go, just reach out and take what you need...."

"I want to make you greedy, too," she breathed, easing herself into his lap so she was astride him, knees clamped around his hips. She slipped her fingers into his hair and kissed him long and hard, ran her mouth down his throat. She moved her hips, caressing him with her body until Tag thought he was going to lose his mind, then sank down over him, taking him fully into her feminine warmth so certainly and deeply that he gasped her name and arched under her, head thrown back against the edge of the tub.

He could hear her laugh very softly, knew by the way she was moving that she intended to please him as selflessly as he'd just pleased her. He caught her hips and held her firmly against him, smiling against her mouth. "You said you bought something for this situation?"

"They're in the other room" Megan whispered, kissing his jawline, his ear. "You don't really want me to get up and get them, do you?"

"Meggie." Tag gritted his teeth, feeling his willpower vanishing. "We should..."

"Next time," she moaned softly, giving an impatient wriggle. "I don't want to stop, even for a minute. I told you I was greedy. And it's all your fault for teaching me what it can be like...."

She moved against him again and Tag had to catch his breath. Laughing quietly, he pushed himself away from the side of the tub and lifted up onto his knees, seeing Megan's eyes widen slightly as he brought their bodies even more tightly together. She wrapped her legs securely around his hips and he grinned at her. "Hang on tight," he whispered.

"What are you going to—Tag!" She clutched his shoulders in astonishment as he stood up, water cascading around them, and stepped cautiously out onto the carpeted floor. Then, still holding her firmly against him, he dropped to his knees again and stretched onto his side.

He braced himself on one elbow and Megan smiled up at him. "I thought you liked swimming."

"I like swimming just fine," he murmured, pulling her thigh up over his hip. "But there are some things I enjoy even more." He punctuated the word with a strong thrust of his hips that made Megan moan. "Buoyancy's great when you're a fish," he whispered, "but there are advantages to being on solid ground, too...." He proved his point with another strong thrust of his pelvis and Megan's fingers dug into the small of his back.

Her head was thrown back and he could see her small white teeth, the tip of her tongue, the tiny frown between her brows. He started to move slowly, deeply within her and she bit her lower lip to stifle a moan, drew her leg even higher over his hip. Her breasts were temptingly near and he lowered his mouth and took the pebbled tip of one into his mouth, heard her soft moan as he tongued it, felt her hands clench and unclench on his hips. The urgency of her movements fueled his own need and it wasn't long before he drew his mouth from her breast and braced himself on his outstretched arm, moving strongly and rhythmically in the embrace of her body, one hand resting on her hip to guide her corresponding movements. He could look down and see the muscles in her flat stomach tighten as she flexed against him, looked up a moment later to see her watching him, her eyes hooded and smoky.

It had once made her shy and flustered to know he was watching her while they made love. But he could tell by her eyes that she was past that now, knew by the way she arched sinuously under him that she knew how erotic it was for him to watch her respond, that she loved the touch of his eyes on her as much as the touch of his hands.

"Witch," he breathed, his body responding fiercely to her awareness of him. "My God, you're like satin and fire, Meggie. I can feel you burning, all wrapped around me...."

"Take what you want," she whispered, her voice no more than a moan of pleasure. "Take what you need, Tag. Please. Please..."

His willpower finally broke, and he felt himself tumble down into a maelstrom of hot, driving desire so strong it made him cry out. He was aware of nothing but the tension within him building until it was almost unbearable. Was gratified to know that even in the taking he was able to give, as he heard her sharp, breathless little moan, felt a sudden, fierce tremor run through her, then another behind it, and yet a third.

It was as though his body was waiting for that signal to simply let go, and he finally stopped fighting it and lost himself in the sheer physical wonder of it. Her mouth was hot under his and he kissed her roughly, hungrily, then tore his mouth from hers as the urgency grew that last desperate distance and he was panting her name, plunging against her until that final, cataclysmic moment when everything just vanished in one all-encompassing uprush of sensation.

It left him spent, and he cradled her against him, wondering how in God's name he'd ever thought he could live without her. How he'd ever thought himself whole before experiencing the wholeness he felt at this moment. She'd come into his life by accident, a tiny, wide-eyed gamine who'd made him laugh when he'd thought he'd never laugh again, who'd reached inside and touched places he'd never had touched before. He felt like both laughing and crying. For the first time in his life he knew what men meant when they spoke of that wondrous moment when the act of love transcends mere physicality and becomes something else, something deep and profound and achingly sweet. He knew he'd never be the same again.

Not just the *act* of love. But *love*. Whole. Pure. Real.

He covered her mouth with his and kissed her deeply, dazed by the simple reality of it. He loved her. He'd known it all along at some deep unconscious level, had married her knowing it, had made love to her that first night knowing it. Had come to her bed last night knowing it.

"Megan..." He raised himself on his elbows and gazed down at her wonderingly, cradling her face between his hands. "Meggie, I—"

Her eyes were the color of dark chocolate and he could see his own reflection in them. He frowned slightly. Damn it, he shouldn't hit her with this now. He could be dead tomorrow. She'd opened herself to him too trustingly as it was. If he admitted he loved her, she'd let down those last barriers around her heart and be even more vulnerable than she was now.

"What were you going to say?" She brushed a tangle of hair off his forehead, looking up at him with a puzzled half smile.

"Nothing, angel," he murmured, lowering his head to kiss her lightly. "I was just thinking about grabbing some shut-eye before dinner."

"Great idea," she murmured drowsily, her voice already slurred. "Can't keep my eyes open...."

"That's what great sex does for you," he said with a chuckle against her ear.

Megan smiled sleepily and wrapped her arms around his neck as he picked her up and carried her into the bedroom. "It's never been anything *but* great with you," she murmured, kissing the curve of his ear. "Every time I think it's as wonderful as it can get, you take me somewhere I've never been before."

Tag drew the bedspread and covers back on the huge bed and slipped Megan between the cool sheets, then slid in beside her. He wrapped his arms around her and pulled her against him, resting his chin on the top of her head. "Me too, Meggie," he whispered, doubting she was even awake enough to hear him. "Me too."

Chapter 13

They spent the rest of the afternoon like that, naked and warm, sleeping a bit, then waking to talk or simply lie there in companionable silence. They made love again in the dim light of late afternoon, very slowly and lazily this time, making it last for nearly an hour. Neither of them said a thing the whole time, not needing words to express what they saw in each other's eyes, and when the end finally came it was the best it had ever been for Megan.

They lay there for a long, peaceful while afterward, then got up and shared a leisurely shower before getting dressed and walking to a nearby restaurant. Megan had intended to come back to the motel room and talk to Tag about their strategy for the next day or two, but they wound up making love again, on the floor just inside the door of their room this time. They'd come tumbling in so ready for each other they barely had time to get out of their clothes before Tag had brought them together with a powerful thrust of his body. They'd made love with a fierce, wild urgency that left them both spent and breathless.

It was only when they were finally in bed that Megan remembered to ask Tag what his plans were for the following day. But he just slipped his arms around her and murmured something vague and reassuring, already half asleep, and in a few minutes Megan forgot all about Lucas and the Black Dragon as she, too, slid toward sleep.

Tag was already up and dressed when she finally awoke the next morning, and she sat up to find pieces of the field-stripped M16 laid out across his side of the bed. He was putting it together, wiping each piece of gleaming metal with an oily rag before sliding it into place, and she subdued a little shiver at the intent, almost anticipatory expression on his face.

She showered and got dressed, and when she came back into the bedroom the M16 was reassembled and Tag was standing by the window, staring thoughtfully down at the pool. She looked around at their few scattered belongings. "Are we staying here again tonight or should I pack this stuff?"

"I'm staying," he said quietly, not looking at her. "You're not." His face was lean and hard in the harsh light from the window, and when his eyes met hers, they were cool, shuttered. "I called Cantrell this morning. He and his wife have a place in upstate New York, and you can stay with them for as long it takes me to sort this out. You'll be safe there. Griff was a good friend of Rick's, and I trust him."

Megan stared at him in shock. "New York?" she whispered. "But I thought—" *You thought what?* her mind urged. That he really loved you this time?

"I'll have a better chance alone, Megan. I have to get down to Las Vegas—Rick and I agreed to use general delivery at the post office there as an emergency drop. I'll have to move fast and quiet, Meg. Alone. And if you're here I'll be spending valuable time worrying about you—time should be spending worrying about Lucas."

His voice was crisp and matter-of-fact, with none of the gentleness she'd come to expect, none of the warmth. In fact, everything about him was different this morning: the quick, catlike way he moved, the impatience in his eyes when he looked at her, the hint of hardness around his mouth. It was as though she'd gone to bed with a lover last night, and had awakened this morning in a stranger's arms.

"I see." She felt awkward and self-conscious for some reason, like a party guest who looks up and suddenly realizes everyone else has gone home. She turned away and picked up the small carryall she'd bought the previous day, then started to put her toiletries and clothing into it, feeling numb. Her throat ached and she had to keep swallowing, but it was only when a tear landed on the back of her hand that she realized she was crying.

Don't you *dare* cry, she told herself fiercely, trying to blink back the tears. He never made any promises. He never once said he loved you, or that you'd be together after this was over. You were the one who kept reading things into the relationship that weren't there, just like on the cruise. And the only reason you wound up in bed together both times was because *you* insisted on it, not because he'd planned it that way! In fact, you were the one who said you didn't want to think about tomorrow, that you just wanted today....

"Meggie?" His voice was very soft, and very close.

When his hands settled on her shoulders she stiffened slightly, but kept her face turned resolutely away, damned if she'd let him see her cry. There were limits to how much vulnerability she was willing to admit to!

"Meg, it's better this way, trust me." She could feel his breath on her hair.

"You're probably right," she said lightly, reaching for the next garment. It was the black nightie the women at the Val-U-Save had given her amid much giggling and teasing, and she hastily stuffed it down in a corner of the carryall, cheeks burning. My God, she'd acted like such an idiot! You'd think she'd have learned the first time, when he'd simply vanished out of her life. What in heaven's name had made her think it was going to be different this time?

Tag sighed. His hands slipped from her shoulders and he walked away. "I'm giving you most of the money O'Dell gave me yesterday. It'll get you to New York, and I'll have Cantrell make sure you've got what you need—it's too risky for you to contact anyone in Des Moines, even your bank."

He handed her the money, his eyes troubled, and Megan took it and tucked it into the carryall. "There's no need for that. I'll call Adam Cambie and have him send me what I need."

"The fewer people who know where you are, the better, angel. Until this whole thing is over, you're still in danger."

"I'd trust Adam with my life," Megan said quietly. "And he'll do whatever I tell him—including not mentioning a word of what he's doing to anyone, not even his brother."

"How can you be sure he'll do what you ask?"

Megan looked around the room for anything she might have forgotten, then looked straight at Tag. "Because he loves me," she said simply. "He's been in love with me for years."

Tag's eyes narrowed slightly. Something shifted in them then was gone before Megan could identify it. "Do you love him?"

"No." *I love you,* she felt like screaming at him. But she didn't. There was no point. He'd shut himself off so completely that it was doubtful he could ever love anyone. Lucas had taught him too well, that was the problem. *"Don't stand in one place and let them draw a bead on you."*

"Are you going to...marry him?" Again, there was that odd expression in his eyes, a flash of what—in anyone else—might have been pain.

"He's asked me." It wasn't what he wanted to know, but she quite honestly didn't know the answer herself. There had been a time, not too long ago, when she could have said 'no' and meant it. But she'd still been waiting for a dream bac

en, waiting for her tall, green-eyed slayer of dragons.
ow...who knew? "I'm already married, remember?"

To her surprise, he winced. He raked his hand through his
air and turned away to stare down at the pool again.
When you're up in New York, tell Griff what happened.
sk him to help you find a good lawyer, and get the paper-
ork under way. If I make it back, we can get a quick, clean
ivorce. And if I don't make it back..." he shrugged,
oking around at her. "Either way, angel, I'll be out of
ur life for good." He gave her a fleeting smile. "And I
romise to stay out this time."

There didn't seem to be a lot to say. She simply nodded
fter a moment, feeling empty and numb. At least he was
aying goodbye this time, she reminded herself. At least she
ouldn't simply turn around one day and find him gone.

"There's a plane leaving for New York in a couple of
ours. I'll drive you to the airport, then head down to Las
egas to pick up the stuff Rick sent."

"I'd rather take a cab," Megan said softly, pretending to
ave trouble with the zipper on the carryall. "I hate airport
oodbyes. And it would be too dangerous for you, anyway.
ven if Lucas doesn't have a handful of his men out there,
m sure he'd have alerted the security police."

"Megan..."

"Please, Tag—I'd really rather do it this way, all right?"
o you can't see me crying, she added to herself. "In fact,
's probably safer if I just go down to the lobby and call a
b from there." If she didn't get out of that damned room
e was going to make a fool of herself, she just knew it.
ther by bursting into tears or telling him she loved him or
eaven knows what! She picked up the carryall and turned
look at him, smiling. "I guess I never have thanked you,
ve I?"

His mouth warmed for a moment, one corner lifting in
at lopsided smile she loved so much. His eyes held hers,
led with a thousand memories. "I think you have, Meg-
e."

She managed to hold onto the smile, but she did drop her gaze so he couldn't see the hurt in her eyes. Had that been what he'd thought these last two nights were—just her way of saying thanks? But then again, what had she expected? She'd told him she hadn't wanted promises he couldn't keep. Deep down, she must have known that it would end this way.

She started to walk to the door, then suddenly stopped and put the carryall down. Surprised at how easy it was, after all, she stepped across to where he was standing and lifted onto her toes to kiss him lightly on the mouth. "Be careful, all right?"

"I'll be careful," he growled as he slipped his arm around her and drew her against him tightly. "I always am, angel." He eased his embrace and lowered his mouth to hers. It was a gentle, lingering kiss, saying more, probably than he'd intended to say.

"Just take care of yourself," she whispered fiercely. "Just don't get yourself killed or anything silly like that, hear me?"

"Loud and clear, angel," he told her with a chuckle. "And don't *you* go talking to any strangers. Griff will meet you at La Guardia, he knows what you look like—and knowing Griff, he'll probably have a couple of buddies along just in case. You'll be fine up there."

She nodded as she slipped out of his embrace, turned to pick up the carryall. One thing she'd always thank Taggart Welles for, she thought as she walked out the door, was making her strong. Strong enough to keep walking without looking back even though she knew he was standing at the door watching her, strong enough to make it all the way to the motel office without stumbling even though she was blinded by tears. Strong enough to say goodbye to the one man she'd loved in her entire life . . .

* * *

Tag didn't know how he'd let her go. Watching her walk way, back straight, stride firm, without even a backward ance, was the toughest thing he'd ever done in his life.

He eased his breath between his teeth, not realizing until en that he'd been holding it. Damn it, it wasn't supposed hurt like this! He'd known right from the beginning that had to end, yet he'd allowed all those silly dreams to get etween him and reality.

But she'd said it herself: no plans for tomorrow, no com- itments, no promises. And he had enough dead bodies on s conscience now; he couldn't risk adding Megan's name the list.

Their faces still haunted him some nights. And their ames. On his first tour in Nam, he'd made it his business learn the name of every man in his unit, to know some- ing about each of them: where he was from, if he was arried, how many kids he had. He'd figured it helped them t through the rough days, having a C.O. who cared ough about you to know your girlfriend's name and that ur old man sold used cars in Duluth.

But finally there came a time when he had to stop know- g, when the burden of all those names, all those private, timate details of dead men's lives, became too much. hen he'd come back to the real world that first time, ey'd followed him—faceless dead men, whispering their ay through his dreams. And when he hadn't been able to and them anymore, when he'd had to go back and find the eces of himself he'd left behind, they'd called him Ice- an. The man with no heart.

But, damn it, he'd kept most of them alive! That whole cond tour was just to vindicate the deaths he'd seen on his rst. He hadn't been fighting VC that tour as much as he'd en fighting Death itself, using the things he'd learned to ep other young men alive. It had been some sort of emo- nal payback, and it had worked to a degree. At least af-

ter that tour, back in the real world again, he'd been able t
sleep.

But the one thing he'd learned almost too well, was tha
it didn't pay to care too much.

He turned and walked back into the motel unit, swearin
angrily at nothing in particular. The rumpled bed seemed t
fill the room, silently rebuking him. He pulled the sheets up
catching the faint, musky scent of their lovemaking, and hi
mind was suddenly flooded with images that he impatientl
ignored. He rammed the M16 into the duffel bag and zippe
it up, then grabbed his small canvas pack and the car key
and strode out into the sunshine.

A cab was just pulling away from the office as he walke
across to the Camaro. He tried not to look but couldn't hel
himself, caught just a glimpse of a silky cap of dark hair an
a pale oval face. Then she was gone.

Megan was standing in line waiting to board her plan
when she saw Spence O'Dell. He was striding down th
corridor beyond the boarding area with one of the airpo
security police, gesturing angrily as he talked. Two othe
men trailed behind them, both looking grim and busines
like in identical dark suits, everything about them scream
ing "government agent."

"Excuse me, Miss Kirkwood?"

The woman's voice at her elbow startled Megan. Sl
turned to find one of the airline staff standing beside he
"Miss Kirkwood, would you come with me, please?"

Megan's heart gave a thump. Who in God's name ha
spotted her? O'Dell? Had the Black Dragon's people di
tributed pictures of her to the security staff of every airpo
in the country as they had Tag's? *Bluff it out,* she told he
self fiercely. She looked at the woman with what she hope
was the right amount of bewilderment. "I'm sorry, but yo
have the wrong person. My name is Peggy Walker."
wasn't very original, but it had been the first name that ha
popped into her mind when she'd bought her ticket.

The woman smiled reassuringly. "Please, Miss Kirkwood. He said it was most important that he talk with you."

"He?" Megan glanced around uneasily, wondering how far she'd get if she made a run for it.

"Colonel Childress. He's with the—"

"Childress?" It surprised her for some reason. Somehow she'd expected it would be O'Dell. She saw him then, striding purposefully toward her, thin hair windblown, camel-hair coat open, gloved hands clenched. He had two large men in tow who could have been twins to the pair that had been with O'Dell only minutes earlier.

Megan took two steps backward, and Childress stopped abruptly, holding his hands out as though to reassure her. "Miss Kirkwood, I don't want to alarm you, but you've got to come with me right now. You're in extreme danger. My people have a place where you can stay until this whole thing is wrapped up—it's secure, and you'll be completely safe there."

Megan wet her lips, nervously eyeing the two men behind him. "Tag said—"

Childress made an impatient gesture. "With due respect to Welles, he simply does not have the full picture! I don't think he realizes just what kind of danger he's put you in." He looked at her intently. "Let me be frank, Miss Kirkwood. If you get hurt or—God forbid—even killed on this operation, the people I work with are going to be *very* upset. Government agencies like mine are supposed to be protecting the citizens of this country, not allowing them to get killed because some amateur like Welles—as good as he may be—decides to take the bad guys on singlehandedly."

"And just who *are* the guys you work with, Colonel?"

He smiled. "Let's just say we're the guys in the white hats."

Megan hesitated, her mind awhirl with possibilities and confusion. What he said made a distressing amount of sense—if he was telling the truth. If he wasn't, she was walking into a trap. Tag said she'd be safe in New York with

Cantrell. *If* she got there in one piece, she reminded herself grimly. And if Griff Cantrell was still alive himself. Whoever killed Rick might have gone after Cantrell. She could be walking into a trap whichever way she went....

There was a shout behind them. Megan glanced around to see O'Dell gesturing furiously toward her, his mouth twisting as he shouted something she couldn't hear.

"Get down! Get down!" someone bellowed. "He's got a gun!"

A woman screamed. Then, suddenly, people were diving in all directions and Megan could hear the sharp crack of gunfire, heard another scream, more shouts. There seemed to be dozens of people milling around, all of them large, broad-shouldered men with cold eyes, and Megan just stood there paralyzed in the middle of it all, staring at O'Dell. Those dark, icy eyes seemed to bore into hers, freezing her where she stood as he swung the gun around toward her.

One of Childress's men clamped a meaty hand around her wrist and wrenched her toward a nearby door, and in the next instant someone slammed into her from behind, propelling her through the door so violently she nearly fell. Someone else grabbed her by the arm and pulled her upright, and then she was running as hard as she'd ever run in her life, Childress in front of her and two armed men behind. They were out the far door and into the chill air in seconds, across the wide sidewalk, people scattering before them like windblown leaves.

And then they were at the car and Childress was pushing her safely inside and they were under way, tires shrieking as the driver floored the accelerator. A luggage cart appeared in front of them and the driver wrenched the wheel to avoid it, caught it with the tip of his bumper and sent it flying, baggage spilling across the road while the porter and a bevy of tourists dived for cover.

She flinched instinctively at the crack of distant gunfire. Then it was lost under the roar of the engine as the driver gunned it and headed for open highway. Childress leaned back in the seat beside her and wiped his forehead with a gloved hand, managing a weak smile. "Sorry if I frightened you, Miss Kirkwood, but it seemed more expedient to push you through that door than stand there talking about it. Are you all right?"

"I'm...fine." She was shaken up and frightened half out of her wits, Megan realized, but not hurt. "My God, that was O'Dell! W-what was he doing?"

"Spence O'Dell is either the Black Dragon himself, or he knows who is. We've suspected it for some time, but we won't know for certain until Welles gets that information Rick sent to him." He looked at her curiously. "Welles *has* gone after the information, hasn't he?"

"Yes." Megan brushed her hair back with a trembling hand. "At least," she added as an afterthought, "I guess he has. He didn't actually say what he was doing. Or where he was going." She didn't know why she was being so cautious, but Megan suddenly knew exactly how Tag felt. You didn't dare trust anybody. "H-how did you know where to find me?"

Childress smiled. "Dumb luck. One of my men spotted you coming into the airport. And I hope this has convinced you to take me up on that offer of protection. At least until Welles gets back and can look after you himself."

Megan nodded and clasped her trembling hands together. "Why didn't O'Dell just kill us in the mountains?" she whispered. "Why bring us back?"

"He wants that information Rick pulled together as badly as we do—and Welles is the only man who knows where it is. I suspect he intended to kidnap you again to force Welles to turn the information over when he finds it."

"And now?" Megan whispered.

"Now I'll take you someplace where you'll be out of sight and completely safe, and we'll wait for Welles to get back."

"What the hell do you mean, you don't know where she is?" Tag bellowed, shoving his face close to O'Dell's. "You said she went with Childress—does that mean you and Childress *aren't* working together on this?''

O'Dell's eyes glittered coldly. ''If you ever want to see Megan Kirkwood alive again, Welles, you'd better start listening to me!''

Tag fought down the urge to plant his fist squarely in the middle of O'Dell's lean face and stepped back, dragging a deep breath between his clenched teeth. ''Talk!''

O'Dell seemed to be having the same difficulty holding onto his temper. ''I'll take care of your wife,'' he said in a dangerously soft voice, ''and you take care of business.''

''And if I don't?''

''Do you want to get Megan back or not?''

''That sounds like blackmail to me, O'Dell.''

''It is.'' O'Dell's thin lips twisted. ''Childress may be our Black Dragon, Welles. If he is, your wife is in considerable danger. I can get her out. But I want that information Rick sent. It's that simple.''

''Unless *you're* the Black Dragon,'' Tag rumbled menacingly, ''and Childress has Megan tucked away safely so you can't get her. You've never told me what you were doing at the airport.''

''I could ask you the same thing,'' O'Dell snapped. ''You're supposed to be picking up that information Rick sent, not out at the airport harassing my men.''

''I wasn't harassing anybody! I was trying to find out why my wife didn't board the flight she was booked on, and why the whole place was sealed off like a—''

''Don't get confused about who's giving the orders around here, Welles, and who's taking them.'' O'Dell's voice was deceptively mild.

''I quit taking orders from guys like you a long time ago. Don't get in my face, O'Dell. I don't really give a damn *who* the Black Dragon is—I just want Megan back. Alive and unhurt.'' He took a step forward, muscles relaxed. ''Because I swear, O'Dell, if she gets hurt, people are going to pay. And pay *hard*.''

"If you do as you're told, she won't get hurt." O'Dell turned away, motioning for his men to take Tag out. "Just get the information, Welles. And I'll make sure you get your wife back."

They drove him back to the airport parking lot where he'd left the Camaro in his fruitless attempt to catch Megan before she left. It had been one of those crazy impulses that comes out of nowhere, but he'd suddenly known it couldn't end that way between them. So he'd gone tearing out to the airport to stop her from leaving, only to find the place cordoned off and surrounded by an armed and very serious assault force. A slight security problem, they'd said. Nothing to worry about.

Tag gave a snort. The place had been under siege. And no one was talking. All he knew was that Megan had been here, and now she wasn't.

He stared through the windshield at nothing, trying to fit the pieces together. What the hell was going on? It was hard to believe that O'Dell had gone bad, but money could make a man do strange things.

And China White made money! Tons of it. It took around two thousand poppies to make a kilo of opium gum, and ten kilos of gum to make a kilo brick of the finest China White. The farmer up in the hills of Thailand would sell those ten kilos of gum for the equivalent of seven hundred dollars. The kilo of refined heroin would go for around nine hundred dollars in Marseilles, resell in New York for close to a million, and by the time it hit the streets, it was worth somewhere around seven million dollars.

Considering that the hills of Burma and Thailand and Laos were literally teeming with the infamous *papaver omniferum* poppy, and that in an average year a farmer could produce fifteen hundred kilos of gum—weather and bandits and DEA raids permitting—it didn't take a genius to figure out that the Black Dragon's cartel was worth billions. Enough, perhaps, to corrupt the strongest man.

Rick had trusted O'Dell, and now Rick was dead. Megan was *somewhere* with Childress, maybe safe and maybe not.

He swore softly and reached down to turn the key in the car's ignition. Eighteen months of playing hide-and-seek with Lucas and the Black Dragon were enough. If they wanted him, they were, by God, going to get him. Only they just might wish that they'd left well enough alone.

The small efficiency motel unit where Childress had left Megan was comfortable enough, but she was too keyed up to do more than pace restlessly. She'd tried to phone the motel where she and Tag had spent the night, hoping against hope that he might still be there, but her call hadn't been put through. Instead, one of Childress's men had poked his head in and had told her, gently but firmly, that outgoing phone calls were not allowed.

If she only knew what was going on! It was almost worse than being held prisoner in that dingy basement—at least then she'd known who her enemies were. And she hadn't had Tag to worry about then, either. But now she could hardly think of anything else but what kind of trouble he could be in—seeing him lying hurt or even dying while she sat there unable to do a thing to help him. Finally, exhausted by sheer tension and worry, she curled up on the bed and tried to sleep.

It was a shout that awakened her. She sat up, groggy and disoriented. The room was dark and she turned the bedside lamp on, then slid off the bed and went across to the window. She turned the corner of the curtain back and was shocked to see it was well after sundown.

The motel parking lot was brightly lit, and even as she stared out, frowning, someone darted between two parked cars. He stayed there, crouched low in the shadows, and she felt a prickle of alarm. Someone else moved to the left of the first person and she blinked, the last vestiges of sleepiness vanishing abruptly as the dark figure eased himself for ward and, for the briefest instant, she could clearly see his face. Spence O'Dell!

Her heart gave a thump and she recoiled from the window as thought she'd been stung, her mind whirling. How in God's name had he found her?

There was another shout, more muffled than the first, then something hit the door of her unit with a thump. There was silence, then a spate of hurried whispers too low for her to decipher and the sound of something heavy being dragged away from the door. Like a body, Megan found herself thinking numbly. Like a guard who had just been knocked out or killed and was being quietly disposed of.

It was that possibility that galvanized Megan into action. She shoved her feet into her sneakers, then grabbed her light cotton jacket and headed for the bathroom at a dead run. At the moment, she didn't give a damn who was out there. She'd rather be on the run, on foot and alone, than cooped up in here waiting for something to happen. She'd find someplace safe to hole up where no one could find her, and figure out what to do. But whatever it was, she'd do it alone.

She clambered up onto the vanity and eased the bathroom window open, then peered out gingerly. To her surprise, no one was waiting for her. It was a tight fit, but she managed to wriggle through, and she was balanced precariously on the window sill when she heard the front door open with a crash. She dropped into the deep shadows in the laneway behind the units, paused just long enough to get her bearings, then sprinted for the lamplit street at the end of the long, dark alley.

She didn't even see the car until it turned its headlights on. They pinned her against the darkness like a deer caught in a jacklight and she skidded to a stop, arm thrown up to shield her eyes from the blinding glare. A car door opened and she could hear footsteps running on gravel. She turned to bolt back up the alley when three figures materialized in the distance and came charging noisily toward her.

There was a snarled oath from right behind her, then a gunshot. One of the distant figures stumbled and fell and the remaining two melted into the deep shadows, then a hand clamped on her shoulder and pulled her sharply to one side. There was a tiny puff of sound where she'd just been standing, and one of the car headlights exploded as the bullet hit it squarely.

Chapter 14

he hand pulled Megan back into the shadows so vio-
tly that she lost her footing and fell, knocking the breath
t of her. "Stay out of the light, damn it! What are you
ing to do, get yourself killed?"

'T-Tag?" Her voice squeaked with astonishment.

The tall, faceless figure reached down and grabbed her by
collar, hauling her to her feet. His free arm went around
· and he hugged her so fiercely she couldn't breathe. "It's
, angel," came Tag's warm, husky baritone. "Just can't
y out of trouble, can you? I turn my back on you for a
ple of hours, and look what happens." Then he gave her
erocious shove toward the car. "Get in there and stay
wn!"

She scrambled into the car, and a second or two later Tag
ung into the driver's seat. He rammed the car into re-
se and floored it, and they shot backward out of the al-
and into the street like a cork out of a bottle. "What the
/ are you doing, running around out here in the dark?"
demanded furiously. He shifted into forward and accel-

erated so abruptly that Megan was flung back against t
seat. "Damn it, Megan, I came within a cat's whisker
shooting you!"

"What the hell are *you* doing s-sneaking around back
leys with your lights off?" she countered just as furious
trying to find the seat belt and keep from bursting into tea
of fright at the same time. She found the buckle finally, b
her hands were trembling so badly she couldn't fasten it.

He gave her a sharp look, his face lean and dangerous
the glow from the dashboard. Then he gave a snort
laughter, shaking his head. "Fair enough, angel. Poi
taken. I was there trying to find you, as a matter of fact. I
followed O'Dell to the motel and was sitting in the all
trying to figure out what to do next when you appeared rig
in front of me. Where the hell did you come from ar
way?"

"I sneaked out the bathroom window," she muttered, st
trying to get the belt secured.

"Who brought you here? Childress?"

"Yeah. Right after O'Dell tried to kill me at the a
port."

"After O'Dell *what*?"

She tossed her hair out of her eyes to look at him. "The
was a lot of shooting and yelling and running around. Ch
dress grabbed me and brought me here."

Tag swore under his breath. "So Childress is okay?"

"I don't know!" Megan snapped, patience frayed nea
through. "You need a scorecard to tell the good guys fro
the bad guys around here! I just know I'm sick and tired
the whole lot of them."

"Amen," Tag breathed, glancing into the rearview m
ror.

Megan looked up suddenly. "Why were you looking
me at all? As far as you knew, I was on that plane to N
York."

"I went out to the airport after you," he said quietly.

"You did?" Megan blinked.

"Yeah." He turned to look at her, eyes serious. "Meg, _"

"Look out!"

Tag spotted the car at the same instant Megan screamed r warning, and her voice was all but drowned out by the riek of tires as Tag slammed the brake pedal to the floor. aught with her seat belt still undone, she was thrown vio-ntly forward as their car plowed into the one that had pped out of a side street right in front of them. She skated f the seat and wound up on the floor under the dash-ard, shaken up and bruised but surprisingly unhurt. She s just going to crawl out when Tag threw himself across e seat with a shout of warning. The entire windshield ex-oded in a spray of automatic-weapon fire, showering them th nuggets of glass, and Megan covered her head with her ms and curled up as far under the dash as she could.

She was still blinking in shock when both doors were enched open and the beam from a high-powered flash-ht blinded her. A large hand grabbed her wrist and agged her out of the car, her feet crunching through bro-n glass and bits of metal as she stumbled after the man. 1other car came to a screeching stop behind the accident, es smoking. Someone flung himself out of it and strode grily toward them.

"Damn it, I told you to *stop* him, not smash into him!" 1e voice crackled with anger, and was chillingly familiar. f he's dead, I swear I'll shoot you myself!"

"He's not dead, sir," came another voice, just as famil-.

"No, but you'll wish I was." Tag's voice whispered rough the shadows just beyond the harsh beam of the one adlight still working. "You'll pay for this, Lucas, you son a—" There was a soft thump, then a groan and the sound a body falling.

Tiger Jack stepped into the light, grinning evilly, and stured with his M16. "He won't be giving you any trou-e for a while."

"If you hurt him—" Megan stepped toward him but t
hand gripping her upper arm wrenched her back.

Tiger Jack grinned. "I didn't hurt him half as bad
Khiem's going to," he said with a threatening laugh th
chilled her to the bone. "I just owed him that." The grin le
his mouth abruptly, turning his eyes hard and cold as
stepped close to her. "I owe you, too," he said softly. "I'
still got a lump on my head where you hit me with th
chunk of firewood."

"Save it," Lucas snapped. "You deserved a crack acro
that thick skull of yours for being dumb enough to let Well
sucker you into that room in the first place. She just sav
me the trouble of doing it."

Tiger Jack glared down at her for another moment
two, then turned and walked away into the darkness. Luc
gazed at the two damaged cars, then swore under his breat
"Let's get out of here. Nelgaard, strip these cars of an
thing that can identify us or Welles. Let's move, gentl
men!"

Jammed between Lucas and Tiger Jack in the front se
of the car, Megan didn't move a muscle during the enti
ride, although her mind was whirling like a pinwheel. T
only thing she could think of was to grab the wheel and ste
them off the road or into a parked car, but she couldn't i
agine for a moment what that would accomplish besid
giving Tiger Jack the opening he seemed to be waiting fo
He kept glancing down at her as though wishing she'd
something careless, his fingers never ceasing their gent
caress of the M16's gleaming barrel. And then there was T
to consider. He was in the back seat, conscious but grogg
and she doubted he was in any shape to take advantage
whatever distraction she could create.

So they'd just have to wait, she told herself with forc
calm. There would be a way out of this. There was *alway*
way out....

The warehouse was dark and seemingly deserted, with
couple of tall, feeble lights overlooking the loading ba

ing their best to hold back the night. The air stank of en-
e oil and salt water and rusting metal, and Megan could
the outline of a big freighter moored by the docks, a
ck silhouette against a dark gray sky, moving very gently
ainst the ebbing tide.

Lucas stopped in front of the big loading doors and
ped the horn twice, and a moment or two later the huge
or slid ponderously open. Lucas drove the car inside and
egan heard the door groan closed behind them, shutting
m in.

She was pulled out of the car and she stood there, taking
ck of her surroundings. The place was dimly lit. Every
nd echoed and reechoed, magnified in the vast empty
ces. The ceiling was lost in a maze of shadows and steel
ders and crane booms. Mountains of stacked crates,
ding pallets and big overseas-shipping containers rose like
red stone temples, immense and mysterious in the shad-
s.

Her gaze was drawn to one corner that was relatively well
There was a table and a couple of chairs there, and three
ned men, waiting. One of them was a tall, slender Ori-
al with shoulder-length graying hair and a wide black
tton band tied around his forehead. His eyes were as cold
a snake's, and Megan shivered when they met hers.
Khiem.

There was a scuffle behind her and Megan looked around
t as Tag wrenched free of the two men who had dragged
n out of the car. He strode into the circle of light where
cas was standing. Rubbing his wrist, he looked around
h a cold, calculating stare that made Tiger Jack lift the
16 slightly. He carried himself like a street fighter, walk-
; lightly on the balls of his feet, shoulders down and back,
d there was something in his expression that made at least
o of Lucas's men take an involuntary step backward.

"Welles, you have caused me a *lot* of trouble over the past
ar." Lucas's voice was conversational, almost amused.

"Glad to hear it." Tag smiled humorlessly. He glance
around again, seemingly casually, although he was takin
everything in, every shadow and angle, estimating, sizi
up. The odds were bad, but he'd gotten out of tougher spot

Alone, he reminded himself brutally. But he wasn't alo
now. He had Meggie to care for. No matter what else ha
pened, he had to get her out of this.

"Of course, you always were a troublemaker," Lucas wa
saying. "I should have remembered that. I should ha
killed you in Bangkok when I had the chance."

"Like you killed Russ?"

Lucas shrugged. "Russ Hammond was an idiot."

"Russ Hammond was a friend of mine."

"You shouldn't have wasted your time. He had troub
written all over him, right from Nam."

"And Rick Jarvis?"

"I don't know what happened to Jarvis—none of n
people knows anything about his death."

Tag didn't say anything. He simply stood there ar
looked around him, apparently relaxed and unconcerne
He let his gaze brush Megan's. She was standing quietly
one side, looking very small and defenseless, her face as pa
as alabaster in the harsh light. But in that heartbeat of e
contact, he realized that shrewd accountant's mind of he
wasn't missing a thing. He could see the fear in her eyes, b
she had it well under control, was assessing and calculati
and estimating just as he was. Then he looked at Luc
again, eyes narrowed slightly. "How are we going to pl
this?"

Again, Lucas shrugged. "Easy or hard. Depends
you."

"Let Megan go, and we'll talk."

Lucas gave a long, lazy laugh. "No, I don't think ;
She's my ace card, Welles." He turned serious. "Get me t
information that Rick Jarvis sent you, and you can ha
Megan back."

"No dice. She walks out of here now or we don't have a al."

"You know I won't do that, Welles," Lucas said quietly, so let's stop wasting time. She won't get hurt if you coop- ate. All I want is that information."

"And you'll let the two of us walk out of here alive if I ing it to you, right?" He didn't even bother to keep the rcasm out of his voice.

"If I get your word that you'll back off, yes. We'll have e heat taken off you and clear your name, and you can go ack to living a normal life. Without that information of rvis's, you can't prove a damned thing anyway."

Tag glanced idly at Megan. She was looking at some- ing behind Lucas, frowning very slightly as though not re of what she was seeing. He let his own gaze drift that ay, thought he saw movement in the deep shadows but uldn't be sure. "And I'm just supposed to forget about uss Hammond and Rick Jarvis and all the other people u've murdered over the years."

Lucas sighed. "There's no room in the world today for roes, Welles. Corruption and greed and murder are on an ternational scale now. Whole governments are involved. o you think my men and I could have spirited away all ose artifacts and temple baubles without the cooperation government officials? And who do you think is financ- g the armies patrolling the hills of Thailand and Burma, otecting the opium farmers from bandits?"

He strolled across to the table and sat on the edge of it, ossing his arms and looking at Tag with a faint smile. Hell, Welles, we're just businessmen. There's a need out ere and we fill it. And while we're filling it, we employ ousands of people and provide economic stability to untries which couldn't otherwise compete in today's world arket."

"I'm sure the cotton kings in the South once used the me logic to rationalize slavery, Lucas," Tag said dryly. "It dn't wash then; it won't wash now."

"And heroic rhetoric may sound good if you're runnir for political office, Welles, but dead is still dead." He mad an impatient gesture. "It's just like in Nam—us again them. We survived because we took care of each other. An that's all we're doing now, just taking care of our own." H looked at Tag for a long, contemplative moment. "You' as good as you ever were, Welles. We could use you. Aft all, you were one of us, once. You could be again."

"I was never one of you," Tag said softly.

Lucas stared at him. "I used to think you were pret smart, Welles. I guess I was wrong. I was giving you an o portunity to keep yourself and your lady alive, but you' not leaving me much choice. I guess it'll have to be Khie after all."

The single rifle shot snapped through the silence like tl crack of a bullwhip, and a bullet ricocheted off the met wall a scant inch above Lucas's head and went singing o into the darkness. Instinct sent Tag into a fast dive to h right. He rolled hard and came up off his shoulder in crouch, found himself staring into the barrel of a heavy a sault rifle held by one of Lucas's men. He froze, his ba exposed to whoever had shot at them, and the spot betwee his shoulder blades crawled. Everyone else had taken cov and was crouched in the shadows, weapons out, scannir the girders crisscrossing the roof for some telltale mov ment.

Tag looked around frantically for Megan. She was hu dled between two wooden packing crates across from hir seemingly unhurt but obviously shaken. Tiger Ja crouched behind her, one hand on her shoulder to keep h down while he cradled the M16 in the other, moving tl barrel in lazy arabesques above her head as he tried to s where the ambushing shot had come from.

"Who the hell was that!" Lucas's voice sounded tight.

The next shot hit the wooden pallet by Tiger Jack's le ear. Splintered wood went flying, and Tiger Jack gave animallike snarl and was on his feet, the M16 braced in fro of him and on full automatic as he sprayed fire in sweeping arcs across the darkness above them. Megan clapped her hands over her ears and curled up at his feet as a hail of spent cartridges rang down around her, bouncing and clanging on the concrete floor.

Then he was empty and in the sudden silence Tag could hear Tiger Jack's harsh breathing, the click as he released the spent magazine. It dropped beside Megan and she flinched, and Tiger Jack slapped another one home.

Even braced for it, Tag flinched, too, when the next shot came. The bare bulb above the table exploded in a shower of glass and sparks, plunging them into near darkness, and Tag could hear someone give a bawl of profanity. He didn't even bother looking around. He grabbed the rifle barrel in front of him with one hand and shoved it aside even as he brought his other fist around with every ounce of strength he had. It hit his opponent in a perfect uppercut that sent both of them sprawling across the floor, and he'd grabbed the rifle and was on his feet in one movement, diving low and fast for cover. Someone was shouting orders, then someone else opened up with what sounded like an AK47 and all hell broke loose.

It was the break Megan had been waiting for. The entire place erupted in a madhouse of shouting men and gunfire. Some of Lucas's people dived for cover and others started firing wildly into the darkness, and in that instant of confusion she was on her feet and down a long alley between rows of stacked crates like a shot.

She dodged left down another alley, then right, left again, her new sneakers giving little squeaks of protest at every sharp turn. The big warehouse was a maze of passageways, some wide enough for a forklift truck, others so narrow her shoulders brushed the crates on either side. It was also poorly lit, and the farther away she got from the main loading doors, the darker it got, especially in some of the narrower passages where the high stacks of crates blocked what little light there was.

She could still hear angry shouting and sporadic gunfire
but they were far enough behind her now that she ignored
them, concentrating instead on figuring out what to do next.
Part of her wanted to get out of the warehouse and as far
away from it as possible, but another more practical part
reminded her that she'd be a sitting duck out there. Besides, Tag was still inside somewhere. She'd caught a
glimpse of him vaulting a stack of crates and vanishing into
the darkness just before she'd scrambled for cover herself,
but there was no point in trying to find him in this rat's nest.

Winded and completely lost, she squeezed into a dark
cranny between two giant shipping containers and sat on the
edge of a wooden pallet to catch her breath. She could hear
indistinct shouts in the distance, a spate of irate profanity,
a couple of gunshots that resulted in another burst of angry
shouting. They were chasing each other, by the sound of it,
whoever had caused the disturbance either gone or simply
in hiding.

Now and then she could catch the sound of running
footsteps or see huge, distorted shadows bobbing along the
walls of crates surrounding her. At least twice someone
raced by the narrow entrance to her little hideaway, too
quickly for her to make out who it was. Someone was moving stealthily in the maze of girders and steel cross-beams
above her, too. She'd caught glimpses of shadowy figures up
there, gone before she could focus on them, and now and
again a fine tracery of dust would drift down as though dis-
lodged by a careless foot.

Some movement above her made her look up just then,
and she swallowed a scream as Tiger Jack's face loomed
over the edge of the crate above her. She recoiled with a
muffled gasp, realized she was trapped, and bolted the other
way. There was a roar of gunfire and the crate beside her
exploded in a shower of wood and packing material, startling her so badly she stumbled and fell headlong into the
passageway, half-deafened and stunned with shock. A
shadow moved across her and she tried to scramble to her

eet, knowing he was going to fire again and that she was
never going to be able to get clear in time....

"Hold it!"

Megan froze before realizing the shout wasn't meant for
her. Panting for breath, she dared a quick glance over her
shoulder. But Tiger Jack wasn't even looking at her. He was
staring at something above and behind him, every line of his
body tensed, then he gave a bellow of rage and swung the
gun up. There were two shots, so close together they were
almost one, and before Megan even fully comprehended
what had happened, Tiger Jack had vanished. It was only
when she heard something large and heavy crash to the floor
that she realized he'd been hit.

She simply lay sprawled there, too stunned to do more
than watch as a lone figure detached itself from the darkness above her and quickly and effortlessly lowered himself
hand over hand down the dangling chain of a nearby roof
crane.

For a dazed moment or two she thought it was Tag. He
was tall and rangy and tow-haired, dressed in black combat
gear, a heavy weapon slung over one shoulder. He dropped
the last few feet, stumbling slightly, and it was only when he
jogged awkwardly toward her that she realized his left leg
was badly injured.

His face was a bizarre mask of multihued camouflage
paint and as he came toward her, Megan stiffened. But to
her amazement, he honored her with a broad, cheerful grin
completely at odds with his fierce garb and war paint. "I'll
bet you're Meggie." He squatted beside her with a wince,
keeping his left leg straight. "You okay?"

"I'm ... fine," she whispered, too bemused to do more
than blink owlishly at him. "You saved my life."

He smiled and put out a large, rough hand and cupped
her chin with surprising gentleness, lifting her face so the
light fell on it. He gazed down at her for a moment or two,
then nodded with satisfaction. "Welles always did have a
nell of an eye for a good-lookin' woman."

It all made so little sense that she didn't even bother trying to answer, and instead sat up a trifle unsteadily. She noticed his left pant leg was shot to tatters just then, and she sucked in a horrified breath. "Your leg...!"

"Oh. Yeah." He chuckled and started rolling up what was left of the fabric. "I'm going to catch hell for this for damn sure. The VA hospital gets real upset when you bust up one of their legs. Wait till they get a load of this!"

It took Megan a moment to comprehend why there wasn't any blood, and when it finally hit her she simply stared at it. His left leg was made of molded plastic, although one of Lucas's goons had done his best to shoot most of it away. Chunks of plastic had been torn away to reveal the thin metal supports running through it, and he poked at it with a shake of his head. "Not much loss, actually. Damn knee jammed on me—I've been hobbling around all week like I'm crippled or something."

Megan blinked, then lifted her gaze from the battle scarred leg to the hard-hewn, paint-smeared face. "You're Rick Jarvis."

"In the flesh," he said with another grin. "So to speak."

"But... you're dead."

"That's a long story, Meggie," he replied, easing himself to his feet. There was a low, trilling whistle above them and he glanced up, then trilled an answering whistle. A figure padded into sight along a steel beam just above them, seemingly unconcerned by the fact he was a good forty feet in the air. Rick flashed him a thumbs-up, and the figure lifted his hand in casual acknowledgement, then vanished into the shadows.

Megan looked at Rick and he smiled. It was a cold, inward smile, and Megan remembered Tag saying *"he got that look he used to get just before a night patrol—the kind of look a wolf gets when it scents a rabbit."*

"I brought along a few friends," he said, the smile taking on an edge that made Megan shiver. "Tag's a buddy of ours. And buddies help each other out..."

There was a sudden flurry of gunfire on the other side of he warehouse, and Rick looked around, his eyes narrowing. Then he picked up his rifle and nodded toward the narrow, dark niche between two walls of wooden crates behind er. "Get back in there and stay low. As soon as the cavlry gets here, I'll come and get you."

"Cavalry?"

"Drug Enforcement, probably. Maybe FBI. I called them bout an hour ago when I realized what was going down, ut it takes forever sometimes for those government types o mobilize." He gave that wolfish grin again. "That's why ay buddies and me decided to liven things up a bit. We'll eep them busy until the good guys get here—you just keep our head down and stay out of trouble." He gave her houlder a reassuring squeeze, then eased himself caubously around a corner and was gone.

"But—" Megan was left staring after him, mouth halfpen around a thousand unasked questions. Then she heard unning footsteps heading her way, and the spell broke. She ucked into the shadows at the back of the little hidey-hole hat Rick had spotted, and settled down to wait.

And then, suddenly and silently, Tag was there. She saw is shadow first, thin and grotesque as it loomed on the side f the crate across from her, and a moment later he stepped ato her line of view. He paused there for a moment, as hough getting his bearings, and Megan's breath left her vith a huff of sheer relief as she stepped out of the shadws. "Tag!"

He crouched and wheeled around in one fluid motion, nd Megan found herself staring into the muzzle of his M16. he raised her eyes to meet his, and they simply stared at ach other in shock for a paralyzed moment. Then Tag relxed with a soft, heartfelt oath, closing his eyes for an intant as though offering a silent prayer.

He stepped forward then and wrapped his arm around her a fierce hug. "My God, you're really doing your best to-ay to scare me out of about twenty years, aren't you?"

"I've scared myself out of a decade or so, too," she as
sured him with an unsteady laugh. "Are you all right?"

"That's supposed to be my line, sweetheart." He grinne
down at her and gave her another quick hug. Then he so
bered, glancing around uneasily. "I think we got caught i
the middle of a drug war between Lucas and one of hi
competitors, angel. It took the heat off us, but we've still go
to get out of here alive." He reached for her hand. "Let's ge
moving."

"It's not—"

"Welles!"

The bellowed voice was behind them and Tag wheele
around. Megan caught a glimpse of two of Lucas's men
then Tag was firing, the staccato roar of the M16 nearl
deafening in the confined passageway. They dodged out o
sight and Tag shoved Megan in the opposite direct. "Run!"

She didn't need further encouragement. She sprinte
down the long, narrow passageway with Tag right on he
heels, trying not to flinch at the intermittent bark of the M1
as he fired a burst or two back down the passage as they ran

Lucas stepped in front of her so abruptly that Mega
didn't even have time to shout a warning before the stubb
little weapon in his hand started to chatter and a row o
holes stitched the crate right beside her. She recoiled in
stinctively and careened heavily into Tag, who gave her
ferocious push that sent her sprawling across the floor s
hard she cracked her chin. Her teeth snapped down acros
the end of her tongue and she tasted blood, tried to blink th
sudden tears of pain from her eyes, recoiled again, sti
blinded, as something tore into the floor beside her chee
and ricocheted off with a whine, spraying her with slivers o
concrete. She could hear the maniacal clatter of Tag's M1
right above her, a snarl of pain, the crash of somethin
heavy hitting the crates across from them.

And then it was over. A hand clasped her upper arm an
dragged her to her feet and in the sudden silence Mega
could hear her own heart slamming against her ribs. Luca

as sprawled on his back, unmoving, and Tag gave her a hove in the opposite direction. "Don't look," he snapped, is breath rasping noisily. "Keep moving, Meg!"

Half-stunned, she started to run in the direction he'd ushed her. She stumbled to a stop about halfway down the ong aisle where it intersected another one, glancing around t Tag for directions. He caught up to her, panting heavily, hen staggered slightly and leaned against the nearest wall of rates as though to catch his breath. His face was slick with weat and he had his teeth clenched, and it was only then hat Megan realized that something was terribly wrong.

"Oh, my God," she whispered, grabbing him instinc- vely as his knees buckled and he started to sag. "Tag, lease . . . no!"

"Sorry, angel." He managed a rough laugh that turned) a groan of pain halfway through. "I zigged when I should ave zagged back there, and he nicked me good."

"Where . . . oh, God!" It was more prayer than anything lse as she pulled his jacket open and saw the blood. Too uch blood! She braced him against the crates and looked round frantically for help, had her mouth half open to cream for Rick before she realized that chances were it ould bring Lucas's men instead. She took a deep gulp of reath instead and wedged her shoulder against him. 'Come on . . . in here."

He managed to stagger the few steps into the sheltered pace between two huge shipping containers stenciled in ome language Megan had never seen before, then sagged) the floor before Megan could catch him. "Go," he whis- ered. "Meggie, get out of here before—"

"Be quiet." The words snapped out with a strength and uthority that surprised her, and she pulled his jacket open. le'd been hit low on the right side, just above the waist- and of his jeans, and was bleeding heavily. She whipped er own jacket off and looked at it for a moment, then pped the cotton lining out of it in one violent motion and

folded the torn fabric into a thick pad that she presse
firmly down on the wound.

"Hold this," she ordered him, taking his hand and put
ting it on the rough dressing. "Press hard!"

He struggled to get up, his face gray. "Meg, you've go
to—"

"Damn it, sit down and shut up!" Her voice made hin
blink, and she smiled grimly as she pushed him back down
"You've been ordering me around all week—now it's m
turn!" She grabbed the big knife from the sheath at his bel
and started to cut up her jacket, managing to get three lon
strips of cotton from the back of the garment before turn
ing to the sleeves. When she was finished, she tied all th
strips together into one long, makeshift dressing and woun
it around him to hold the pressure bandage tightly in place

"It won't win any awards for neatness, but it seems to b
working." She glanced up at his face, frightened by what sh
saw. "Damn you, Taggart Wells, don't you *dare* die on me
If you think you're getting away from me this easily..."

"Look on the bright side," he whispered, opening pain
filled eyes. "At least it'll save you the trouble of divorcin
me."

"I don't *want* to be your widow," she sobbed, the sud
den tears catching her by surprise. "I don't even want to b
your ex-wife!"

"Do you mean that, or are you just saying it because yo
figure I won't live to hold you to it?"

"Yes, I mean it!"

He reached up and cupped her cheek in his hand. "I lov
you, lady," he whispered.

"Tag, please!" She had to fight to hold her tears bacl
"We don't have time for that right now. I've got to g
help!"

She started to stand up but he caught her by the wrist an
held her firmly beside him. "How the hell I ever thought
could make you a part of this and not make you a part c
me, too, I'll never know." He licked his lips, breathin

uickly. "I've loved you right from the start, Meg. But I've
een fighting it all along...scared to open up. Scared to let
ou get too close..." He clenched his teeth together, breath
issing with pain.

"Tag, please, I've got to—"

"Meggie, if I get out of this, I want to marry you. Again.
roperly, I mean."

"Do you mean that," Megan said with a sob of laughter,
or are you just saying it because you think you might not
ave to deliver?"

He managed a fleeting grin. "I mean it, angel. That's why
went out to the airport after you—to tell you I want it for-
er between us. Will you marry me?"

"As many times as you want."

"Once will do." He stopped, closing his eyes for a mo-
ent, then opening them again to hold hers in a searching
ok. "I love you, Megan Kirkwood Walker," he whis-
red, his voice slurring slightly. "Always remember that. I
ve you...."

"Taggart, damn you, stay awake!"

She heard the scuff of running footsteps just then and
oked around in time to see Buck Childress hurry by their
ding place. He must have seen her at the same instant,
cause she'd barely even opened her mouth to call out to
m when he appeared again and peered into the shadows in
tonishment.

"Thank God you finally got here! We need help...."

"What's happened?" He kneeled beside Megan, frown-
g down at Tag. "Is he dead?"

"Not yet," Megan said tightly, "but he needs a hospital,
d he needs it right now. We—"

"This is the FBI," someone bellowed over a megaphone
st then. "Everybody stay where you are. Weapons down
d hands up!"

Childress whispered something under his breath, glanc-
g around. Then he looked back at Tag and pulled his

jacket open, eyeing the blood-soaked dressing. "He's in ba
shape."

"I know that!" Megan nearly shouted in exasperation
She started to stand up again. "I'm going to get someor
to—"

"No!" He caught her arm and pulled her down sharpl;
"That won't be necessary. I'll take care of everything."

"But he—" Megan stopped dead, eyes widening slight
as she stared down at the hand still clamped around her arn
Buck Childress's hand. "Gloves," she whispered. "You'v
always been wearing gloves..."

"What?" He looked at her sharply.

"Your ring." She swallowed, staring at the heavy gol
ring on his right hand. It was set with a large black stor
that was polished until it gleamed like ebony; a stone carve
into the shape of a dragon. It was intricately worked, ever
detail of its gleaming coils done with extravagant precisic
right down to the individual scales on its back and wings, th
tiny clawed feet, the flaring nostrils. The artist had used a
inlay of red coral for the burst of flame issuing from th
dragon's mouth, and two tiny, oval emeralds for its eye
They glittered malevolently at her now, gently mocking,
Childress moved his hand.

"It was you," she whispered. "You were the other ma
with Lucas, the one who kept asking me questions. I mu
have seen the ring, but I was drugged and it was all
fuzzy...."

Childress sighed, frowning very slightly as he gazed dow
at the ring. "Lucas always said it was too distinctive. I kno
it's a foolish risk, wearing it. A vanity, really. But I am for
of it. Maybe too fond..." He looked up at her. "I alwa
suspected you were a little more clever than Lucas gave ye
credit for. I told him he should just kill you then and the
and get it over with, but he wanted to make certain
caught Welles before disposing of the bait. Now I'll have
do it." He smiled very faintly. "With Jarvis dead, you're th
only two people who can present any kind of threat to m

elles won't last the night, so you're my last problem. My st bit of tidying up."

"No," Megan said very calmly, "I don't think so." Tag's 16 was heavier than she expected, but it felt comforting in r hands. She aimed it straight at his heart. "Get up."

He smiled almost companionably. "Spare me the dra- atics. I admire your spirit, but you're not going to shoot e."

"Colonel Childress," she said in a flat, even voice, "I've en kidnapped, shot at, chased, lied to, threatened, half- zen and frightened out of my wits over the past few days, d now the man I love is lying here bleeding to death. I've en pushed just about as far as I'll go—*get on your feet!*"

"And if she doesn't kill you, Childress," a chillingly fa- liar voice told him matter-of-factly, "I'll be happy to lige." Spence O'Dell stepped lightly around the end of the ites. "It's over, Buck."

"What the hell are you talking about?" Childress stood impatiently. "I was just—"

"Jarvis finished tracing the codes through the Pentagon mputer," O'Dell said quietly. "It leads right to you, ck."

"Jarvis?" Childress looked pale. "You told me he was ad."

"He lied." Rick Jarvis appeared just then, looking hot d dirty and angry. He glared at O'Dell. "It's damned well out time you showed up! What did you do, take the sce- route?"

"And just what the *hell* do you think you're doing?" Dell glared right back. "I told you to stay in New York. ld you—"

"*Stop it!*" Megan lunged to her feet and in the startled nce, she could hear the distant whoop of police sirens. Vhile you idiots are standing here arguing with each other, g is bleeding to death! Now will someone arrest Chil- ss or whatever you're going to do, and the rest of you *p* me!"

O'Dell looked at her with something that was very clos to amused respect. Then he started machine-gunning o ders, and within minutes Childress was in handcuffs and Ta was in the back of one of the ambulances that had com screaming in behind the police.

Epilogue

he room was dark and still. Tag heard the rhythmic,
ctronic beep of his own heartbeat and smiled to himself,
ssured to discover that he was, contrary to expectations,
l alive.

It gave him a feeling of smug satisfaction, knowing he'd
tsmarted Death, O'Dell *and* the doctors. Of course, none
them had known how much he had to live for.

He turned his head and saw her there as he had so often
ring the past ninety-six hours. She was sitting on the chair
ide him, arms crossed on the bed, head resting on them.
r eyes were closed and he realized she was asleep.

Vorn out, poor kid. She hadn't left his side for more than
nutes at a time, was always there, close enough to touch,
enever he'd opened his eyes. It had gotten him through
se first few bad hours, knowing she was there. Even
en he hadn't been fully conscious, when all he'd been
are of was the pain, he'd sensed her there in the shadows
he room, touching him with her heart if not her hands.
he'd been the first thing he'd seen when he'd regained
sciousness after surgery, smiling down at him as though

she'd never had a doubt in the world that he was going
make it. The thought made him smile again. She must ha
been the only one, then, because all the medical wiza
O'Dell had brought in hadn't given him much hope. A
there had been a time or two when he'd wondered hims
if he was going to be able to hang on. But then he'd think
Meggie waiting patiently for him to come back, and h
fight the nearing darkness a little harder.

She stirred slightly, frowning in her sleep, and Tag cupp
her cheek with his hand. Sleep, Meggie, he told her silen
letting his own eyes slide closed. I'm here. I'll always
right here....

Morning.
Again.
Megan pulled the pale yellow curtains open, and ga
out across the hospital parking lot to the distant, s
brushed cone of Mount Rainier rising serene and untr
bled against the eastern sky. It had become almost a rit
with her, greeting that distant mountain each dawn,
omen that they'd gotten through another night safely.

She turned around and walked back to the bed, and br
into a smile when she realized that Tag was awake. She
beside him and put her hands around his. "Hi. How are y
doing?"

"I feel like hell," he muttered, "so I guess I'm still aliv
Then he smiled at her, fingers tightening around hers. "H
about you, angel?"

"I'm okay." Especially now, she added to herself. He
still very pale, unshaven cheeks almost gaunt. But with
the clutter of breathing tubes and monitor wires that I
been removed just that morning, he looked reassurir
normal. There was a strength to his voice that hadn't b
there the few times he'd spoken before, and his eyes,
clouded by the fog of pain and drugs, looked at her wi
warmth and vitality that made her heart sing.

"You saved my life back there, Meggie."

"I had my reasons," she whispered. "Selfish reasons

'You're pretty handy to have around when a man gets
self into trouble.'' He grinned at her. ''Quite a little
gon slayer yourself when the chips are down, aren't
?''

'As I said, I had my reasons.'' She reached up and
ched his cheek, smiling.

ag turned his face and kissed her fingertips. ''When was
last time you got some sleep? And I don't mean a cat-
here beside me—I mean a real, honest-to-God twelve
rs of sack time?''

'Don't worry about me. Spence rented a room for me at
otel just down the street, so I've had somewhere to
wer and freshen up—and sleep.''

'Spence?'' He arched an eyebrow. ''Getting pretty
ndly with the guy you once thought was the Black
gon, aren't you?''

he gave a quiet laugh. ''He'd probably kill me if he knew
ld you. He tries so hard to play the role of the cold-
rted government agent, but he's been like a mother hen
the past four days. He sat in that waiting room for
nty straight hours after they brought you in.'' And held
when I cried, she added silently, for those long three or
r hours when we thought you weren't going to make it.
e even sent a government jet down to Houston to bring
r parents up. They're over at the suite right now, get-
a bit of sleep.''

Are they okay?''

They're both fine. Spence has been telling them what
d of a hero you are, breaking the biggest drug ring in
ory wide open all by yourself, how you're going to get all
s of awards and commendations. Even an invitation to
White House. Your dad's so proud he's bursting at the
ns. Spence sugarcoated some of the worst parts. He let
hat you've been working with the government all along
that the story about your being wanted for the murder
hose three agents was concocted for cover. And *that's*
you haven't contacted them over the past year and a

half." Megan smiled. "He figures you can tell them as m
of the truth as you want later."

Tag gave a grunt. "Never thought of O'Dell as bein
soft touch."

"You gave him a scare, dragon slayer." She smiled at h
reaching out to brush a lock of hair from his pale forehe
"In fact, you gave us *all* a scare."

"I love you."

His words wrapped around her like melted butter
Megan's smile widened. "I know. It was the first thing
said when you came out of surgery—you gave the h
nurse quite a thrill. In fact, it's been just about the c
thing you've *been* saying for four days, aside from sc
fairly unrepeatable comments about O'Dell and Lucas."

He smiled sleepily. "I just wanted to make sure you k
I meant it." Then his fingers tightened around hers. "
still haven't said how you feel about that."

Megan gave a soft, surprised laugh. "You idiot! I thou
it showed every time I looked at you."

"So tell me, anyway."

"I love you, Taggart Welles," she whispered. "I n
stopped loving you."

"You never gave up, did you?" he asked softly. "You
ways knew I loved you. That I'd finally realize it and
back for you someday." He untangled his fingers from I
and stroked her hair. "You're the best thing that's
happened to me, angel. I've been living in the shadows si
Nam, afraid to really open up and be alive again. But
changed all that. You brought the sun back into my
Meggie."

"I do love you."

"How would you like to prove that?" he murmured. "
not against hospital regulations to kiss the patients, is i

"Oh, probably," Megan said with a laugh. "They s
to have regulations against everything else." She lea
across and kissed him gently, then less gently as his h
moved up to cradle her head and his mouth moved gree
under hers, pliant and warm and very much alive.

She sat on the edge of the bed and rested her forearms on ne pillow on either side of his head, smiling down at him. "We're probably going to have a nurse down here in a min-te," she murmured. She nodded toward the array of elec-ronic equipment surrounding the bed. "I think your heart ate just went all erratic and silly."

"Kiss me again," he whispered, "and let's see if we can't et off every damn alarm in the place."

She started to do just that when a movement at the door nade her glance around. "Hi!" She smiled in pleasure. "Come on in. We were just discussing . . . medical proce-ures."

Rick Jarvis grinned broadly as he came through the door. "I thought the doctors said he was past the point of need-g mouth-to-mouth."

"Just a precautionary measure," she said with a laugh. "We don't want to take any chances on a relapse."

"Well, I'll be damned," Tag drawled, grinning. "You ally *are* alive. I thought I'd just been hallucinating."

"Hell, no, old buddy." Rick swung a chair around and raddled it, reaching out to clasp Tag's hand strongly. "They tried their best, but we're the good guys, remem-r?"

"So it was just a setup?"

"It was O'Dell's idea," Megan said quietly. "He figured e only way to keep Rick alive was to pretend he was *dead*."

"Yeah," Rick growled darkly. "He made it look as ough I'd been killed, then shipped me off to stay with antrell. That put all the heat onto *you*, old buddy. O'Dell gured while the Black Dragon's people were busy chasing u and Meg around the Cascades, I'd be able to concen-ate on deciphering those last computer codes."

"And all that time I thought O'Dell was the Black agon," Megan said ruefully.

"Which sure as hell didn't make it easy trying to keep an e on you," O'Dell snapped as he strode into the room.

"If you'd told me what the hell you were up to," Tag snapped right back, "you wouldn't have *needed* to keep an eye on her."

"You were never in any real danger. I had no proof that Childress was involved, but my instincts told me to keep him under surveillance."

"Which is why you were able to find me after Childress grabbed me at the airport," Megan said.

O'Dell shook his head impatiently. "By then, Rick had contacted me and I *knew* Childress was the Black Dragon. I was out at the airport that afternoon making sure my men were in place to follow Welles if *he* turned up, and I turned around and saw you and Childress! I tried to warn you, but you took off like a startled cat. Fortunately, I had a couple of mobile units outside and they were able to follow you to that motel."

"Oh." Megan winced.

"Yes." He raised an eyebrow. "I was trying to get in quietly so if Childress had someone with you, we could take him by surprise. But by the time we got inside, you'd shot out the bathroom window." He gave a bark of laughter. "I've tackled some difficult cases in my life, but trying to keep you under surveillance beats them all!"

"But you shot at us in the alley!"

O'Dell's thin face flushed slightly. "An unfortunate case of overreaction on the part of my men—Welles had taken one of them down, and they shot back." Those cold eyes turned onto Tag. "One of my best, as a matter of fact. And he's going to be out of action for another month."

"All I saw were three men trying to grab my woman," Tag growled. "By that time I didn't give a damn who the Black Dragon was. I just wanted Megan safe."

"And the information that Rick supposedly sent Tag?" Megan asked. "It never existed, did it?"

"No. But I wanted the Black Dragon to *think* that information existed. As long as it did, he had to keep Welles alive."

"You used me," Tag rumbled.

"I knew you could handle it," O'Dell replied mildly.

"And Megan? Did you think she could handle it too?"

O'Dell's face darkened. "She was never part of the plan, 'elles. You were *supposed* to agree to Childress's offer of fekeeping—I was going to smuggle her up to Cantrell's ithout Childress even knowing what was going on. But you t paranoid and went outlaw on me. Which reminds me," added with some hostility, "you owe the government one ay, four-door sedan."

"Bill me."

"And speaking of outlaws," O'Dell said with a look in ick's direction, "you still haven't told me what you were ing at that warehouse. I told you to stay out of it."

"I don't like the way you operate, O'Dell," Rick said lmly. "You were using Tag as a decoy to take the heat off e, but you were just letting him twist in the wind out there ithout a net." He shrugged. "The boys and me were the fety net, that's all. I left Cantrell's two days ago, picked a few friends, and came out here to make sure Tag and s lady didn't get left out in the cold if anything went rong."

"Damned cowboys," O'Dell muttered. "The whole inch of you always were more trouble than you were orth—Cantrell, you, Welles."

Megan merely smiled. "And Childress's little empire?"

"Coming down like a house of cards," O'Dell said with tisfaction. "He had people working everywhere—moniring everything. He knew when the DEA was planning an vestigation or raid that could hurt him, or if any of his erseas contacts or routes were in danger. He also planted formation about his competitors' activities, crippling them badly that he was just about able to wrap up the world roin trade." He gave Megan a smile. "That tip you gave about some of the shipments coming in through Van-uver tied up a few loose ends, too." Then he looked at g. "And if you hadn't gone blundering around looking Russ Hammond, we'd probably never have uncovered "

"Forget the handshakes and cigars," Tag muttered, "ju[st] get me off the CIA hit list! It's going to be years before I ca[n] walk down a street without looking over my shoulder for [a] guy with a bad haircut and shiny shoes."

O'Dell's mouth twisted. "Your name's been cleared of a[ll] charges and warrants, and the Department will be compe[n]sating you generously for the illegal confiscation of you[r] home, business and finances. There were a few ruffl[ed] feathers to smooth regarding a falsified passport in the nam[e] of Michael Walker, but I took care of that too. I'll leave th[e] matter of the fraudulent marriage up to Miss Kirkwood."

"I think Miss Kirkwood and I have come to an agre[e]ment," Tag murmured, squeezing Megan's fingers gentl[y.] "How about it, angel? Still game to marry me? I'm a littl[e] worse for wear, I don't have a job or even a place to live ye[t,] and I have no idea what the future holds. But I do lo[ve] you."

Megan smiled and leaned across to kiss him. "I'll mar[ry] you on one condition."

"Name it."

"That we have a nice, quiet honeymoon this time."

Tag's mouth curved. "How about a South Seas cruise?["]

"How about Des Moines," she murmured. "We can bu[y] a king-size bed and lock the doors and close the drapes a[nd] not come out for a month."

"Angel, you've got yourself a deal."

Megan glanced around just then and realized that Ri[ck] and O'Dell had gracefully withdrawn. The sun had broke[n] through the light cloud cover, and the room was floode[d] with golden light, the shadows banished. She smiled, a[nd] turned back to kiss Tag gently. Gone, too, was the Shado[w] Warrior who had come into her life a year and a half ag[o.] In his place was this gentle, giving man who loved her eve[ry] bit as much as she loved him. And now, dragons slai[n,] shadows gone, they had the rest of their lives to teach eac[h] other just how deep and lasting that love could be.

*   *   *   *   *

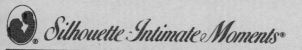
Silhouette Intimate Moments®

COMING
NEXT MONTH

#325 ACCUSED—Beverly Sommers

Anne Larkin was assigned to defend her former law professor, Jack Quintana, on a murder charge. Jack was innocent, but Anne was guilty—guilty of falling in love with her client. When the verdict was handed down, would it be life without parole—in each other's arms?

#326 SUTTER'S WIFE—Lee Magner

When Alex Sutter and Sarah Dunning met, the air crackled with electricity. If only they could find a way to merge their lives.... Could a cynical, semiretired intelligence agent who was accustomed to a no-strings-attached lifestyle and an independent, settled young woman find permanent happiness together?

#327 BLACK HORSE ISLAND—
Dee Holmes

Keely Lockwood was stuck between a rock and a hard place. She was determined to fulfill her father's lifelong dream to work with troubled boys, but she got more than she bargained for when she hired Jed Corey. Could she mix business with pleasure and succeed at both?

#328 A PERILOUS EDEN—
Heather Graham Pozzessere

What do you do when the man you've fallen in love with may be a traitor to your country? That question haunts Amber Larkspur when she finds herself held hostage in a terrorist plot. Suddenly she has to trust Michael Adams, not only with her heart but with her life.

AVAILABLE THIS MONTH:

#321 SPECIAL GIFTS
Anne Stuart

#322 LOVE AND OTHER SURPRISES
Kathleen Creighton

#323 STRANGERS NO MORE
Naomi Horton

#324 CASE DISMISSED
Linda Shaw

Silhouette Special Edition

proudly presents

Taming Natasha
by
NORA ROBERTS

In March, award-winning author Nora Roberts weaves her speci[al]
brand of magic in TAMING NATASHA (SSE #583). Natasha
Stanislaski was a pussycat with Spence Kimball's little girl, but t[o]
Spence himself she was as ornery as a caged tiger. Would some
cautious loving sheath her claws and free her heart from
captivity?

TAMING NATASHA, by Nora Roberts, has been selected to receiv[e]
a special laurel—the Award of Excellence. Look for the
distinctive emblem on the cover. It lets you know there's
something truly special inside.

You'll flip . . . your pages won't!
Read paperbacks *hands-free* with

Book Mate · I

The perfect "mate" for all your romance paperbacks

Traveling • Vacationing • At Work • In Bed • Studying • Cooking • Eating

Perfect size for all standard paperbacks, this wonderful invention makes reading a pure pleasure! Ingenious design holds paperback books OPEN and FLAT so even wind can't ruffle pages — leaves your hands free to do other things. Reinforced, wipe-clean vinyl-covered holder flexes to let you turn pages without undoing the strap . . . supports paperbacks so well, they have the strength of hardcovers!

SEE-THROUGH STRAP

Reinforced back stays flat.

Pages turn WITHOUT opening the strap

Built in bookmark

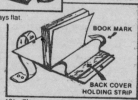

BOOK MARK

BACK COVER HOLDING STRIP

10˝ x 7¼˝, opened.
Snaps closed for easy carrying, too

At long last, the books you've been waiting for by one of America's top romance authors!

DIANA PALMER
DUETS

Ten years ago Diana Palmer published her very first romances. Powerful and dramatic, these gripping tales of love are everything you have come to expect from Diana Palmer.

In March, some of these titles will be available again in DIANA PALMER DUETS—a special three-book collection. Each book will have two wonderful stories plus an introduction by the author. You won't want to miss them

Book 1
SWEET ENEMY
LOVE ON TRIAL

Book 2
STORM OVER THE LAKE
TO LOVE AND CHERISH

Book 3
IF WINTER COMES
NOW AND FOREVER

 Silhouette Books®